Just the Three of Us

An Erotic Romantic Comedy for the Commitment-Challenged

LORI L. SCHAFER

First Edition

DEDICATION

To the two young men without whom this book would not have been possible – Sam and Ted.

CONTENTS

CONTENTS

CHAPTER 1

"Wow, you're fast!" he said with admiration, gawking at me with wide eyes through a plastic face-shield thick with fog.

I turned to look behind me but I was the last player on the bench; this unfamiliar young man with the friendly face appeared to be talking to me.

"Uh, thank you," I said, returning my eyes to the ice and uncomfortably shifting my grip on my stick.

"I mean it," he assured me. "You are very fast, especially for, you know, a – Hey!"

The exclamation caught my attention more than the unfinished remark. I turned again and saw another young man sitting beside this one, elbow out as if he'd just used it to nudge his friend into silence.

"For a what?" I said shrewdly, watching in amusement as my neighbor struggled to solicit a polite response out of an apparently unresponsive brain. "For a woman? Or perhaps you meant for an older woman?" I concluded, putting extra emphasis on the "older." At thirty-seven I was hardly ancient, but there was no doubt in my mind that these fellows were a good ten years my junior, a fact that gave me the indisputable right to tease them mercilessly.

His face, already beet-red from the exertion, flushed scarlet. "I wouldn't say older!" he fibbed unconvincingly. "You're what, like twenty-eight, twenty-nine?"

"Don't mind my friend," the other fellow said, leaning across him towards me and grinning. "He's really a nice guy. Sometimes just a bit of a dumbass."

"It was a compliment!" the nearer man stuttered before being abruptly rescued from his consternation by the return of the other left wing. He stumbled over the boards and onto the ice and his buddy slid over next to me.

"I'm Ted," he said, extending his arm in my direction. "And that's Sam."

"Kathy," I replied, bumping my glove against his by way of a handshake.

"I haven't seen you here before," he said. But before I could answer, I saw the one of the defensemen hurtling towards the boards and sprang to my feet to take his place. Ted followed hard on my heels to replace the other wing, who had just lurched, panting, over to the bench.

I hadn't even noticed them before – possibly because I'd been too busy trying not to embarrass myself my first time on the ice in my latest new town. But now I couldn't stop watching them skating around in front of me; two of my nameless, faceless teammates had turned into people. Of course, meeting people wasn't always as great as it sounded, as I'd discovered in the course of my many travels. You don't worry so much about making a good impression when you're an unknown member of an anonymous crowd. I pondered that as I forced my legs to an inhuman effort in chasing down the next breakaway when it came. I didn't want to lose my newly established reputation for speed, after all.

"Nice job," Sam said when I flung my body back over the boards a minute later, fresh sweat trickling coolly down my spine.

"Thanks," I gasped, plunking my butt down on the bench and taking a deep swig of my water. My partner for the day was still nowhere in sight and I wished he'd hurry up and finish dressing; it was exhausting playing with only three D.

The guy named Ted leaned over again. "So are you new here?" he said, picking up our conversation right where we'd left off. It's customary for hockey players to chat in fragmented one-minute intervals.

"Just moved to town," I nodded, starting to catch my breath. "I was in a women's league the last place I lived, but there isn't one in town here. Thought I'd give this group a try, if it's not too tough."

"You're tough enough!" Sam exclaimed. "I've seen the way you skate."

"Trust me, I have no skills," I countered, pleased in spite of myself. I wasn't being modest; I was a poor puck-handler and had no shot to speak of, and it had already become apparent that my rather abundant apportionment of feminine muscle wasn't quite as useful among these men, most of whom were younger and a lot bigger than me. And apart from my speed, I had few real skills as a skater, and already I was struggling a lot harder to keep up than I had in my last league. Ever heard the expression "tripping-over-your-tongue-tired?" That was me.

"Pshaw!" he answered, dismissing my critical assessment with a wave of his glove. I turned to look more closely at my new acquaintance. Along with that broad, boyish face and welcoming eye went the kind of personality that could use an expression that went out with the previous century without an iota of shame.

"Pshaw?" Ted echoed, making a motion as if scratching his helmet with his padded glove.

"Pshaw!" Sam repeated, unabashed.

"Okay," Ted said, clearing his throat audibly and leaning towards me again. "So where are you from?"

"Um, well... New England, originally. Most recently, California," I answered. "Up north, near San Francisco."

Sam laughed. "So what the hell are you doing here? Sick of the beautiful weather?"

"Something like that," I chuckled back. I wasn't about to try to tell my life story to two strangers in the ten seconds before I had to be on the ice again.

"Well, welcome to Minnesota, eh?" Ted replied in a heavy and decidedly phony accent. I looked askance at him. He had the agreeable look of a young man who hasn't quite reached his prime; I guessed he would be downright handsome about five years down the line. Slimmer, more serious-looking than Sam, with dark hair and deep brown eyes and a neatly trimmed beard that ran the length of his chin.

"Yeah, you're welcome, eh?" Sam agreed.

"We don't actually talk like that," Ted assured me. "It's just an affectation put on for outsiders, so they'll think they're in Canada or something."

"You'd better start working on yours, too," Sam said seriously. "Here, I'll teach you," he began, but fortunately I was rescued from a lesson in Northern American linguistics by the return of the entire forward line, which sent my new acquaintances scurrying for their positions.

My defensive partner finally arrived, plopping his enormous

body down next to mine and effectively cutting me off from further conversational efforts with Sam and Ted. I couldn't decide whether or not I should be sorry about that. But as the game continued, I watched them weaving in tandem along the ice, passing the puck to one another seemingly without effort, to all appearances like two balls on the ends of the same chain. They must have been teammates for a long time, I thought; they made such a good wing pair. I wouldn't have said that they were great athletes; I mean, they were both obviously competent, but not spectacular in any way. But there was something in the way they played together that made them better, much better than their skill levels alone would have suggested. Almost as if they knew each other so well that one was an extension of the other; two minds and bodies separated only by twenty feet of ice.

Following the closing handshakes, I was surprised to find them both skating beside me back to the bench.

"Okay, so we know you're not a native, but do you drink beer?" Sam inquired, as if it were a beverage endemic only to Milwaukee and cities of similar latitude.

"Of course!" I answered. I was actually very fond of beer, although I'd found, as I often did, that the styles that were popular in Minnesota weren't the same as those that dominated other markets.

"Good," Ted replied. "We usually go out for a beer after the game, and we think you should come."

I was taken aback. They seemed like nice enough fellows and all, but I really saw no point in going overboard with the acquaintance. Sure, I was a little lonely. It's never easy being the new kid in town, no matter how old you are, and I hadn't exactly been a ball of social fire in any of the many places I'd lived in the wandering course of my adult life. But really, what besides hockey could I, a relatively mature woman, possibly have in common with two twenty-something-year-olds? Boys, practically, to my mind.

I guess my lack of enthusiasm showed, because while I hesitated in answering I heard Sam saying, "I don't think she likes us, Ted."

"Well, you shouldn't have made that comment about her skating like a, 'you know,' " Ted replied, shaking his head dolefully.

"Please just come have a beer with us!" Sam pleaded. "Otherwise Ted will never let me hear the end of it."

"Unless you really don't like us," Ted said, narrowing his dark brows at me. I wasn't short, especially with my skates on, but standing up he still towered a good six inches over me, and I might have been intimidated had he not had such an indisputably gentle face.

"We wouldn't blame you much," Sam chimed in. "We are kind of obnoxious."

I looked from one to the other. There was something refreshingly youthful in their earnestness and a part of me was touched. It was sweet, really, the way they'd taken pity on me. After all, I probably seemed as old to them as they seemed young to me.

"It's not that," I answered finally, weighing my words carefully. "I was just surprised that you're old enough to drink."

"Oh-ho, she got you back, Sam!" Ted said with a laugh.

"Says you!" he shot back. "Ted's just jealous because I'm more mature."

"You're only six months older than me!" Ted said. "And older does not mean more mature!"

That was certainly the truth. Here I was in my late thirties, with no husband or children and no particular desire for either yet. In a new city with a new job that I wasn't even sure I was going to like because I still hadn't decided what I wanted to be when I grew up. Plus I was living in a one-room apartment with cardboard-box furniture and a mattress on the floor. What did I know about mature? Maybe my mistake all along had been in trying to meet people my own age: settled, adult, grown-up people. I'd be right at home with these guys.

"Twenty-six is mature!" Sam retorted. "Isn't it, Kathy?"

"Hmm, sorry, I can't remember back that far," I joked. "It's been a long decade."

We retreated to the locker room to undress. As usual I kept my head down so I could pretend not to notice those few bold fellows who stripped down to their bare asses before changing into clean clothes. Me, I never bothered. I was always way too sweaty after a game to even think about forcing fresh pants on over my sticky thighs. I did wonder, though, how the other players would react if one day I, too, decided to strip down naked and wander around the locker room with all my goods hanging out like it was no big deal.

That was one way to make an impression, I thought. I'd never been what you'd call beautiful, even when I was younger, but I wasn't bad to look at, either, especially since hockey had sculpted my once-flabby form into a passably pleasing shape. I hoped that having a decent figure helped to distract the interested observer from my other physical flaws, which weren't too tough to overlook if you didn't look too closely. I had very plain brown hair that I wore cut to the shoulders, and kind of a square face that was rescued from dullness by deep dimples, rosy cheeks, and big green eyes that I simply adored. Most days I didn't mind not being gorgeous. It was much easier to blend into the background when you were average-looking, and I'd spent most of my adulthood trying not to be noticed. And I could still clean up pretty cute when I wanted to, although I knew those days were rapidly drawing to an end. Hmm, I thought as I glanced around the room full of strangers and contemplated the cold and lonely bed waiting for me at my apartment. Maybe I should flaunt it while I still had it.

I hauled my gear out to my car and then, with some trepidation, headed upstairs to the sports pub. Sam and Ted were waiting for me in the doorway and that relieved me somewhat; I always felt hopelessly awkward walking into a place alone. I nonchalantly looked them over. Unlike me, who was twice my normal size with gear on, they didn't look that different without it. Sam, I saw now, had golden blond hair that he wore in a buzz-cut all over his rather round head; it added to the general impression of constant cheerfulness that he radiated like sunbeams off of every edge of his person. He had a solid, stocky build and was several inches shorter than Ted. With his fair skin and bright smile, I'd describe him as cute more than handsome; he seemed to ooze a boyish sort of charm that made him appear pleasant and harmless. Ted, by contrast, had a darker, almost olive complexion, and seemed the quieter of the two; something in the set of his jaw suggested a level of reserve his friend seemed to lack. He had a narrow face that went well with his lean form, and seeing him in his street-clothes, I would have sworn he didn't have an ounce of fat on him; only lithe, long muscles that ran like thick wires over his elongated limbs.

"Shall we?" Sam said, extending an arm as if to offer it to me with old-fashioned courtesy. When I hesitated, he seemed to think better of the idea and hurriedly retracted it. I pretended not to notice.

I followed them inside. A few of the other guys from the team were up there and nodded to Sam and Ted. Then I caught them looking bemusedly at me and I blushed. Self-consciously I raised my hands to my head and felt my hair all utterly disheveled into sweaty locks, as it always was after hockey. I'd never gotten in the habit of showering after a game, either. I figured since I was always going straight home afterwards, what was the point in enduring the fungus-ridden locker room shower?

This is why you don't have a boyfriend, I thought as I plunked myself down at the small, circular table Sam selected while Ted went up to the bar to buy us a pitcher.

"So why did you move here, Kathy? Was it for work?" Sam asked as Ted poured our beers and I slipped him a five for my share. He pushed it back across the table with a pleading little wave of his hand. I shoved it back towards him with a bigger, more insistent wave. His eye caught mine and I watched it crinkle in amusement. Then he nodded and, conceding defeat, tucked the bill into his pocket. It was very rare that I lost the battle over going dutch with men. I hadn't been independent all these years for nothing, after all.

"Was it for work?" Sam was repeating.

"Oh! Well, sort of," I answered, jerking my attention back to the conversation at hand. "Not really."

I took a sip of my beer while he stared at me as if expecting me to continue talking. Ted was peering at me keenly through narrow-rimmed glasses he had not been wearing during the game. I liked them. They did something for the shape of his face.

"No shutting her up, is there?" Sam said at last into the silence.

"So are you naturally not very talkative, or do you just have a lot to hide?" Ted inquired.

I chuckled. "A little from Column A…"

"Well, what do you do? For work, I mean?" Ted said.

"Oh," I hedged. "This and that."

They looked at one another.

"Wait right here," Sam said. "I left my good dental extractor in the car and I think we're gonna need the big one if we want to get any information out of this girl." His voice was husky, and a little edgy, as if he spent a lot of time joking around; it rather pleasantly complemented Ted's deep, gravelly rumble.

I laughed. "Really, there's not much to tell. I have a Bachelor's in Film Studies, which, as you might imagine, is pretty close to worthless."

"Film Studies?" Ted interrupted. "That sounds interesting!"

"It was!" I answered enthusiastically. "Oh, I really enjoyed it. It's not what people think, criticism and all that, it's more like a sociological study, looking at the culture behind movies and so on. You do a lot of reading on the history of the time and write a lot of papers – it was really fun. Kind of useless in the real world, though. There wasn't much I could do with it except get a doctorate and then teach, and I don't really have the personality for that. It looks good on my resume, though; proves I was smart enough to finish college."

"Why'd you choose it, then, if you didn't want to make a career out of it?" Sam inquired curiously.

"I dunno," I answered vaguely. "There wasn't really anything else I wanted to do, I guess."

"Huh," Ted replied, resting his head on his hand as if seriously considering the meaning of what I had said.

I gave up attempting to describe what was obviously a foreign concept and hurried on with my speech. "Anyway," I said, "I haven't got what you'd call a career. I've done all kinds of work: office jobs, waitressing, copyediting… I was even an online retailer of out-of-print videos for a while. Right now I'm working as a bank teller."

"Well, that's cool!" Sam said without much enthusiasm.

I shrugged. "I like math," I said. "It's one of the better jobs I've had. I actually did it once before, back in New Jersey, but then I got promoted to New Accounts and I didn't like it as much. Dealing with people… It can be really irritating, you know. And when I moved to North Carolina, I decided to try something else so I never advanced any further in banking."

"Why did you move to North Carolina?" Ted inquired, his eyebrows raised as if he thought it a strange destination.

I shrugged again and let out an awkward laugh. "No real reason, I guess. Just felt like a change."

"How many places have you lived exactly?" Sam asked, furrowing his brow. It forced his forehead into shallow, barely perceptible wrinkles that made mine look like the walls of the Grand Canyon but without all the pretty colors.

I smoothed my wet hair down over my forehead uneasily. "Oh, I don't know," I said. "I guess on average I move every couple of years."

"Every couple of years?" Sam replied, astonished, drawing back to peek underneath the table at my lower half. "No moss grows beneath your feet, I see."

"I guess we shouldn't get too attached, eh, Sam?" Ted said.

"Why so often?" Sam asked me.

"I can't stand cleaning," I said seriously. "It's easier just to move when the apartment gets dirty."

They frowned at me skeptically and took big swigs of their beer.

"Well, I think that's great," Ted said defensively. "You know that except when I was in college, Sam and I have only lived two places our whole lives?"

"Really?!" It was my turn to be shocked.

"Yup. We moved here from the country right after school and have been in the same apartment ever since."

"Wow!" I said. "Don't you get tired of being in the same place all the time?"

"Well, one day we'd like to move out to the suburbs. Have a place we can call our own."

"I really want a house with space in the yard for a vegetable garden this big," Sam said eagerly, spreading his arms wide to illustrate the size he had in mind. "And that's not happening here in town."

I guess they realized that I was starting to wonder, because all at once they said together, "No, we're not gay."

"And if we were, I still wouldn't want to go out with him," Ted said seriously, peering across the table at me. "He just isn't my type."

"Oh, you would, too!" Sam objected. "You'd be lucky to have me!"

"That's not what your mom says!" Ted replied.

"It's true," Sam conceded, turning to me. "My mom's been hoping for years to get Ted for a son-in-law, and since I'm an only child…"

I couldn't tell if he was serious or not, so I tactfully decided not to comment. "So what do you guys do?" I asked, hurriedly changing the subject.

"I'm a carpenter," Sam announced with pride. "A Lead Carpenter, in fact. Just got promoted last year."

"What's that?" I asked.

"Sort of like a foreman."

"I know what that is!" I answered. "I was a foreman once."

"Really?" They stared at me in disbelief.

"Yup. Up in Alaska when I was nineteen. I'd gone up to clean fish for the summer and was put in charge of the vacuum-packing machine. I had one person under me. I was so proud." I clasped a hand to my chest to express the sweetness of the memory of being in charge.

"Who'd you get to go with you all the way up to Alaska?" Ted wanted to know.

"Oh, I went up alone," I answered, thinking it a strange question. Why would I have brought anyone with me?

"All by yourself?" Sam squeaked, jumping a little in his chair as if something small and furry had just scurried underneath it.

"I don't travel that well with others," I confided. "Most people kind of drive me crazy after a while."

"Huh," Ted said again, scrutinizing me as if I were as mysterious as the Mona Lisa and only half as congenial.

That's it, I thought. From now on I stay home in my apartment with the door locked and the windows bolted shut.

"So what do you do, Ted?" I said, taking one last desperate shot at trying to sound like a well-adjusted woman having a normal conversation with people she wanted to befriend.

He shrugged. "Something with computers," he said. "You don't want to hear about it. Boring."

"Don't you like it?"

"Yeah, I do," he admitted. "It's just not my dream job. But I've got student loans to pay off."

"So what is your dream job?" I started to say, reaching for my glass and finding it empty. I always drank faster in the company of strangers.

"Hey, you want another?" Sam said, standing up to go and fetch a fresh pitcher.

"No, thanks, I really gotta run," I said.

"Big date?" Ted said.

"Just me and my showerhead," I chuckled. They frowned at me again in that half-serious manner and for a moment I felt like the young and immature one. "No, I just get really nervous about drinking and driving. I don't like to have more than one if I have to drive afterwards. But I can't stand sitting around with an empty beer, either."

"I hear that," Sam said.

"Well, will we see you next week?" Ted said, standing up by way of farewell. I wasn't sure if he meant at the game or afterwards, so I played it safe.

"I think so," I said vaguely.

"Come again when you can stay longer!" Sam called as I made my way to the door. I turned to wave at them and thought that I would never see those two outside of hockey again.

But I was wrong. I didn't see how anyone who'd had to endure twenty minutes of my dull and dreary conversation could be inclined to sample more of it, but they didn't seem bored with me at all. Indeed, had I not been an on-the-spot witness to my poor social performance, I would have sworn that they actually liked me. It seemed impossible, but the following week they cornered me again, and the week after that, and before I knew it, meeting those two for a beer after the game had become a routine that I looked forward to as much as the game itself. They had such easy-going personalities that, somewhere between the post-game drinks and the bits of chatter on the bench, even I began to relax around them. In a weird way, I thought the age difference also helped. I mean, I knew it wasn't the biggest spread ever, but between that and the fact that I only ever saw the two of them together, I was fairly confident that this wasn't some elaborate pickup scheme, and that took most of the pressure off me. Of course, if they'd ever been tempted to think along those lines, they would have stopped once they'd gotten to know me.

"So why did you leave California, anyway?" Sam still wanted to know during about the sixth week of our acquaintance.

"It's complicated," I muttered.

"Complicated how?" Ted prodded.

"Oh..." I said reluctantly, trying to remember that these were my only friends. "I was seeing this guy, and he wanted me to move in with him. I thought that was crazy, because we'd only been going together six months, but he kept trying to convince me, and I don't know... I couldn't decide. And I'd been sorta looking around for a new job and then this position came up, so, well, I figured that made the decision for me."

They both gawked at me as if I was speaking a little-known dialect of ancient Swahili.

"Um, couldn't you get a job as a bank teller anywhere?" Ted

said.

"I suppose… Yeah, I guess I could."

"And how did you happen to even be looking for a job in Minnesota, anyway?"

"Well, I wasn't, really. I just put some feelers out… I mean, I don't really care where I live."

"I have a question," Sam announced. "Most women your – I mean, most women would be delighted if a man they were seeing wanted to move in with her. Aren't you starting to worry… I mean, don't you want to get married?"

"Not really," I said. "I mean, I'm not planning on having any children, so I don't really see any point in it."

"You don't want kids?" Ted said, surprised. I could swear there was a bit of a crack in his usual calm, and Sam appeared downright shocked, his jaw hanging open like I'd just announced I was next in line to be the Queen of England.

"Kids are a lifetime commitment," I said seriously. "It's not like a marriage; there's no walking away from that."

"Well," Sam said, at last recovering his ability to speak, "I think we finally understand why Kathy prefers to hang out with us after hockey."

"Don't worry, Kathy," Ted said. "I promise we won't be pressuring you to move in with us or anything."

"Phew!" I said, wiping a warm hand across my still-sweaty brow. "I was worried there for a second."

"But we do want something from you," Sam said enigmatically as he stood up to hug me goodbye. "Something that will require a serious commitment on your part."

"If it involves planning a bank heist, I'm not interested," I replied.

He glared back at me. "One of these days we're going to come pick you up so you can come out with us for some real beers and you won't have to drive. There's this great place near our apartment and we usually go there on Fridays."

"Where do you live anyway, Kathy?" Ted inquired. I guess it had never come up before. I told them.

"Do you know where Delaney's is?" Sam said excitedly.

"Sure," I said, surprised to realize that I actually recognized a landmark. Although I'd been in town nearly three months by then, I still didn't know my way around very well, probably because I never went anywhere but work or home or the ice rink. "It's like a mile down the street from my place."

"We live just a few blocks from there!" he exclaimed.

"Well, whaddya know?" I marveled. "We're practically neighbors."

"Now you have no excuses," Ted threatened ominously, lowering his glasses down to the bridge of his nose and peering forbiddingly down at me. I cowered in mock intimidation.

"You will come for a beer with us," Sam said, waving his fingers at my face as if attempting to perform some sort of supernatural mind-meld. "Next Friday. Deal?"

"Deal," I agreed. It was nice having something to look forward to on a Friday night for a change.

But of course one Friday led to another, and before I knew it, that, too, was a standing engagement. Just three friends meeting for beers; nothing unusual about that. Except for the fact that social-moth me was one of them. But I admit it; I fell in with those two as splendidly as feathers fill out a peacock and without all the fuss. I had a great time hanging out with them, a great time. They were so full of youth and vitality; everything was exciting to them, from a new ale on the beer list to an old-fashioned roadster driving by; even my dull, repetitive work stories seemed to interest them. And they had stories, too, endless, joyous reams of them, as if everything that had ever happened in their short, unchanging lives was novel and fascinating and worthy of telling. And there was something in the banter between them that I enjoyed listening to and watching; it was the kind of relationship the guys I had known growing up had had with their close friends and I found it amusing and comforting somehow.

And it wasn't long before I could say, with undeniable honesty, that "my boys," as I liked to call them secretly in my mind, had become my closest friends; probably the best friends I'd had in a very long time. Soon we weren't just meeting for beers on Friday nights; sometimes it was dinner on Saturday or a movie on Sunday, and then the following summer, when we'd known each other about six months, one day it happened, the unthinkable.

"We wanted to ask you something," Ted said, one dark eye on me, the other monitoring the level of head in his glass. "Something important," he added mysteriously.

"Oh?" I answered, raising my eyebrows in dubious disbelief.

"We're serious!" Sam declared. "This could mean a big step forward in our relationship!" He winked coyly at Ted.

I looked at them appraisingly. "Your mom is right; you would make a pretty cute couple," I observed.

"Kathy!" Sam objected. "I meant our relationship," he clarified, spreading his arms as if to encompass the three of us.

"Huh," I answered, narrowing my eyes at them in mock suspicion. "What exactly did you have in mind?"

"See, you're totally giving her the wrong impression," Ted said.

"What? No – no, I'm not!" Sam added hastily. "I didn't mean – I didn't mean that!"

"Don't be scared," Ted said reassuringly to me. "He's basically harmless. Just kind of an idiot."

"Not that you aren't... I mean... not that we wouldn't be lucky to...well, you know..." Sam continued, his neck reddening.

"How deep do you think he'll get into that hole before he shuts up?" I inquired of Ted.

"But we would never... You're our friend!" Sam spluttered, flecking both Ted and I with a spray of saliva.

"Pretty deep, I think," Ted said disgustedly, wiping his cheek with his napkin. "Are you going to ask her or what?"

"Well, I'm not sure I want to, now!"

"Of course you do! You haven't stopped talking about it all week!"

"But that was before..."

" 'We should ask Kathy,' " Ted quoted. " 'Don't you think we should ask her? It would be fun, right?' "

For one crazy, wild moment I wondered if they actually were referring to the thought that had inevitably crossed my mind in the midst of this roundabout conversation. You know what thought I mean.

"Nah," I said to myself, shaking my head. "It couldn't be."

"Just ask her!" Ted prompted.

"Oh, all right," Sam said as his face gradually faded from maroon to pink. "Kathy," he began momentously, turning to face me with a pronounced aura of solemnity. "Kathy... we'd like you to go away with us for the weekend."

I hesitated a long moment before answering. They sat across

from me, watching me intently, evidently anxious for my response.

"Do you really think we're ready for that?" I said quietly at last. "I mean, first it's weekends away, then suddenly we're shacking up together. Before you know it, we're starring in our own reality TV show."

Sam began humming the theme from *Three's Company*.

Ted flicked a coaster at him; sent it bouncing hard off his wrist and onto the floor. "It's just a camping trip," he explained. "We go once or twice a year with some of the guys from Sam's work."

"There'll be beer there," Sam said hopefully. "Lots of beer!" he wheedled, nudging Ted with his elbow as if to emphasize the point.

"Hmmm…" I pretended to think. "Bunch of drunk people I don't even know? Doesn't sound like my cup of tea." They stared at me uncomprehendingly. "Pint of beer," I said, translating my metaphor into language they could understand.

"They're good guys," Ted assured me. "Not at all creepy."

"Plus we'll be there to protect you," Sam added, flexing his big bicep at me as if I should be reassured by its length and depth.

"Not that you'll need it," Ted chipped in hastily.

"You won't be the only girl," Sam asserted. "There are always at least a few at the campground."

"A very few," Ted said under his breath.

"But see, we know you can hold your beer. That's why you should come."

I mulled it over. "When and where is this camping trip?" I asked.

They told me. It was in two weeks, at a lake a couple of hours north of us.

"We guarantee you'll have a good time," Sam promised.

"What do I get if I don't?" I wondered.

"You get to smack Sam upside the head," Ted answered, demonstrating with a light whack against his friend's skull.

"I can do that anyway," I argued, responding in kind and causing Sam to exclaim "Hey!" and withdraw, sulking, to the corner of the table with his glass.

"We'll buy you a beer," Ted offered. "No, two beers," he said, emphasizing the "two."

"Way to sweeten the deal, Ted," Sam replied, rolling his eyes.

"Well," I sighed, "I suppose it would be kind of a long weekend, me here at home all by myself while the two of you are away."

"Aw!" Sam exclaimed. "You'd miss us!"

"Hmph!" I snorted contemptuously.

But I would, I realized to my unending chagrin as I listened to them regaling me with tales from prior camping trips. Although I'd begun to have dates here and there, the majority of my social life really revolved around these two young men, and sometimes I even got the feeling that a huge part of their lives revolved around me, too. Why didn't they ever seem to go out with women their own age? I almost began to wonder if they saw me as a girlfriend-substitute of some sort. Without the sex, of course.

I was still thinking about that when we met up at the pub the following week. That and the disastrous first date I'd had myself the previous evening.

"Loser," Ted was saying, shaking his head disappointedly as I described the miserable lack of chemistry between me and my co-worker's cousin, a deep, thoughtful man whom she had assured me would appeal to my sensitive side.

"I'm just not sure I have a sensitive side," I said uncomfortably, recollecting the unfortunate fellow's unfortunate monologue on the nature of romantic love. "Isn't love mostly about screwing, anyway?"

"Kathy, please!!" Sam objected. "My virgin ears!"

"Your ears are virgins?" Ted said quizzically. "That's a relief."

"Plus he was just no fun," I went on, ignoring them. "Talk about stodgy... it was like being out with somebody's invalid great-great-grandfather, only the conversation wasn't as lively."

"We've spoiled you," Sam said. "It's hard for you to hang out with anyone else now that you've experienced our awesomeness."

"Do you guys ever date?" I said suddenly.

It suddenly got so quiet that a feather falling off of a pigeon's butt would have broken the silence.

"Oh sure," Sam said hurriedly into the void. "We go cruising for chicks all the time. Ted's a great wing man."

"I thought you were the wing man," Ted replied.

"No, you're the wing man. And the straight man. I'm what you would call the main man."

"That explains all the empty space in your little black book."

"Hey, I get around!" Sam exclaimed. "You're just never around to see the bevy of beauties I'm always bringing home."

"But we live in the same apartment," Ted countered.

"So you two don't date much either, I take it?" I interjected.

There was another long, silent pause. "It's been a while," Ted admitted. "My last relationship experience... didn't end so well."

"You were too good for her," Sam snarled defensively. Ted shrugged. "You were. She was nothing but a... but a hoochie-mama!"

"A hoochie-mama?" Ted repeated, frowning. "What century are you living in, Sam?"

"I am living in a century in which girls like that stay away from my friends," he huffed.

"Sam's last girlfriend wasn't exactly a shining example of womanhood, either," Ted confided to me.

"She sure wasn't," Sam agreed. "Good-looking but cold, real cold at the core. Our kitchen table treats me with more affection than she ever did. She didn't even blink when I finally broke up with her."

"Ten years later," Ted muttered.

"You were together ten years?" I said, astounded.

"That's not so long," Sam said, shrugging as if all men in their twenties had had relationships that had lasted a decade.

"It is to me," I insisted. "I've never had a relationship that lasted more than a year."

"That's funny," Ted said. "I've never had one that lasted less than a year."

"Huh," I said wonderingly. "You guys are all like, good at commitment and stuff." It certainly wasn't one of my particular skills, and not one I was sure I was all that interested in honing, either.

"Especially Sam," Ted answered. "He's a one-woman man."

I shuttled my eyes back and forth between the two of them. Ted was gazing at Sam, who stared unabashedly back at him and then glanced back at me.

"That's right," he said vehemently, coloring only slightly, as if uncertain whether to be proud or defensive in light of this unexpected revelation. "I've only been with one woman. We were high school sweethearts, you know."

"When did you break up?" I inquired, thinking that he seemed awfully uninterested in dating for a twenty-six-year-old man who'd only had one girlfriend.

"I dunno...eight or nine months ago," Sam replied.

"Not long before we met you," Ted clarified.

"And you haven't found anyone new, I take it?" I said.

"Nah... nah," he said. "Girls my age, you know, they're just so immature. They don't even want to think about settling down yet."

I stared at him for a moment in stunned disbelief. That settled it; I simply didn't understand the younger generation.

"How about you, Ted?" I continued at last.

He shrugged. "Haven't met anyone who interests me lately."

"Sorry, guys," I said. "I don't really have any girlfriends I can set you up with."

"Don't worry about it," Ted replied. "We're in no hurry."

"Someone's bound to come along someday," Sam agreed.

"Well," I said seriously. "At least we have each other."

"See, you're totally sensitive," Sam said, grinning. "From time to time."

"And on that charming observation..." Ted intervened, "Let's have a toast. Here's to the three of us."

"To the three of us," Sam and I agreed.

We clinked.

CHAPTER 2

As it turned out, the camping trip actually was a pretty good time. It was a lazy weekend spent lounging on the beach and paddling around the lake and sitting about the campfire while the men cooked and I took charge of handing out beers. It was, in fact, a good group of guys, as I should have known it would be. I really appreciated the fact that no one treated me any differently because I was a girl, if you know what I mean. I understand that men are just trying to be polite when they do things like apologize for farting or swearing in front of you, but I think it's silly. Really, we women aren't that delicate, and you'd have to come up with some amazingly rancid gas or creative cursing to offend me in a noteworthy fashion. And I know they mean well when they offer to help you carry your luggage or your groceries, but personally, I don't like it much; it's as if they think I can't take care of my own crap. I, who had moved single-handedly in and out of more apartments in fifteen years than most people occupy in a lifetime. If I can manhandle a mattress in and out of the back of my pickup with my own two hands, then surely I ought to be allowed to carry a case of beer out to the car. But these guys seemed perfectly at ease with cursing freely and letting me haul coolers full of beer and ice into the shade to my heart's content. And nobody gawked or laid it on thick with cheesy compliments, either, as men sometimes seem to feel the need to do with women, even ones they aren't trying to get into bed. Nobody except for Sam, that is.

"You really look lovely today, Kathy," he said sincerely when I emerged from my tent in a simple sundress, looking, perhaps, more feminine than I usually did when I was bundled up in my bulky winter jacket or my enormous chest pads.

"Uh, thank you," I answered, startled but not displeased by the compliment.

"Hey, Ted," he called over his shoulder, "Doesn't Kathy look nice today?"

Ted let go of the bundle of firewood he'd been rearranging and stood up to glance at me.

"You look very nice," he replied, then bent again to his chore.

"What does Ted know?" Sam said in exasperation. "Trust me, you look good."

Just as I was about to make a smart remark asking whether he was flirting with me, he got up to join his friends in a game of washoes and didn't mention it again. But for the rest of the summer I did notice that he looked at me a little differently when I was more scantily clad in a skirt or a dress, and maybe I was a little surprised to realize that he was aware that besides being a friend, I was also a woman, and a not unattractive one, at that. Not that I thought anything of it, of course. You don't suddenly become immune to the charms of the opposite sex just because the charmer happens to be your pal, after all. But that doesn't mean you plan on making anything of it, either. I guess mostly it struck me as odd because of the age difference. Friends or not, I wouldn't have expected even cursory admiration from a man who was so much younger than me. I did find it reassuring, though, particularly considering that I wasn't exactly burning up the romantic scene. Maybe I even found it so reassuring that I started putting a little extra effort into dressing things up a bit. I frequently found myself choosing skirts that were cut an inch or two shorter and tops an inch or two lower when I went out with them. I couldn't help myself; it was flattering to watch Sam's eyes tripping delicately over my body in that appraising way before settling themselves again firmly on my face, as if he'd snapped himself out of a pleasant but fleeting daydream.

But if Sam could be beguiled by thighs and cleavage, Ted appeared as immune to such shallow physical qualities as ever; never once did I catch him glancing at my bared flesh the way Sam did, not at mine, nor, as far as I could determine, at anyone else's.

"Oooh, look at her, Ted," I'd say, pointing out a particularly fine specimen perched on the nearest barstool, her shapely figure encased in a dress that emphasized each one of her well-rounded curves.

"Eh," he'd shrug. "She's trying too hard. I mean, really, does anyone need that much makeup?"

And I'd brush my hand against my own perpetually unpainted face and wonder if he'd given me a backhanded compliment after all.

But these changes in our friendship were subtle, at best. The overriding difference was really the comfort level we began to develop with one another, which expressed itself in a myriad of ways. The way we lounged together on their sofa, watching a movie, Sam with his arm extended around me while I crooked my elbow through Ted's. The stories I relayed to them of my unending dating woes while they clucked sympathetically and threatened any man who treated me shabbily. The way we crammed all together at our bar around a table built for two, our knees and elbows overlapping one another's like spokes on a bicycle wheel. The tales they told, of their families and their childhoods; their lost loves and faded dreams. Although I was sure there were secrets they didn't share with me, I would have been hard-pressed to guess what they were. Indeed, as time went on, I began to feel almost as if the lifelong friendship they'd had with one other had itself expanded to include me; as if they'd allowed me into their own cozy circle and made me a part of the bond that was Sam and Ted.

So early that fall, when the next camping trip rolled around, they didn't even have to ask me if I wanted to go.

"You're free that weekend, aren't you?" Sam inquired anxiously, consulting the calendar on his phone.

"For you guys?" I said with affection. "Of course."

"Good," he answered. "It wouldn't be the same without you. Right, Ted?"

"Right," Ted agreed.

They were right. It wouldn't have been the same without me. And after it was over, none of us would ever be the same, either.

CHAPTER 3

"Ew!!" I howled, crossing to my tent and finding, by the faint firelight and strong stench, that someone else's vomit was spewed all over the front flap. "Who puked on my tent?" I yelled to the campground at large and got no answer. Admittedly, I wasn't too surprised. The puker was probably passed out already and was unlikely to 'fess up even if he wasn't.

"What's the matter, Kathy?" Sam said, unzipping the flap of the tent he shared with Ted and poking his head out in alarm.

"Somebody barfed all over my tent!" I grumbled. He slipped on a pair of flip-flops and stumbled out to investigate.

"Aw, man, they got you good!" he said, laughing.

"I'm so glad you're amused," I answered icily. "Perhaps you'd like to sleep in the puke house?"

"Noooo, no thank you! But hey, you know, since you're hard up and all, you can come and sleep with us if you want. Wait, I totally didn't mean it like that!" I'd shot him my frostiest stare. Although I wasn't quite what you'd call hard up yet, I hadn't had any masculine companionship of the naked kind in over a year, and I was really starting to feel the pinch of not being pinched. Secretly I liked to blame Sam and Ted. They made lousy wing men for a single girl.

"Seriously, I'm sure Ted won't mind if you stay with us. We've got plenty of room. You'd better watch out for Ted, though; sleeping outdoors makes him frisky. Man, I can't tell you how many times I've woken up to find him crawling into my sleeping bag looking for a little action."

"Don't you know that mesh isn't soundproof, dumbass?" I heard Ted call out, perfectly audible from within their tent.

"Don't worry about him," Sam assured me. "He gets cranky when I've been away too long."

"Kathy, why don't you come and sleep with me and put Sam in the puke-tent where he belongs?"

"Oh-ho, you'd like that, wouldn't you?" he yelled to Ted before turning back to me. "He's trying to get you alone, I see. Just because you're prettier and a little more feminine than I am. I'm heartbroken, I tell you." He wiped a phony tear from dry eyes and looked coyly at me from underneath his long eyelashes.

"Shut up, sweetie," I said. "Can we please just get to bed before I have to pee again?"

"Oh, sure. Just be careful where you let it go. I mean, me, I'm broadminded, but I don't know if Ted's gonna be cool with the whole golden shower thing."

I shoved him unapologetically in the direction of their tent and followed the noise of his yelping to my new lodgings for the night.

"So, now, Kathy," Sam said once we'd ducked inside the darkened canvas, "Not to put any pressure on you or anything, but which one of us would you rather sleep next to?"

"I dunno," I replied. "Which one of you is the bedwetter?"

"Funny, funny, ha ha ha. That would be Ted, of course, so I guess that means you're sleeping next to me."

"I don't think so," Ted snorted from the corner, where we could see the dim outline of his slim form. "Because then I'd have to sleep right next to you, too, and that ain't happening. Besides, Kathy's the girl, so she should sleep in the middle."

"Ted!" Sam exclaimed in mock horror, positioning himself in front of me like a shield; a knight in shining armor preparing to duel in defense of a hapless maiden. "Are you planning on attacking our sweet, innocent Kathy with vile intentions?"

"No," Ted answered evenly while I snorted my disbelief. "But I'm going to attack you if you don't shut up." He had sat up and was unzipping their sleeping bags. "I only meant that since we're going to have to share our sleeping bags, she should be in the middle so she won't get cold."

"Thanks, Ted," I replied. I slipped off my shoes and shorts, unhooked my bra, and climbed in awkwardly next to him in the darkness, trying to ignore the body heat I felt emanating from his side of the bed and being careful not to let our limbs touch. Whatever levels of intimacy we had achieved in recent months, getting into bed together was not among them. I heard the jingling of keys and zippers and knew that Sam was getting undressed, too.

"Here, take my pillow," he whispered as he lay down at the far edge of our shared blankets, shoving it towards me like a pushy waiter with a tray of cocktail weenies at a wedding.

"I'm fine without one," I fibbed.

"Just take it," he whispered urgently. "It's too firm for me anyways; I was just going to put my head on my jacket," he lied in return.

"Well, all right," I said. "Thanks, Sam,"

"You're welcome," he said earnestly. He could be almost charming when he wasn't trying to be funny. "Good night, Kathy," he said, reaching out to pat my elbow in a friendly fashion before rolling onto his side away from me. "Good night, Ted."

" 'Night, Sam," Ted replied. "Good night, Kathy," he said, a bit more softly, before also rolling over onto his side away from me.

I don't know how long that sleeping arrangement lasted, because thanks to all of the sun and beer I slept straight through the long, cool night. But when I woke up in the morning, I found that I had wrapped my arm tight around Sam, Ted had circled his tight around me, and we were nestled all together as cozy as three silver spoons in a velvet-lined drawer. Even then, I might have escaped without the idea insinuating itself into my mind except that I couldn't help but notice that Ted was holding me in a most peculiar and unexpected fashion. Just beneath the tiny beer belly that was so determinedly beginning to take hold around my waistline, his arm was stretched out, so close to my crotch that the edge of his hand brushed up against the pubic hairs that were peeking over the top of my underwear, which had become slightly disarranged while I slept. I didn't mean to do it, but I couldn't help myself; instinctively I shifted upward and that hand slipped down just barely onto my mound. That urge I knew so well bubbled up unbidden within me, as exciting as a geyser of newly tapped oil and half as controllable.

For a long time afterwards I wondered what it was that made me respond the way I did. Another woman would have withdrawn from the embrace of a friend, or would have shunned all together the touch of one man while another lay beside her. Even a rather kinky female inclined to give in to such a filthy temptation would at least have rolled away from the one into the arms of the other; could have derived her satisfaction from the naughtiness of clandestine cuddling and fondling alone. But neither of these very logical courses of action even occurred to me as I lay there squeezed between them. Instead I pulled Sam closer; pressed my breasts into his back and felt them swell in response as he stirred. And then I felt Ted's fingers twitch where they rested so near to the most enjoyable parts of my body and right then I was inexplicably overwhelmed with the desire to fuck them both back into unconsciousness.

And then Ted woke up, realized with a start where his hand lay and jerked it away, mumbling something apologetic and incomprehensible, while Sam jumped out from underneath my arm, hopped into his shorts and dashed out the door of the tent like the bed was on fire. And me? I just lay there quietly turned away from Ted while we both pretended to sleep until Sam returned, looking much more at ease and not in the least aware of how close he had come to enjoying a costarring role in the wild and wicked feminine fantasy in which I had nearly indulged. But he didn't come back to our nice warm bed, and when Ted rose soon after, they both politely left me alone to dress in private.

"Oh, hush," I whispered to my whining breasts as I nuzzled them, lonely and naked, back into their wiry cage. "Stop even thinking about it!"

But of course I didn't stop thinking about it.

We rode home in peace, though, and it was obvious from their usual free and easygoing manner that the moment I had so fiercely experienced hadn't happened for them; had probably never even entered into the most recessed parts of their subconscious minds. I was relieved. It was bad enough that I had thought it, but if they had known about it... I could only envision disaster.

Over the months that followed, I made a studied effort not to alter my behavior towards them, and this was made easier by the fact that their conduct towards me hadn't changed in the slightest. We continued to go out for beers together on Friday nights. We saw each other at hockey and hung out afterwards. We went for hikes and kicked around the dead leaves until the autumn ended, and then built mini-forts and threw snowballs at each other all through the winter. But I was conscious now, when we were cuddled up together on the couch or at the bar, of something more than a close but benign friendship, of the masculinity that now seemed to emanate from each of them like a radiant force pulling me towards them. Now I couldn't help but notice, when I peeked out of the corner of my eye at them undressing after a game, how well-built they were; Sam's big arms and broad chest, Ted's lanky sensuousness. And suddenly I didn't see them as merely boys anymore, much too young for a woman my age; they were men, two very appealing, very attractive men that I would have had a very hard time resisting, if only they'd been inclined to give me cause to attempt to resist them.

Routinely I promised myself not to think about it. And in their carefree innocence, I doubt that they ever even came close to suspecting. If once or twice one of them caught my eye trained upon areas of their bodies where I should not have been looking, they probably chalked that up merely to lack of attention on my part to where I was blankly staring. If my hugs were longer, more frequent, and more fully-frontal, they no doubt attributed that more to my ongoing singledom, my lack of romantic masculine companionship than to any unsavory desires cropping up in my straight-laced mind. I shelved away that hunger I so often felt now, the desirous greed kept so carefully in check in their presence, leaking out only in dark, devious daydreams that I pretended belonged to someone else. I could never let on, I knew. It would ruin everything. What would they think of me, if they knew what I was thinking? Likely they'd be thoroughly disgusted; maybe even repulsed to the point of forsaking me entirely. There was simply no way. It was certainly possible that the idea of being with me in that way had crossed one or both of their minds at some point in time. Maybe it wasn't even so far-fetched to think that one of them might be willing to risk our friendship in order to turn it into something more. They might consider a Kathy and Sam or a Kathy and Ted if that was what I wanted. But I had no interest in either of those combinations. I simply couldn't separate them in my mind; couldn't see myself with one without the other close by. It had to be Kathy and Sam and Ted, or nothing at all. And the idea of that, I knew, would never, ever fly.

But time flew, and before I'd even finished dusting the snowflakes off my heavy winter jacket, spring had come, and with it the dreaded annual ritual that these days usually left me as desolate and cold as a midwinter dawn: my birthday. Not only was I rapidly heading towards the downhill side of the getting older coaster, it had been years since I'd had anyone with whom I even wanted to celebrate such questionable milestones. In consequence, as with most other holidays, I'd made a practice of ignoring the event entirely, and I'd gotten pretty darn good at it, too. As it happened, that year it fell on a Friday night. Since I was happy to let this particular occasion slip by unnoticed, I didn't mention it to the guys, but arrived at their place as usual for our Friday night beers, only a little less cheerful than usual.

You can therefore imagine my very great surprise when they both sprang to the door, grinning like two mad Christmas elves, holding a vast bouquet of brightly colored balloons and a highly mysterious cylindrical package wrapped in tissue paper and tied with curled ribbons all around it.

"Happy Birthday!" they cried, releasing the balloons and permitting them to drift joyfully to the ceiling as if they'd been imprisoned far too long.

"How did you know?" I inquired, gently shaking the cold, damp present as if trying to guess what it could possibly be.

"Ted remembered," Sam burst out proudly, as if he himself were somehow responsible for his friend's recollection. "You told us last year when we all went out for my birthday, remember?"

"Not really," I admitted. Sam's last birthday was the first time I'd had a hangover in years. I didn't feel too bad about it, though. As I recalled, he hadn't gotten up at all the next day.

"We know you don't like to make a fuss," Ted assured me. "But we wanted to get you a little present. Something we hope you'll want to share with both of us."

I felt that intoxicating burbling in my loins again and for one crazy moment I almost dared to hope that my birthday wish was going to be granted after all.

"Open it," Ted said, grinning and nodding towards the cool package that was warming in my fevered hands. I managed it with only a bit of shaking.

"Why, it's a beer!" I exclaimed, poorly feigning surprise. "But what a beer!" I added, examining the bottle. It was an oak-aged Imperial Stout from a prestigious craft brewery. This was a rare and ridiculously expensive beer.

"Thanks, guys!" I said enthusiastically, internally rebuffing my surging hormones into silence while I pecked each of them on the cheek in turn. "What do you say we crack this puppy open right now?"

It was as delicious as anyone could have hoped and strong, very strong, and when we finally lumbered out into the street towards the bar, I didn't feel the slightest compunction about positioning myself cozily between my friends and locking my arms about their waists.

"You guys are the best," I said, drawing them towards me.

"Eh, we kinda like you, too," Ted conceded, eyeing me affectionately and squeezing me back ever so slightly.

"Not me!" Sam interjected. "I just put up with you for Ted's sake."

"Good. I only put up with you for Ted's sake, too," I shot back, sticking my tongue out at him.

"Oh, I'm hurt!" he cried, half-pulling away and forcing me to draw him in tighter, my breast pressing against his ribs like a cheerful ambassador from the pools of my passion.

"You know I was joking, right, Kathy? I really do like you," he added anxiously a moment later, peering at me with concern.

"I know," I said. "Being a jerk is part of your charm."

"Did you hear that, Ted? Kathy says I'm charming."

"Sure she did," Ted answered skeptically. "Dumbass."

"Speaking of asses," Sam said to me, seemingly apropos of nothing. "You're what, thirty-nine now?"

"Don't remind me," I grunted.

And with that he drew back his hand and slapped my butt hard with the flat of his palm.

"There's one!" he cried.

My internal simmer rapidly threatened to boil over and for a moment I couldn't even walk; I stood stock-still in the middle of the sidewalk while they halted beside me, staring at me curiously. And then Ted drew back his hand and whack! my other cheek was stinging delightfully in turn.

"There's two!" he shouted.

"Stop that!" I muttered unconvincingly, wondering whether they could see me blushing beneath the streetlights.

"Huh," Sam said, grabbing my hand and dragging me back along the sidewalk. "You know what I think, Ted?"

"Um, that Kathy likes being spanked?" he replied without hesitation.

"You picked up on that, too, huh?"

And before I could even mount a half-hearted protest, they had both slapped me again hard, smack in the middle of my ass.

"Does that count as one or two?" Ted inquired.

"Two, I think," Sam answered cheerfully. "Only thirty-five to go!"

"Plus one to grow on," Ted reminded him, pulling back for another strike.

"Catch me if you can!" I cried, wiggling out of their grasp and bolting down the street towards the bar while they chased me with threatening palms.

It may have been the best night I'd ever spent with them. We joked and talked and laughed and sat close together at the bar, each of them angling to get another crack at my butt every time I shifted in my seat or got up to go to the bathroom. And I don't know whether it was the stout that did it or the three beers that followed, but by the time we tumbled in a pile out onto the sidewalk I was definitely feeling tipsier than usual and said so.

"You're just punch-drunk from all the spanking," Sam replied, landing another solid one on my buttocks while my back was turned.

"That was what, nineteen?" Ted said, winding up for another pitch. "We'd better get busy; there's a long way to go."

"Did I say I was turning thirty-nine?" I said playfully, edging away from them. "I meant forty-nine."

Again we ran most of the way home until at last, landing on their doorstep, they cornered me; set me face-first against the wall and gave it to me good while I screamed and laughed.

"Twenty-eight! Twenty-nine!"

They eased up for a second and I broke free; scrambled out from between them and ran shrieking through the apartment.

"Look out!" Sam cried as I tore off my jacket and hurled it behind me like a wild animal net.

"Booby trap!" Ted yelled, tripping over the hard, flat shoes I'd smoothly slipped out of and left in my wake.

When I reached Ted's bedroom at the end of the hall, I was forced to a halt. I'd only been in here once before, when he'd wanted to show me the oil paintings that hung on his wall, and I felt vaguely as if I'd entered some very private space and wondered whether I really ought to be there. But I was cornered now, and I had no choice but to duck behind the king-sized bed and stand there waiting while they prowled menacingly around the perimeter.

One man, of course, I might have held off. But with two there was no chance.

Finally tiring of toying with me, they sprung, one on each side, throwing me laughing onto the bed. Undaunted by my half-hearted struggles, Sam sat down on the edge of the mattress and together they forced me upside-down onto his lap, my skirt riding up to my thighs and allowing a cool breeze to flush against my burning cheeks.

They took turns while I whimpered and groaned, naughtily shifting my hips so that my skirt rode up higher, exposing the lace panties already damp with my dew.

"Forty-nine, and fifty!" Sam said, releasing me at last. But I simply lay there in blissful abandon, my face pressed against his thigh, not looking at either of them except in my mind.

"Look, we wore her out!" he observed, noting my lassitude.

"You know I'm really only thirty-nine, right?"

"Guess we'll have to start over!" Ted threatened, leaning over me with palm extended.

"No!" I yelled, grabbing his hand and yanking him down onto the bed beside us. He went over laughing, and then I pushed hard against Sam and he went over, too, with me lying between them while we all panted from the exertion.

"That wore me out, too!" Sam said, lying down on his back, closing his eyes and turning his face towards me and Ted, who now lay on his side behind me.

Subtly I scooted my backside closer to Ted. I could feel his fingertips on my back and I reached around and grabbed his hand and drew his arm snugly around me, letting his hand fall either accidentally or subconsciously onto my right-hand breast.

Being too thoughtful to point out my little mishap, he didn't jerk his hand away, but rather tightened it into a fist that hovered just above the flesh of my breast. I inhaled deeply and felt his knuckles tickling my nipple.

"Comfortable?" he murmured.

"Mm-hmm," I sighed, trying and failing to keep the longing out of my tone.

Suddenly Sam's eyes popped wide open and then bulged as he saw us lying there so close together. "Hey, how come Ted gets to feel you up and I don't?" he teased.

"I'm not feeling her up!" Ted protested. But he didn't move that errant hand as I wiggled my chest more thoroughly into it.

I looked at Sam and patted the bed right beside me, indicating that he should come closer. "Are you sure you two wouldn't rather be alone?" he teased again. I didn't answer but patted the sheet again, more vigorously this time. He grinned and scootched over half a foot.

"Closer," I said, patting an area an inch in front of my thigh. He laughed and pulled in, so close to me that the hair on his legs tickled mine. He lifted his hand to my hip and dabbed at it with playful fingers.

"Close enough?" he inquired.

"Almost," I agreed. And then I took hold of his hand and planted it firmly upon my left breast.

"Whoa!" they said together. For a moment nobody moved.

Then Ted muttered into my ear, "Um, Kathy? Are you drunk?" In the excitement he'd forgotten to keep that fist going and now his palm lay flat upon my breast, which was silently begging to be clutched.

I couldn't help myself. I tilted my body and snuggled further into the hands that were touching me from before and behind.

"I don't think so," I answered tentatively, uncertain which answer was most likely to get me the action I so desperately wanted. Neither man had let go of the breast I'd given him and they both seemed to be poised there, waiting uncertainly to see what would happen next.

I looked at Sam, whose eyes were just inches from mine. His hand twitched on my tit and involuntarily my hips jerked in response, pressing against the delicious warmth of the thighs on my thighs, the belly and back on my belly and back.

"Aw, shit," he said softly.

I felt my hindside grow cool as Ted retreated behind me, but he only withdrew far enough to push me gently onto my back, where I lay snugly between them while they gazed down at me with a mix of wonder and apprehension. Their arms were still criss-crossed over my chest and I felt trapped like a full-grown butterfly in a silk cocoon, waiting to flutter beautifully into life.

I inhaled audibly and heard them breathe deeply in turn. They gazed intently at one another, as if talking without speaking, and then nodded in unison, as if they'd come to some unspoken mutual agreement. I waited.

As one man they released their hands from my breasts and began unhooking the buttons of my blouse, one starting from the top, and the other from the bottom. With bated breath I watched as they gently pulled the cloth aside, leaving me nearly bare in a hot pink brassiere that nearly matched the color rising in their cheeks. Slowly they unhooked the front clasp, and pulled the bra aside, releasing me into the wild. I moaned gratefully. For a long moment they gazed down at my naked breasts, not moving, not speaking. Then they both smiled broadly, bent their heads to my breasts, and took them into their mouths as if they'd been expecting this all along.

It was ecstasy; every bit as glorious as I'd dreamed it would be, and I watched with ardor the tongues on my tits while unseen hands crept further down my trembling torso, my shivering hips, and my shaking thighs. They sucked harder and I groaned and wiggled my hips in response as I felt a different man's fingers grasping at each edge of my panties, tugging them softly, surely away from my body while they both looked up at me with warm, tender eyes.

Eagerly I lifted my rear and my undies broke free. And all at once, I was exposed to them, these, my two closest friends, and as they smiled up at me I was no longer afraid of what this might do to our friendship, no longer worried about their disgust over my unusual desire. I let my legs fall open wider and smiled as they bent to glance down at it, my most private of parts, one of the very few sides of me they had never yet seen. And gently the fingers of two hands crept across my hips and thighs; met in the middle at the juncture of my holiest crevice, and again, as if by that unspoken mutual agreement, silently parted. They bent to my breasts with renewed vigor, and I cried out in my joy and desire and pulled them even more tightly to me. And then I felt them at last, the hands exploring my underside, the fingers slipping into my hole and stroking my clitoris and I couldn't help it; abruptly I burst into a frenzied, frantic, flailing finish while they hung on by their teeth to my still-swollen breasts and gazed up at me with a hint of amusement filling their eyes.

Slowly they withdrew; let go of my breasts and leaned back on their elbows while I waited, flushed and panting with pleasure and wondering what to do next. Ted looked over at Sam, and Sam looked over at Ted, and they nodded at one another again in silent understanding. Then Sam sat up, awkwardly shimmied my panties back up over my body, stripped down to his boxers, and again lay down beside me, blinking bemusedly at me with his long eyelashes while his hand travelled over the sheet still warm and wet with my sweat. Ted got up to turn off the light, slipped off his pants and then climbed back into bed, nuzzling my ear with his nose and saying "Good night," as if nothing out of the ordinary had happened here, and within minutes they were both fast asleep. I might have lain awake myself, and pondered what was to become of the three of us now, but I was so damned satisfied that I had no energy left for thinking, and merely lay peaceably between them, enjoying the feel of their hot breath on my skin until I too, fell serenely into sleep.

CHAPTER 4

In the morning we didn't speak of what had happened. One by one we rose to use the bathroom and then returned to bed, enjoying the coziness of lying close together against the early spring chill; the laziness of a lax Saturday morning. Ted was still behind me, still wearing a soft T-shirt that accented his fit, firm figure; his fingertips gently brushing the small of my back as if seeking and then finding a convenient place to rest. Sam lay flat on his back, his face turned towards me, his eyes shut tight in a squint that fooled no one. Very slowly, very deliberately, I reached a wandering hand down towards his crotch and then laughed out loud when he jumped.

"Whoops!" I said innocently. "Sorry, Sam, I thought you were sleeping."

"I see!" he exclaimed, flushing furiously. "Planning on taking advantage of me in my sleep, eh?"

"Well," I shrugged, "You're less annoying when you're sleeping."

"Oh, I'm hurt!" Sam said, rolling over sideways towards me and circling a sturdy arm about my waist. "Did you hear what she said to me, Ted?"

"Yes, I did. Of course, she's absolutely right; you are less annoying when you're sleeping."

Sam's mouth fell agape in a pout. "Fine," he sulked, peering slyly at me through half-open eyes. "I'll just go then."

"So long!" Ted answered, coiling his own arm about my torso while I gazed back at Sam in mute defiance.

Abruptly he began to roll but I caught him; yanked him back towards me and Ted with all of the force of my one free arm. He didn't resist very hard, but came back smiling and embracing me more tightly than ever.

"I knew you liked me best," he said.

"I didn't say that!" I protested, clasping Ted's hand across my belly tighter and turning my head to shoot him a look that indubitably indicated that I liked him, too. He gazed steadily back at me with those his deep, dark eyes, half a smile playing about his lips.

"You don't have to," Sam assured me confidently. "I can see it in your eyes. Sorry, Ted," he added as an afterthought.

"Oh, I suppose I'll get over it," Ted said bravely. "It's been nice knowing you, Kathy," he concluded, giving my side a grateful pat and making as if to roll away.

Again I grabbed the hand; brought it back around me. Ted pulled in closer; wrapped one taut leg around mine and pressed his hips forward into my posterior. Sam made a noise of protest and did the same, effectively enclosing me in the very warm middle of those very warm masculine bodies.

All at once I had morning wood pressing into both of my sides. Desire came over me so strong that I swear I had a mini-orgasm just thinking about it. I was so overcome that I didn't know what to do or where to go. I rocked back into one stiffening penis and then forward into the other one and, as if sensing my confusion, they both clutched me harder, pushing their cocks into the crack of my ass and the crevice of my groin while I writhed between them, breathless, one arm clutching at Ted behind me and the other at Sam before me. And then Ted leaned up over me and I caught a glimpse of his perpetually unruffled countenance and then of Sam's boyishly innocent face and I knew I couldn't do it; couldn't despoil the morals of these very nice young men with my filthy perversions and I jumped up and cried, "I have to pee!" and ran into the bathroom without looking back.

I stayed in the bathroom a long time. I guess I don't have to tell you what I did while I was in there. In any case, I was a great deal calmer when I emerged to find them lying on their backs on the bed, watching me expectantly from where they lay a good two feet apart. Just the right amount of room for me to sidle my way into, I couldn't help but notice. But I wasn't going to do that, I told myself determinedly, shutting my eyes before I spoke.

"Well, I'd better get going," I announced, I hoped with more determination than I felt.

"So soon?" Ted said, startled. "You don't want to stay for

breakfast?"

"Sure, sure I do," I replied. "Only I have to work today," I lied unconvincingly.

They glanced at each other, but neither of them spoke.

"Come here, Kathy," Sam said finally, patting the edge of the bed and scooting over closer to Ted so that I would have room to sit. They looked especially adorable, lying next to one another like that, still with that gap between them, a gap just big enough for one sick-minded woman.

He grasped my palm lightly, grazing my fingertips with his workingman's hands. "Are we – cool?" he said.

I softened and smiled down at him; smiled down at them both. "Of course we are!" I answered, and to prove it, I leaned down and kissed Sam squarely on the cheek, and then I leaned over him and did the same to Ted. It was, of course, merely an accident of nature, of my own physical construction that in the course of that lean my breasts fell forward, nearly into Sam's face, that one of them even brushed gently against his nose on my way forward, and more firmly against his cheek as I retreated.

He shuddered slightly and so, I confess, did I. "So I'll see you guys next week?" I said hastily as I struggled into the remainder of my clothes, more to have something to say than because I really wanted to see them the following weekend. I didn't, after all. I wanted to see them now; wanted the full view of those cocks poking unabashedly against the gaps in their boxers; cocks against a warm, fuzzy background of balls and pubic hair; against my own warm, fuzzy background or preferably, deep inside it.

"Right!" Sam rejoindered enthusiastically, jumping up off the bed to bid me goodbye. Ted followed suit.

And then, even then, it still might not have happened but for one small chance, one small act on their part that sent me reeling from their apartment and rushing headlong into a week of wonderful nasty dreams that I could not have refused to fulfill if given even the slightest of openings. Mind you, we had long been affectionate with one another. How many hundreds of times had I hugged them hello and goodbye and just because I felt like it. But I'd always embraced them one at a time, in the usual way among friends – never the two of them at once. But now, now when they took me in their arms to wish me a fond farewell, they did it together, surrounding me tightly on all sides, encompassing me with their strong limbs all the way around my body, as if they were not two men, but one. And as I stood helplessly in the midst of that sweet fulfilling embrace I suddenly knew that we – the three of us – would one day be together.

As to what they were thinking in that final moment of our purest of friendships I could not say; could not even begin to guess. Ted gazed at me with no more and no less than his usual gentle good humor; Sam, for once, made none of his customary wisecracks but merely waved happily at me as I backed through their doorway, my hair still unbrushed, my shirt half-unbuttoned, my body still aching with longing for the naked bodies it had so nearly possessed; that it so dearly still wanted to possess. That it wanted to take together, as one; even as they had embraced me together, as one.

Did I spend the week reflecting, evaluating the quirkiness, the wrongness of my lust? I'm afraid I did not. I spent it buying sexy new underwear, and a wide variety of condoms, and an opaque brassiere trimmed with satin and lace that would let my nipples poke oh-so-perkily out towards the lips of my intendeds. I conditioned my hair and moisturized my skin until they were as soft as the silk between my thighs, thighs that I anticipated Ted's bearded cheeks and Sam's tough, tender hands tingling into excitement. And hardly had I arrived upon their doorstep the following Friday, flush with anticipation, when out it all came: both the lingerie and the naked soft skin it delicately revealed and displayed.

"Pre-beer?" Sam proposed, handing me a glass before I could answer, and downing half of his before I'd swallowed my first sip.

"Thanks," I said gratefully, grabbing onto it with both hands to keep them from shaking. Awkwardly I clinked my glass against theirs and stood thoughtfully between them.

There was none of the usual banter that delightfully filled the hours that we spent together, but I knew we were all thinking the same thing. We didn't speak, but merely gazed shyly down at our beers and occasionally at each other before glancing quickly away.

I've ruined it, I thought to myself as the silence deepened and my glass grew empty. Sam and Ted were staring at the wall as if hoping that some appropriate subject for small talk between three friends who'd almost gotten naked together would be written there. I looked, too, but found nothing that would help me.

"I guess we're not feeling very talkative tonight," I said at last, swirling my final sip around in the bottom of my cup.

Ted shrugged and Sam bit his lip.

"My beer's empty," I noted, draining it. "Shall we – shall we go?" I said uncertainly, wondering if they'd rather I left them alone.

"Ka – Kathy," Sam said, stumbling over the familiar syllables of my name, "We thought we should… you know, that maybe we should…"

Oh, God, no, I thought. They want to talk about it. They want to talk about what happened. Not only am I not going to get laid, I'm about to be subjected to a lecture as to the reasons why. My lacey underthings itched and I cursed myself for wasting my time dolling myself up when apparently no one was going to try to get me naked after all.

"We should what?" I answered, irritation creeping into my voice as I glared, disappointed, at them through the empty walls of my glass.

They nodded almost imperceptibly at each other and I froze, my cup still poised in front of my face like a frosted windshield.

Ted took a step sideways and positioned himself deliberately in front of me. He took hold of my glass, pried it from my clutching fingers, and set it down on the counter. "This," he said.

And then he kissed me, tenderly but firmly, directly on the lips.

I was so surprised that I forgot to be irritated. I kissed him back, harder, then glanced over his shoulder and saw Sam beaming at us with his mouth agape.

I glanced back at Ted. He was beaming, too.

And then I smiled and spread my lips wide and stretched my tongue out into his open mouth and sucked on the tongue he gave me back while he made mmm! noises and I followed suit. And then he stepped away and Sam came up for his turn and suddenly I was no longer sorry I'd put in all that time and effort lacing myself up.

It was delicious. He wrapped one arm around my waist sideways and leaned into me, hard, forcing me backwards against the counter while he pressed his lips against mine with an ardor I hadn't experienced from a man since I'd been in my twenties myself. I could sense Ted standing there watching; the mere thought of it made me prickle all over.

At last Sam released me and stepped back and Ted pulled in closer, so that the two of them were standing squarely in front of me, one on each side. They both seemed to be studying me, so intent were their gazes, and for once I was the one to blush.

"Do you – do you want to…" Sam began and then trailed off, his eyes growing wide.

"We could…we could go into the bedroom," Ted finished, placing his hand on my arm as if to hold me steady.

I swallowed and opened my mouth to speak, but nothing came out.

"Only if you…" Sam said.

I nodded and took hold of his arm as well. His hands were shaking, too.

Ted led. Guided the two of us all the way back into his bedroom, the site of the previous week's crime. Unhurriedly he lay down on top of the blankets, fully dressed, and pulled me down after him. Sam meekly followed. I could feel his body trembling against my backside as Ted drew me into a tight embrace and another long, luscious kiss. When he finally released me, I rolled over and took Sam's mouth again with mine. For several minutes I probed him thoroughly with my drooling tongue and when I finally rolled over back towards Ted, I thought he seemed to have relaxed a bit.

Ted lay quite calmly beside me, his hand resting lightly on my hip, seeming perfectly at ease. His fingers took a few tentative steps down my thighs and warmth flooded into them. I guess it showed because he smiled meaningfully at me. I smiled back, my knees parting subtly in welcoming expectation.

I heard heavy breathing in my other ear. I turned to look and saw that Sam was hyperventilating.

"Are you all right?" I said, stroking my fingers against his chest.

"Are we going to…?" he choked, panting with the effort of speaking. "We are, aren't we?"

"We don't have to," I said uncertainly.

"We don't?"

I put on my bravest face and tried to swallow my eagerness. I felt Ted's fingers pressing into my thigh and disappointment overcame me again. I forced it down. We were friends first, after all. Even if I could pressure him into this, I wouldn't.

"Not if you don't want to," I assured him.

He swallowed and gazed thoughtfully into my eyes. Behind my back, Ted remained silent.

"But you want to, don't you?"

I shrugged away my ardor with effort. "It's not all about me," I said.

I saw him glance over my shoulder and knew he was looking at Ted.

"It's not that I don't want to," he mumbled. "I'm just... I'm just not sure I'm ready."

Ted laughed loudly behind my back, breaking the tension, and I swiveled towards him, startled.

"This is all you've talked about all week!" he roared, rolling his body forward into mine.

"What?!" I said, turning back to look at Sam. He was grinning rather sheepishly.

"Night and day," Ted confirmed, his hand abandoning my thigh and tightly circling my waist instead. "How he absolutely couldn't wait one more minute and couldn't we get you to come over sooner and did I think you'd really go through with it."

"Well, I..." Sam protested feebly, his cheeks coloring as he lapsed again into that sheepish grin.

"So the truth comes out!" I laughed.

"Hey, it's totally different now that you're actually here! I still can't believe..."

"Believe it, buddy!" I interrupted and he gaped at me, surprised by my sudden change in tone. "Now get your butt over here before I lose my temper. It's not polite to keep a woman waiting," I said severely.

"Yes, ma'am!" he said, sliding into me with all of the force and enthusiasm of mud on a California hillside. "Miss!" he hurriedly corrected himself.

"That's better!" I asserted. "Now by the time I count ten, I expect to be in bed with two very handsome and very naked young men. No more dilly-dallying!" I threatened, wagging my finger at them. "One..."

Abruptly they both jerked away from me, and I rolled onto my backside and watched as polo shirts and boxers went flying across the room like kites snapping in a spring breeze.

"Eight," I breathed, but they were already done. They rolled sideways against me where I still lay flat on my back and then snuggled up close to each side of me, their cheeks pink with excitement. I sensed the weight of their bodies pushing against me from my chest to my legs; felt the sweat forming where their skin was pressed against mine. And into each of my hips poked something hard but soft; deliciously promising and hopelessly decadent, and I gulped, uncertain whether to savor the sensation or run away from it.

Maybe I, too, had the tiniest of doubts about this.

And then Sam said softly, "Well, that's not fair. One of us is still dressed. What do you think we ought to do about that, Ted?"

He hesitated, stroking his fuzzy chin as if in thought.

"Spanking," he answered finally, abruptly rolling me over and threatening my behind with his fist.

"Hey!" I cried, feeling his hands hard on my ass.

"Get the zipper, Sam!" he yelled, and Sam leapt across me and straddled my butt like a rodeo cowboy while he worked my dress with fumbling fingers.

"You got it?" Ted whispered after a minute. I could still feel tugging across the middle of my back.

"Yeah, yeah, only… See how it's stuck here? I don't want to wreck it."

"Ooh, right," Ted answered. "Here, let me hold it here…"

At last it broke free and there was a sudden silence. My backside was bared to the ceiling and I turned my head sideways but I couldn't see them. What were they doing back there?

"Everything okay back there?" I said at last, wondering whether I should tell them to zip me up again.

"Just admiring your form, my love," Sam answered.

And then I felt fingertips on the hooks of my bra and the sudden release of straps and then hands were rolling me over, rolling me forward.

"Sit up a second," Ted whispered and without thinking I obeyed. I let them scoot my dress up over my head, release my bra straps over my shoulders and then lower me back down to the mattress.

For some moments we remained in that position, the two of them kneeling smiling before me; me smiling back at them. And then they each reached out a hand towards my panties and shimmied them awkwardly down my thighs and calves down to my ankles, and as they raked their eyes over my bared body I was overcome with a peculiar sensation. Somehow I thought I'd never felt quite so naked before. Almost as if the extra set of eyes made me twice as exposed.

I liked it.

It seemed they did, too. They knelt there grinning and looking me up and down for what felt like several minutes and then they both reached out and stroked my breasts gently with the backs of their hands almost as if afraid of touching them.

"Boobies," Sam said in a whisper.

"Boobies," I agreed, rubbing my fingers over my nipples.

They looked at one another and bent their heads to my chest and I felt again the incredible sensation of their lips on my breasts. Sam was working my nipple with his mouth open wide, as if he were trying to swallow my breast whole, while Ted was running his tongue along the tip, taking it every so often gently between his teeth and giving it a little tug, causing me to moan with pleasure.

For some minutes I held them to me, the backs of their heads clenched hard in my palms, while they nibbled and sucked and I grew more and more aroused. Finally they paused for a moment, both of them resting their chins on my chest and staring up at me with sly smiles, and that was when I said it.

"Shall we…move on?"

They turned to one another and nodded, and then stood up abruptly, leaving me lying alone on the bed and more excited than ever.

"We'll be right back," Sam assured me. He went over to the nightstand and fumbled with something in the top drawer. His back was to me, but from the way his naked ass was bobbing up and down I guessed he was putting on a condom. Ted hopped back up on the bed and knelt beside me, tenderly holding my hand and patiently watching Sam get ready. And then Sam returned and planted his feet on the floor before me, waving his hands over his rather large erection as if not quite certain what to do with it. And then he glanced at Ted, who nodded as if it were a signal, and that was when I knew that they had planned this, too, even down to the detail of who would take me first, and I laughed out loud and said, "Come here, Ted," and pulled him down beside me where I greeted him with a lush, lingering kiss. And then I spread my legs wide and said, "Come here, Sam," and as he leant over me I grabbed hold of his ass and pressed him hard into me.

"Sweet Jesus," he said softly. I was tight, very tight from the many long months of celibacy and it didn't slide in easily; oh, no, I had to fight for every inch of it.

"My God, you are so... Jesus," he said again, moaning slightly and taking my calves in his hands in order to raise my legs up higher.

Ted glanced back over his head and then turned back to me. "Is it okay?" he whispered.

I moaned in answer.

"Not... too much?" he whispered again.

I shook my head. "Just...lack of use," I said.

He nodded comprehendingly.

I gave my hips a jerk and felt cock slipping into me at last, cock filling every inch of my crevice, and with joy and relief I caught myself yelling.

"Hallelujah!" I cried.

Sam withdrew halfway and then thrust his penis into me all at once, harder. I gasped and so did he. It felt like a lot of cock. And then the thrusts were coming harder and faster and I felt balls slapping hard against my undersides and before I was even ready for it to be over he was squeezing my thighs and shuddering like he'd had an attack of the heebie-jeebies and had decided he liked it.

"Jesus," he said again, fumbling to remove the wiener-wrapper with unsteady fingers. He was breathing heavily, his mouth hanging open slightly, and I could feel his hands trembling on my thighs. For once he didn't laugh or smile, but instead looked down between my still-open legs as if it was the most serious sight he'd ever seen. And then he gave my mound a friendly little pat with his hand and nodded to Ted, who rolled his way over to the nightstand to get himself prepared.

Slowly Sam crawled over and sprawled out beside me. He cupped my breast in his hand and lay prone at my side, his eyelids half-closed. He didn't speak and his eyes, they were different now; there was something in them I couldn't quite describe or define.

And then I heard Ted saying, "Are you ready, Kathy?" and I looked up and he was standing now between my legs, poised as if to make a dive, and I recalled with sudden delight that however quick the first round had been, I was guaranteed at least one more and I was so thrilled that I hollered out "YES!" and threw my legs wide with such vigor that Ted laughed and Sam snapped back into wakefulness.

"Oh dear God," I said as he pressed his penis into me, much

more smoothly this time, and then held it inside me, letting me absorb the feel of every precious inch of it. Then he withdrew and I said "Oh!" disappointedly and he smiled and put it back in. And then he closed his eyes halfway and proceeded to rock me with a slow but steady rhythm. In – out – in – out, without speeding up or slowing down, and somehow the regularity of it excited me further. I couldn't believe it; I thought I could feel myself coming close to a peak and as he slid his cock back and forth inside of me, I turned to look at Sam. I was breathing heavily and my mouth was hanging open and he understood at once. He slid his hand the length of my chest and torso and came to rest with two fingers on my clit.

"Now, Ted!" he called out, and Ted began pounding furiously at me while Sam rubbed me in oh, just the right spot, and watching them I suddenly cried out in pure ecstasy because I was coming, joyfully, gleefully coming while Ted stiffened inside of me and then fell, at last, hard and sweaty onto my chest as if utterly drained.

Sam half-lifted himself up on my other side and for some time we lay all together like that, in a wet, breathless bundle while I stared happily at the ceiling and felt the coolness growing between my legs as my juices evaporated. And then I felt thirsty and I remembered to my great joy that it was Friday night and I suddenly sat up, sending Ted sprawling overboard.

"Who wants a beer?" I cried eagerly.

Their faces lit up like a laser light show. "I do! I do!" they hollered back, and before you could count ten we were struggling our sticky bodies back into our clothes and heading out into the warm evening air.

CHAPTER 5

I know what you're thinking. You're thinking, okay, this is where it finally gets weird; where the three of us acknowledge of strange kinkiness of what we've done and get all freaked out about it and then the friendship is ruined and we all – mainly me – live unhappily ever after in lustless, lonely solitude until the end of time.

But none of that happened. We went to Delaney's. We sat at our usual table. We drank our usual beers. We were even served by our usual waitress. We laughed and chatted as usual. In fact, as far as I could tell, absolutely nothing had changed.

Oh, there may have been a few very subtle differences, detectable only to the most astute of observers. Our server Maureen, for instance, when she came to take our order, made a telling remark.

"How many pre-beers did you guys have exactly?" she said with a smirk, flicking the latest beer list down on our table with all of the grace and precision of a professional Frisbee athlete.

We looked at one another. "One," we said, surprised by the question.

"Huh," she answered. "Then how come you look all, like, glow-y and stuff?"

"Well..." Ted said, stroking his bearded chin to cover up a smile while Sam choked on his beer and I sat silently agape, terrified of what might come out of my mouth if I tried to answer. "Well," he said again.

"Never mind," she answered, rolling her eyes skyward. "I don't think I want to know."

"Hey, would you take our picture?" Sam said suddenly, holding out his phone.

"Sam!" I objected. I was not a fan of having my picture taken, even when I wasn't all soaked with sweat and other bodily fluids.

"Aw, come on, Kathy! Look at you, you look great!" He gestured towards the mirror behind the bar and I glanced at it. He was right, and so was Maureen. The three of us were glowing.

"Besides, I want to remember this night!" He looked meaningfully at me.

"Because without the photo you might forget it?" I retorted in kind, causing him to flush from the neck up and the waitress to stare at us even more curiously. "All right," I acquiesced, "Take the picture!"

I snuggled even closer to the two of them and she snapped it, three goofy grins sitting side by side on three jubilant faces.

But apart from that, things were the same between us as they had ever been. Except that I spent the entire evening with two hands on my knees and occasionally on my thighs. And that when we got home we got naked again and didn't get dressed until late the next morning.

"Are you sure you have to go?" Sam whined, rolling over sideways to watch me pack up my things. "The least you could do is spend the day with us!"

Typical, I thought. It's not enough that I spent the night; now they want me to waste the whole day hanging around with them, too.

"I'm sure Kathy has other things to do," Ted said complacently, fetching my jacket from the hallway. Instantly my suspicions were aroused.

"Trying to get rid of me, are you?" I snapped, turning my back to him so he could zip me up. "Here's your jacket; what's your hurry?"

"Of course not," he answered smoothly. "You're welcome to stay as long as you like. That was true before, and it's true now."

It was difficult even for me to feel insecure in the face of such calm reason.

"Hmph," I answered noncommittally. "Well, I really do need to be going."

Really. I'd already lingered far too long following the post-coital act. Acts. If I wasn't careful they might start to think I liked them or something.

"So does that mean we won't see you again until Friday?" Sam said wistfully.

"I – I guess not," I answered, creasing my brows together in an attempt to shut out that disquieting thought. It had never fazed me before, going a week at a time without seeing them. Now, suddenly, waiting seven whole days for my next nookie seemed interminable, perhaps even cruel to my recently reawakened libido. "Unless…I mean, unless you want…"

"How about Tuesday?" Ted interrupted. "Tuesday's my early day and I always cook. You can come for dinner."

"Okay, then!" I answered brightly, nearly forgetting my customary leave-taking scowl.

"Yay!" Sam exclaimed, giving a little clap of excitement as if I were his favorite new show and had just been renewed for a second season.

They walked me to the door. In the foyer we halted and they came around in front of me and hugged me from each side, as they had lately been wont to do. They didn't let go until I shoved them forcibly away, which grew especially difficult when I began to feel their fresh young stalks blossoming anew against my thighs.

But I did it, and when Ted turned his face towards mine, I took the cue and kissed him, and then turned to Sam and did the same. They both gave me funny little smiles and although I couldn't see it, I was pretty sure I gave them one back.

And then I hurried out into the warm spring morning and began hungrily counting down the hours until Tuesday evening.

There seemed to be a lot of them. Hours, I mean. I should have suggested Monday, I thought irritably as I awoke in my solitary bed on Sunday morning, the bare walls of my apartment staring blankly back at me in silence. Or maybe Sam was right; maybe I should have hung out with them all day Saturday after all. I probably could have stayed over again, and now I'd be waking up with hard wieners between my legs instead of floppy pillows. I tried to thrust these thoughts aside, but since I started drooling every time I thought about thrusting, I was woefully unsuccessful. Even worse, I had a hot dog for lunch and a sausage grinder for dinner and I guess I don't have to tell you how much those magnified my aching hunger. In any case, whatever small amount of cool nonchalance I'd managed to force into my natural character had entirely evaporated before Tuesday arrived, and by the time I landed on their doorstep that evening, it had transformed into outright aggressiveness.

"Gimme," I said, shoving my hosts into the foyer with two

determined fists and dropping heartily to my knees before them.

"Whoa!" Sam exclaimed, clasping his hand to my shoulder as I pressed between them, nuzzling my head between their pantsed penises while I pawed at their zippers. "What's gotten into you today?"

"Hungry!" I said, working my hands through to their underwear and coming to the far more satisfying layer of only half-clothed cock.

I glanced up and saw them looking bemusedly at one another.

"Dinner's almost ready," Ted suggested drily. "If you'd rather wait."

"Hush up, Ted!" Sam answered hastily. "Don't deny the lady!"

I'd gotten both of their pants off – one-handed, mind, which, if you ask me, was a true testament to the depth and determination of my desire – and they were both now standing half-naked before me, their briefs and trousers lying in clumps about their ankles, the sight of which, believe me, did not in any way diminish my eagerness. I was rubbing their cocks hard in my hands, running my palms over their balls, and they had both become very rapidly, very stiffly erect, and I was happy, I was so freaking happy because I couldn't wait, couldn't wait even one second more to inhale that cock.

Wait a minute.

Which cock?

And had I not been so utterly full of the desire to be utterly full of those cocks in my mouth, I think I would have just gotten up and walked away. Because I didn't see any way in heaven or hell that I was going to be able to choose who to suck off first without hurting someone's feelings, and that was the one thing I really, truly did not want to do.

It wasn't as if I particularly cared. I just wanted to feel their penises down my throat and it didn't matter to me in what order that happened. But after the events of the previous weekend, which had seemed so well planned out, it occurred to me that they just might.

And so there I was, my knees dug into the plush carpet, confronted with two very attractive cocks wiggling rock solid right in front of my face and suddenly I found myself paralyzed with apprehension. How was I going to do this?

I looked from one to the other and then back again. Both seemed to be eyeing me hopefully. But still I didn't move; just knelt there with my hands clasping hold of each of them as if afraid to let go.

"Kathy," someone said, but I was too wrapped up in my own thoughts to speak. Without thinking I gave each of their penises a shake by way of response.

"Kathy," someone said again, more gently this time. I glanced up at them, my two closest friends, more naked than I had ever expected to see them, and wondered how I was going to get out of this gracefully.

"We don't have to do this," Ted said, gazing affectionately down at me and tucking a lock of loose hair behind my ear.

"Really, it's okay," Sam agreed.

"You don't want to?" I squealed, squeezing their penises again in my anxiety and causing them instantly to stiffen further.

"Are you sure you do?" Sam replied.

I nodded my head vigorously.

"Then…you know…" He gestured vaguely with his hands in the direction of their cocks but still I didn't take them in.

"See, here's the thing, Kathy," Ted said, resting his hand on the back of my head and stroking it gently. "You say you want to, but since you haven't moved in a good two, three minutes now, we're starting to wonder if you really do."

He made a move like he was about to back slowly away and I panicked. I had to say it if I didn't want to lose my chance.

"I can't decide," I whispered at last.

"What was that?" they said together.

My throat was dry. I could be swallowing something warm and wet by now if I could just get my shit together, I thought absurdly, leaning forward until the smell of cock was so strong I could almost taste it in my empty mouth.

I cleared my throat and croaked the words out. "I can't choose."

"If you're not ready…" Ted said again.

"I am! I am," I assured them. "See, I just don't know who to… to do first," I said at last, bowing my head in my disgrace.

"Huh," Sam said after a moment. He turned to look at Ted in unspoken consultation. "Well, I've never actually been in this situation before," he said as I ran my thumbs over their heads. "But couldn't you just kind of, you know, switch off?"

Their cocks were still throbbing in my hands and again I was nearly overpowered by the urge to swallow them both. So much so that I began to wonder if maybe I should give it a try in spite of the obvious physical limitations.

"She still has to start somewhere, though…" Ted said thoughtfully, finally comprehending my quandary.

"Oh, so that's what it is!" Sam exclaimed. "You don't want to choose, I get it now." He snapped his fingers, causing his penis to jerk in my palm. "Well, we can fix that."

He turned away, and for a brief second I crazily imagined he was taking his own wiener off the table, solving my dilemma with a stunning generosity of spirit. But then he had crossed the room and turned off the light and my world made sense again.

"So what do we do now?" Ted whispered into the darkness. "Spin her around until she's dizzy and doesn't know who's who?"

"I was thinking more like Musical Cocks," Sam answered. There was dead silence, and I could imagine Ted staring at him as incredulously as I was.

"You know, like Musical Chairs?" he continued into the void left by our speechlessness. "When the music stops, whoever is in front of you… Well, you know!"

I did know. I just didn't believe.

"Huh," Ted said skeptically. "You know, the party games I remember were a little tamer. We stuck to the classics, like Spin the Bottle."

"That'll work, too," Sam replied.

I heard a thunking sound and knew that Ted had smacked him.

Suddenly I got a visual. Sam circling around me with his musical cock while Ted spun his bottle. I collapsed so hard into giggles that I nearly lost my grip on their dicks.

"Now look what you made her do!" Ted reproached his partner.

"Me?! It was your Spin-the-Bottle crack that got her going!"

I giggled harder. I guess it was funny because they started laughing, too. Before I knew it we were all three of us rolling around on the floor, laughing, and then I tumbled sideways and found myself face-to-face with someone's penis.

"Hello, what's this?" I said innocently, giving it a little tug with my fist. "Is that a cock? I think it is!"

I licked it and its owner shuddered in response.

"I think we have a wiener," someone whispered from behind my head.

"Shut up, dumbass," someone whispered back, shuddering again as I drew his head hard between my lips. I felt hands on the back of my head and something thrilled inside me. I wanted to feel them pulling me forward, pushing him forward, filling my face with a jerk of his cock, a thrust of his pelvis.

Gimme, I thought again, and swallowed it so hard that it tickled my throat.

He let out such a high-pitched moan that for a second I thought I'd pinched some balls in my enthusiasm but no, he was grasping my head just the tiniest bit harder, drawing me oh-so-gently into him, so delicate, so polite, and I? I inhaled it again all the way down to the shaft.

He shook. I got a rhythm going now: suck, release, suck, release, and as I felt his hips moving beneath my lips it made me feel in a strange way as if I, too, were being fucked; as if there was something in his jerking and thrusting for me after all. And suddenly I understood why my days of desperation had culminated in this, rather than intercourse; why to suck their dicks had been my overwhelming desire. Because a kiss is never just a kiss. Only in this way could I swallow them whole.

Another pair of hands had settled themselves on my back and it spurred me on, somehow, to greater depth and speed, and I felt him moaning and then gasping beneath me and then he said "Here it comes!" and in a flash all of the politeness, all of the reserve was gone and he plunged his whole cock deep into my gullet and held it there while I ran my tongue over its base and felt a slow and seemingly interminable trickle of juice dripping warm down my throat.

For what seemed several minutes he didn't move; merely ran his hands through my hair with trembling fingers while I pulled away from him, releasing his cock through my lips and then taking it in again, licking the remnants of his cum from the tip and curves of his head. At long last he lay back and relaxed with a loud, blissful sigh.

"That was amazing," Sam whispered. He still had his fingers on my back and they were trembling, too. "To watch, I mean."

"It's dark in here," I objected.

"I could see a little bit," he assured me. "Your head moving and Ted's... It was amazing, trust me."

I thought I understood what he meant. Even in the darkness I could sense his mouth hanging agape.

I pivoted my body around to face him. He was still kneeling behind me, still obviously erect, as I could tell from the protruding probe poking my belly.

"Do you want to...?" I said.

"I don't want to wear you out," he answered eagerly, scrambling to get into position as if my offer was nearly due to expire.

"I'm fine," I assured him, gripping my jaw with my hand and stretching it sideways. I dropped down to my belly and kicked Ted in the process, who responded with a half-hearted, "Hey, lookout," and then sank peacefully back onto the floor.

"Well, at least give your jaw break, huh? Spend a minute on my, you know..."

He didn't finish the sentence but wiggled closer to me and then raised his hips so that I had a face full of balls. I stuck my tongue out tentatively and gave one a sweet, salty lick.

"Like that?" I said when he jumped.

"Oh yeah, oh yeah, just like that, only, you know, pull 'em out a little, you know what I mean?"

I did. Softly I took one whole into my mouth and gave it the most gentle of tugs, the most tender of rolls with my tongue.

"Oh, my God, Kathy," he moaned. "Oh, Ted, you gotta try this."

Ted sat up and scootched forward on his side. I could feel his chin on my shoulder.

"Try what?" he said into the blackness.

"Oh, she's got my balls, Ted. Got 'em good!"

I wasn't convinced that this was one of my special skills, but who was I to argue? I ran my tongue over the divide and licked and sucked the other one for a while. Ted hadn't moved but I enjoyed his presence by my side; it made me feel as if he was a part of this, too.

"Okay," Sam was saying, "Okay, now put it in your mouth. Please, I mean," he added hastily.

I obeyed with equal alacrity and nearly gagged on the damned thing. Strangely ashamed, I pulled back a bit. I knew his dick was at most an inch larger than Ted's, a difference that was barely even noticeable in my pussy. In my mouth, however... Well, it was a big pill to swallow.

"Careful, careful there, sweetheart, I don't want you to choke."

He was also holding my head in his hands, but back, as if restraining it. "That's it, that's it, that's a good girl." He applied just the teeniest bit of pressure against my neck and I opened my mouth wider and slid him back in again. "That's right, oh, it's perfect, just like that, just like that…"

For several seconds he was utterly silent and I wondered if something had gone horribly wrong. And then he let out an a explosive breath that sounded like a balloon popping and next thing I knew my mouth was filling with cum and I was swallowing desperately to try to keep up with the flow.

"It's all right, you can spit it out if you want to," he said.

"Ungh!" I answered, semen gurgling noisily in my throat.

"I've been saving up – I knew there was going to be a lot… Man, where did you put it all?" he said with admiration as I finally emerged, like a submarine, for a breath of fresh air.

"Good job, Kathy," Ted said, slapping my ass like a pro football player.

"Seriously, my old girlfriend… Well, I'm impressed is all."

I shrugged, trying to shake off my trembling. "Maybe I was thirsty," I joked.

"Thirsty, huh?" Ted replied, rolling me onto my back to give me a long, tongue-y kiss. I'll admit I was surprised. He didn't seem in the least bit perturbed by the taste of another man's semen on my breath. But then I wondered if it even registered with him that that was something he ought to be bothered by.

"The real question is, are you still hungry?" Sam was saying. He'd gotten up onto his knees again and was prying my panties out from underneath my skirt. Then he began to bend his face down towards my thighs. Suddenly I understood what was going to happen and I threw my legs wide.

"Uh-huh," I nodded vigorously, my knees jerking and twitching in anticipation.

He rose up again and placed steadying hands on my inner thighs. His fingers were rough and callused and they sensuously tickled my skin.

"My, my, my, Ted," he said, "I think we've found another of Kathy's soft spots."

"I thought all of her spots were soft," Ted objected.

"Oh, they are, they are, but this particular one… Oh, wait a minute, maybe I'm being selfish here."

I sighed with relief. I'd been beginning to wonder how long it was going to take before he turned his attention back to my good places.

"I mean, here I was, just going to dive in without even asking Ted. Wasn't that rude of me, Kathy?"

"Um, I guess," I answered, thinking that it wasn't half as rude as leaving me hung out to dry while they discussed it.

"Ted, is it all right with you if I be the first to give Miss Kathy a taste of oral pleasure?" he said magnanimously.

There was a lengthy pause in which Ted seemed to be considering it. I could feel Sam's fingers twitching on my thighs and I suspected he was regretting offering up the option.

"You go ahead," Ted said at last. "I think that's only fair, considering."

"Why, thank you, Ted, that's really very big of you."

"Come on, already!" I whined, hoisting my hips in order to attract attention to them.

"Oh, my, someone is getting impatient, I see," Sam said.

"That's right!" I hissed between closed teeth.

He bent his face halfway to my thighs and paused again.

"You're sure you're okay with this, Ted?"

He bowed down a little closer and I seethed internally.

"Because I don't want you to be..."

"Just do her already, will you?!" Ted exploded. "Can't you see she's dying here?" He stroked my hair reassuringly, as if I were a small, furry pet in the throes of terminal illness, and I whimpered instinctively.

"Oh, I'm so, so sorry, Kathy," Sam said, retreating from my goodies to glance up at me again. "I didn't realize..."

"Sure you didn't," I hissed again. I was quite certain by now that this whole teasing thing was all part of an act.

"Well now, without further ado..."

And without further ado he planted his face between my legs and gave my most intimate curves a going-over such as they had never experienced before. The whole thing was over in about thirty seconds and he seemed disappointed.

"What? You're done already?"

"Well, maybe if you hadn't made me wait so long...!"

"Here, let me just give it another go…"

"NO! It's still – hey! – really sensitive! Hey! Stop that!"

I yanked my body away from his.

"Aww!" he said. "I can't make you go, not even one more time?"

"Not right now!" I insisted. "Besides, aren't you supposed to be cooking?"

"The roast!" Ted cried, jumping up to run into the kitchen and tripping over his pants, which were still wrapped around his ankles. Sam jumped up to help and likewise fell over in a heap. Cursing, they both drew their trousers up to their thighs and lurched across the linoleum, resembling a pair of ill-mated scuttling crabs.

I tranquilly reassembled my garments and followed after them. They were both staring glumly down at a rather crispy-looking tri-tip and three twice-baked potatoes that appeared to have been thrice-baked.

"Ruined," Ted said sadly. "Our first home-cooked meal. Ruined."

"It's probably fine," I said, giving the roast a gentle poke. It didn't move.

He looked at me despondently.

"Let's give it a shot," I said.

He turned deliberately to the knife block and selected a weapon. Then he carved off an end-piece and tore us each off a bite. We chewed them thoughtfully. They were tough but flavorful.

"It's not terrible," he said at last, swallowing with effort. "The middle might be okay."

"It's totally fine, Ted." Sam agreed, stabbing a potato half-heartedly with his fork. "The taters don't seem too bad, either."

"I guess not," he agreed reluctantly. "I'm sorry, Kathy," he said. "I'm usually a pretty good cook."

"It was all my fault," I said. "If I hadn't insisted on appetizers…"

I smiled sideways at him and he shot me half a grin back. "Besides," I said, getting behind him and reaching around for his cock, "I like my meat crispy."

"All right, all right, break it up, you two!" Sam interjected, breaking my grasp on Ted's stiffening cock and forcibly shoving us apart like lonely hound-dogs. "Or dinner really will be ruined!"

It was the first of many such home-cooked meals I shared with the two new men in my life. But never again did Ted let sex get in the way of proper food preparation. "Okay, we've got ten minutes," he would say, consulting his pocket-timer and then jumping up like a volunteer fireman when it went off. Or Sam would tell me, "Ted needs to go first today; he has to tend the sauce." Eventually I got used to this little quirk, even when Ted abruptly withdrew to go and drain the broccoli, leaving Sam to finish for him like a tag-team wrestler given the poke. It was at times like these that I truly felt blessed that my lovers had come in a pair.

CHAPTER 6

"Oh dear God!" I moaned for the third time that day before dissolving into an incoherent cluster of shrieks and groans. Ted had squeezed my tits together and was sucking them with hard and joyful enthusiasm. His head partially blocked my view of where Sam was poised between my legs, but I could tell from his eyes that his mouth was grinning on my pussy.

He popped to the surface, leaving my clit with one last parting lick that sent me into such a spasm that Ted lost his hand- and tongueholds on my breasts and fell over backwards onto the mattress with a grunt.

"Gosh, I love making you come!" Sam exclaimed, giving himself a self-congratulatory pat on the back while Ted struggled back into position.

"Where on earth did you learn to lick pussy like that?" I sighed.

"At the fair," he answered without hesitation. "They had one of those booths where if you pay a dollar you can kiss a girl's…"

"Don't even say it," Ted cut him off.

"What?" Sam protested. "It was a great place to learn! After a while I got so good at it they only charged me fifty cents."

The nature of his training aside, it was certainly one of his more spectacular skills, as I had lately learned to my unending delight. I'd really developed a taste for that wonderful way he had of teasing me just before he went down on me; it always got me so hot and bothered I was almost ready to come before his tongue even made touchdown. I'd know well in advance when he was going to go for it, too. He'd be up by my face, sucking on my tongue or fondling my breasts or watching Ted grunting and forcing his final thrusts deep inside me and then gradually he'd let go; very casually pull free as if he merely wanted a shift in position. And then without turning away he'd slide incredibly slowly down the bed, facing me all the while, dotting my breasts and ribs with slow gentle kisses that tickled and tantalized every fiber of my horniest being. He'd linger a while on my belly, gliding down further with those tender wet kisses until he reached the top of my pubic hair, and then he'd rest his chin there for a while and gaze, smiling, up at me, rubbing his unshaven chin lightly against my own rough hairs until I giggled like a very mature but very naughty schoolgirl.

Then he'd raise up his head, just ever so slightly, and begin his very leisurely descent to the space between my legs, his eyes never leaving mine, not even when a long time later his tongue took its first tentative lick along the length of my clit, and he'd grin as if it were a game that he loved to play and always won. He'd watch my reaction while he lay into it, so very slowly and gently, and he never, ever rushed as if it was the boring salad that preceded the meal, but savored it, as if it was some specially handcrafted dessert that was only available for a limited time. And at the end when I was screaming in ecstasy he somehow never let go a second too soon or hung on a second too long, and he never seemed to mind, either, when my hips crashed into his face in my writhing pleasure. And then he'd slide languidly back up my body and lie down next to me and Ted and kiss me with lips tasting of pussy juice, still smiling into my eyes as if very proud of himself for having done a good deed.

But although Sam was the indisputable master of oral pleasure, Ted was no slouch at it, either, although his methods were very different. He liked to sneak his face into my pussy when I wasn't looking. Literally. One minute he'd be sucking my tit and rubbing my clit and the next he would have vanished without so much as a "See ya later." And of course, since I couldn't see very far with my face full of Sam's dick, I'd have no idea where he'd gone until I felt that damp pressure between my legs and spread them wide to admit him. He took it lower, too, running his tongue almost down to my asshole and then up into my vagina and then he'd tongue-fuck me with his pointed, muscular tongue so hard that if I didn't know it was him down there I would have sworn it was a man with a very small, very wet cock very gently invading my pussy.

Of course, we hadn't gotten this comfortable with one another overnight. It had been three months now since we'd started "seeing" each other, if you could call it that. I wasn't worrying very much about what we should be calling it. I was far too busy learning to appreciate the joys of having two lovers. Especially when they were both working on me at the same time, which they nearly always were. Fortunately I had more than enough good parts to keep two men busy at once. And more than enough drive to want to keep them perpetually occupied.

I can hardly describe what it was like, this unbridled excess of attention. I'd never given it much thought before, I guess, but when it came to sex, there were a lot of things two men could do easily that one was simply incapable of doing. The boob thing, for example. How many times in my life had I had to plead with my one lover to suck on my other tit for a while because it was getting jealous of the one he was on? I rarely had to do that now. Usually they tackled them together, and I'd stroke the backs of their heads, gently nudging my breasts into their open mouths, towards their darting tongues, thinking I had to be the luckiest woman in the world to be receiving such equitable treatment for both halves of my bosom. And those times when only one of my tits was being fondled or sucked, it could only mean one thing: that the other man was doing something even dirtier to some other part of my body.

Yes, we played around a lot in those first months of the three of us; took full advantage of the triangle, if you will. They took to it as if it were the most natural thing in the world, and to be frank, I wasn't terribly shy about taking whatever they wanted to throw my way. And throw they did. One minute we were nearly terrified of seeing one another naked. And it seemed a mere minute later that Sam was sitting on my face while Ted simultaneously plundered my pussy as if it were no big thing. Of course, part of that was because it never seemed right to leave someone hanging – pun intended. I mean, if Sam was doing me doggie-style then it was only natural that I was going to call Ted to come and put his dick in my mouth, wasn't it? What else was he going to do, leave it hanging there all lonely and useless? The very idea was absurd.

One might argue that all this was twice as much work on my end. Ends. Indeed, I'd guess I gave more head in the first three months with my boys than I had in the previous three years combined. On the plus side, I got really good at it. Not only did I build up more jaw stamina, but my mouth turned into a veritable sucking machine, as if I'd finally figured out what to do with that weird-looking brush attachment on my old vacuum cleaner.

And of course, I appreciated their stamina, too. Even had they not still been fairly young men, with all of the explosive sex drive that goes with that age, there were still two of them, which meant I got twice the bang for my fuck without even trying. I had never been the quickest at coming to orgasm and frankly, it took some of the pressure off when I didn't have to worry too much about my hardworking lover getting tired when I was having a slow day. Instead it was like a relay race, with each of them taking a different leg and then going all out for two minutes while I cheered him on with wildly appreciative applause. Of course, I did notice that neither of them was ever willing to give up his spot if I seemed to be getting close. They both wanted credit for the finish, I guess. I didn't really think of it that way, myself; which one of them had brought me to climax. I always considered it a joint venture. But of course there were certain moments in which one of them was sexually dominant. Like that poky fellow pressing into my thigh.

I turned my head slightly in response and Ted pushed his pelvis harder against my leg.

"Ow!" I joked. "There's a thorn in my side."

"What, again?" Sam exclaimed, his dick hanging limply in his protesting fist. "You just did it like five minutes ago!"

They'd already taken turns doing me before Sam had eaten me to my finish. Ted had actually been second to go, but true to form, he was still the first to recover.

"You know I can't help it!" he admonished, tickling my earlobe with his tongue and sending a shiver down the center of my spine.

"I never would have guessed that Ted was such a tireless lover," Sam said to me. "He seems so even-keeled. Would you ever have suspected that he was so passionate?"

"Well, you know what they say," I shrugged. "It's always the quiet ones."

"I don't know how he does it. How do you do it, Ted? Stretching? Squats? Penis lifts?"

"Just naturally gifted, I guess," he answered with a trace of a smirk.

Actually, I had a theory. I'd seen a variety of penises in my years of serial short-term monogamy and it had always seemed to me that, in general, smaller wieners functioned a little better in terms of speed of erection and recovery time. The longer ones just seemed harder to raise into action somehow. I was sure I had learned something in high school physics that would support this, but I was damned if I could remember what it was. Not that either of them was dramatically well-hung, anyway; they were both pretty close to average, as far as my experience indicated. But Ted's was definitely the shorter and skinnier of the two, and I wondered if that was the reason behind his always stunningly quick recovery time.

I flashed a glance at Sam, who was shaking his head glumly. "What?" he said. "Oh, you, too?" he said, catching the way my eyes were glinting and my knees widening. "Well, far be it from me to stand in the way of such a perfect pair…" he sighed. "Don't let me stop you. Have at it!"

Ted was already clambering over my thighs and settling himself between my legs. "Don't worry, Sam," he said kindly as he ripped open the condom wrapper. "You'll be ready to go again in no time, you'll see."

"Come here," I said to Sam, and then inhaled sharply as Ted's penis shoved its way all at once into the depths of my vagina. "C'mere," I said again, breathlessly, reaching out with a beckoning arm.

He scooted closer and lay down beside me. I turned my face towards him and pressed my eager lips against his lackluster ones, then kissed him again harder. Up above Ted raised my legs and pressed my knees together; edged his dick between my thighs and plunged into me with vigor. I gasped and let out a moan.

"Kathy!" Sam said, the beginnings of a mischievous smile playing about his lips as he slipped me his tongue. I glanced sideways at Ted and moaned again, then felt Sam's tongue in my throat and the beginnings of hardness on my opposite thigh.

"See, this is why we have such a great relationship," Sam said a few minutes later as I straddled my goodies over his now fully-erect cock. "The entertainment really can't be beat."

I couldn't tell you if Ted agreed because he'd already fallen into a deep, motionless sleep.

CHAPTER 7

Now I don't want to give the wrong impression. However much of our time together we were spending naked now, it wasn't all about the sex. At bottom we were still friends. And as our physical intimacy increased, in a strange way, our friendship grew, too. Not a week went by when I didn't learn something new about my boys. Like how nosy and inquisitive they could be while they were hanging around with their pants down waiting for it to be time to screw again.

"So why do you always wear that necklace, Kathy?" Sam inquired curiously as I reattached the clasp at the back of my neck. He wasn't exaggerating; the only time I didn't wear the pendant was when I was giving head and it got in my way.

"Oh, I don't know. I just think it's cool-looking," I said, stroking the medallion's intricate geometric design. "And I've been wearing it so long now... I feel naked without it."

"Funny, you look pretty naked even with it on," Ted replied with a grin. I smacked him gently on the chest.

"Seriously, though, I've been wearing this thing for almost twenty-five years now. Since before my mom died, even."

They knew all about my mom already. She'd passed away from cancer during my first year in college.

"Does it remind you of her?" Sam asked quietly.

"Oh, no, not really," I said. "I mean, I bought it myself when I was a teenager. I guess it's more that... Well, it's the only thing in my life that's really been consistent, you know? With all my jobs, and the places I've lived... even my mom I only knew for, what, eighteen years? I know it's silly, but it feels like a part of me. The part that stays with me even when everything around me has changed."

"Interesting chain, too," Ted said, fingering it lightly.

"Yeah, I like that twisty shape," I said. "Plus they're cheap; only five bucks at the department store. Whenever the plating starts to wear off I just buy a new one!"

He laughed. "You sound like Sam. He keeps buying the same carpenter jeans even though the back pockets always tear."

"Hey, I like that style!" Sam said defensively. "Besides, I hardly ever put anything important in those pockets, anyway."

"What's this, then?" I said, stretching my arm down to the floor and retrieving a half-slip of paper lying on the floor by his jeans. I glanced at it before realizing it was a paycheck. I wished I hadn't.

"This is how much you make?" I said, appalled.

"Well, I know it's not nearly as much as Ted," he answered defensively, jerking a shoulder in his friend's direction. "But he's college-educated."

"I'm college-educated," I reminded him. "And I don't make nearly as much as you do. And I'm eleven years older!"

"Oh," he said. "Oh!"

I sat and stared at the gut-wrenching paystub and wondered for the thousandth time what I was doing with my life.

"Well, it's not about the money, is it?" Ted said after a minute. "As long as you're doing something you love?"

I glared at him. I'd known from the start that Sam wasn't the most sensitive man on the planet, but it was rare for Ted to be so clueless.

"Except, of course, that you don't love your job," he added at once. "Right."

"I wouldn't care about the money," I said. "If I were doing something I actually wanted to do."

"So what do you want to do, Kathy?" Sam said, tossing an arm around my belly and blinking curiously at me. It was the super-busy first week of the month again and I'd gone off on another pre-sex rant about how dull and unsatisfying my job was and now, half an hour later, we were apparently picking the subject up again.

"How do you mean?" I responded, confused.

"Like, for your career," he said.

"I dunno," I answered, feeling like a high school kid getting a lecture from her guidance counselor for applying to colleges "undeclared." "Do I have to decide right now?"

"It's just not very common," Ted explained. "A woman your age, with your brains, jumping from job to job like you do."

"What's wrong with that?" I said crossly, yearning to recapture the pleasant stupor that had preceded this state of irritated wakefulness. Why were they interrupting my post-coital bliss with questions about my personal life?

"Nothing, nothing at all," Sam assured me. "Only we were wondering, you know, what you really do want to do with your life."

"When I figure it out, I'll let you know," I snapped.

I wasn't really keeping anything from them. The fact was, there was nothing in particular I really wanted to do. Not forever, anyway. Personally, I liked to blame my apathy on the Cold War. Gen-Xers like me grew up expecting the world to be blown to bits before we reached maturity, and I didn't think that gave us much incentive to plan out long, complicated lives. Sure, I was smart. There were plenty of careers I could have chosen and been successful at; I was just never interested enough in any one field in particular to focus solely on that. There were lots of subjects I found fascinating. History, geology, astronomy, anthropology. I wouldn't have minded becoming a paleontologist, except that I didn't want to spend all those years digging in the desert for bones. And at the other end of the spectrum, literature, the classics, languages. I'd always wanted to learn ancient Greek and read Homer in the original. But I wasn't enthusiastic enough about any of these areas of study to devote my whole life to just one of them. I mean, I liked doing research. I liked writing papers. I guess what I really wanted to be was a perpetual student who was free to pursue a wide variety of interests. But that was a very expensive career, and I hadn't yet found anyone who was convinced enough of my dubious brilliance to fund me in my pursuit of it.

"It's hard," Ted agreed unexpectedly with a shake of his head. "I mean, I like my job and all, but I'm not sure that it's what I want to do for the rest of my life."

Both Sam and I turned to gape at him.

"But you're, like, a high-powered executive!" I responded. He was, too. I'd found it out at his company picnic several weeks before. I could not have been more stunned when his personal secretary referred to him as Vice President. Seemingly simple Ted with his calm demeanor and underlying quirks of humor was in charge of a whole division of a multi-million dollar corporation. I mean, he'd eventually explained to me what he did: statistical data analysis of some sort. I guess I simply hadn't realized what a high-falutin' job it was. Maybe I just assumed that everyone in their late twenties was in the same position I had been, working for slightly better than minimum wage at a series of unsatisfying joe-jobs. Maybe, too, I had a mental block about envisioning Ted as a professional man. It was probably tougher to picture someone in a power tie after you'd seen them naked from a dozen different angles.

He shrugged in reply. "I like to think that someday I could do something else for a while," he said.

Sam was silent, and I suspected he knew more about this subject than I did. I didn't want to pry, but I felt I should say my piece, too. What was the benefit of age, after all, if you couldn't share your perspective with those younger than you?

"Well," I said, "Not to sound like an old lady... But, you know, there does come a point at which change gets harder. A lot harder."

"How do you mean?" Sam inquired.

"Well, it's just... Let's suppose that I decided tomorrow that I wanted to be a doctor." They looked at me curiously. "I don't, of course, but let's pretend. Would it still be possible for me to do that at nearly forty? Technically, I suppose it would. But by the time I finished my residency, I'd be what, close to fifty? What kind of career would I have, starting so late? By the time I really got into the swing of it, it'd be time to retire. Besides, you get tired of busting your ass all the time. I know when I was younger I could work three jobs and not think much of it. But now it just feels like a waste of time – as if I'm squandering what little is left of my youth. So, Ted, I guess my advice would be that if you're considering pursuing another career, don't wait too long to do it."

He nodded thoughtfully to himself and squeezed my breast by way of answer.

"Well, I absolutely love my job!" Sam interjected. "Carpentry is awesome. I get to do different things all the time, so it's never boring, and the quality of work I can turn out now is freakin' amazing."

Ted and I glanced at one another and smiled. Modesty was not one of Sam's defining characteristics. Besides, I'd seen his recent work, and he was right.

"Plus, ever since I got promoted to Lead, I get to manage projects and boss people around and stuff. It's awesome!"

"You mean people actually listen to you?" Ted sneered.

"Hey, I'm a natural leader! Tell him, Kathy, what a commanding presence I've got."

"Eh, maybe later," I said, winking at Ted.

Sam's face flushed. "Well, she's a bad example. You know what you need, young lady? Some discipline!"

He shoved me sideways and lifted a hand as if to thrash my buttocks but I simply yawned and said, "Sorry, not really in the mood."

He stared at me as if dumbstruck. "But you're always in the mood!"

"But not necessarily for that," I asserted.

"Oho!" he said, his eyes shining. "What are you in the mood for then?"

He jumped up to his knees and knelt expectantly beside me like an untrained puppy begging for table scraps from a soft-hearted master. I reached out with my hand and grabbed hold of his penis but he didn't need my help in waking; it had already gotten up on its own.

"What are you in the mood for?" I countered.

"Kathy," he said seriously, "I am in the mood to not waste one second of what's left of my youth."

Me, too, I thought as he spread my legs wide. Me, too.

CHAPTER 8

"Here it comes," Ted said gruffly, his standard warning when he was about to spray my throat with his gizz.

"Mmm!" I said. I said "mmm!" often when I had a mouth full of cock. Of course, to be fair, in that position it was tough to say much else.

I was sitting nearly in Sam's lap at the edge of the bed, my legs wrapped cross-legged around him. He had a firm grasp on two huge handfuls of my ass and was using this handhold to leverage every millimeter of his swollen cock into my deepest recesses with violent, pounding thrusts I could swear I could feel in my gut. Ted was standing beside us with one foot on the floor and one up on the bed, his penis sliding rather sloppily in and out of my mouth as I attempted to suck on it while being fucked by what felt like a very determined rocking chair. It must have worked, though, because Sam was still going full and strong when I felt Ted's dick hardening against the roof of my mouth and heard the tell-tale rumble beginning in his throat.

Sam came to a standstill; he ceased rocking his cock and held it poised, perfectly still, inside of me. They always stopped what they were doing when the other was about to finish, almost as if they didn't want to interrupt the big moment or something. Instead he tightened his hold on my upright torso, allowing me to take my hands off him and hang on to Ted's thighs instead. I yanked him towards me and filled my mouth with his dick. "Mmm!" I said again as his head tickled my palate.

"Oh, God!" he shook, thrusting his cock one, two, three times deep into my throat and finally letting it relax there while his long, loose wad slid languidly down the length of my gullet. His cum was funny like that; it never emerged in a single spurt like other men's did, but seemed rather to gush slowly over the edge of his penis, like a pot boiling over until the fire beneath it is quenched. And it never seemed to run out, either, no matter how frequently we did it. I'd had my face in his balls plenty of times by then, but I still hadn't been able to figure out where he kept it all. I was convinced there had to be a secret reservoir tucked away somewhere in the region of his taint.

Finally he withdrew, dribbling a little of his gizz down my chin as he did so and panting as if he'd just run a half-marathon.

"Mmm!" he said, echoing my sentiments as he sank like a stricken sailboat onto the mattress.

"You've got a little something on your face there," Sam said to me. He reached out with a finger to wipe it away and then stared as if amazed at the wetness gliding over his fingers.

"That's mine," I said, grabbing his hand and licking off the tip of his finger.

He gazed at me bemusedly for a moment. And then shoved me playfully but hard on the shoulders and dropped me to the bed in one quick, smooth motion.

"Come here, you," he said, lifting my legs up high and spreading my thighs wide in the air. "Let's see what you got."

I gave him what I had. And then some.

When it was over, he fell back with a sigh of deep contentment.

"God, I love your hoo-hoo," he said.

"My what?!" I answered, startled.

"Have some respect, dumbass." Ted interrupted, rousing himself from his post-orgasmic stupor. "It's called a vagina."

"Okay, but if I have to call it a vagina, I'm not sure I'm gonna want to do things to it anymore!"

"Why don't we consult the lady, then?" Ted replied.

"All right," Sam agreed. "Kathy, how would you like us to refer to your…" he gestured vaguely towards my lower half.

"My hoo-hoo, you mean?" I said innocently.

"Hoo-hoo," Ted snorted.

"Yes," Sam said, ignoring him, "What term do you prefer for it?"

"Pussy, I think," I answered. "I like pussy."

"Me, too," Sam leered, running his hand down my thigh towards the organ in question and causing Ted to toss a bedpillow at him.

"Weren't we going to discuss our problem with Kathy tonight?" Ted said as Sam ducked.

I leaned up on my elbow and turned towards them. "What problem is this?" I inquired curiously.

Sam sighed. "You remember Ed? That gigantic center on our team last year? He's getting married."

"You were wise to come to me," I nodded approvingly. "You want me to talk him out of making such a terrible mistake. Don't worry; I'll have him scared single in no time."

"No, my dear, sweet commitment-freak," Sam replied patiently. "The problem is, we have to go to his wedding."

"That is a problem," I snickered. Weddings were not my thing.

"Seriously," Sam said, shooting me his most solemn face, which was only half-comical. "It is, because it's plus one for each of us, but only one of us can take you."

"Okay," I answered, still unclear on the dilemma.

"So we have to decide who you're going to go with," he prompted. I glanced at their naked bodies clustered beside me and wondered what made them think I was even interested in choosing between them.

"We'll go, the three of us together, of course," Ted assured me. "We just have to figure out who's going to RSVP with a date."

"And who gets the first dance, and last dance, and so on."

"And what we're going to do if they seat us at different tables."

"Whoa, fellas!" I cried out. "I have the perfect solution to this problem." They looked at me expectantly. "I'll stay home and you can find some nice single girls your own age to go with you."

"Kathy!" Sam cried in horror. "You can't do that to us! It won't be any fun without you."

"We don't want to go with girls our own age," Ted said with uncharacteristic vehemence. "We want to go with you."

"But I don't even like weddings," I whined, surprised at the dramatic turn this conversation was taking.

"Aren't you always trying to convince us to fulfill our social obligations?" Ted prodded.

Inwardly I slapped myself for my good intentions. Even though I was the worst at social obligations, I did have a strong sense of propriety about them, and tried not to let others fall into my lackadaisical ways.

"He's right, you know," Sam agreed. "You're the one who convinced me to attend my work Christmas party last year."

"And you went with us to my company picnic," Ted reminded me.

"But that was different," I insisted. "I didn't have to, like, pick somebody."

Actually, I figured I'd gotten pretty lucky with social events so far. I'd just missed their tenth high-school reunion, and if there was this much fuss over a silly wedding, I couldn't imagine what a scene that would have caused.

"You're not going to hurt anyone's feelings," Ted said evenly. "And you don't have to decide right now. Just give it some thought and let us know."

No one mentioned the subject for the rest of the evening, and inwardly I hoped they'd forgotten all about it. We finished our bedtime beers and Sam got up to go to the bathroom while Ted and I settled, side by side, into bed.

I snuggled backwards up against him, as I always did, my eyes on the door, awaiting Sam's return. I felt Ted move behind me; sensed him leaning up on one elbow behind my back. I felt his lips close about my earlobe and I giggled; lately he'd taken to surprising me with such exquisite nibbles.

I turned my head sideways and he let go of my ear and looked at me. "Good night, Ted," I said sleepily.

"It's okay," he said suddenly, nodding towards the open door. "If you want to go to the wedding with Sam instead of me. I know you like him better." He gave me a weak smile, but it looked more like a grimace he'd put on in contemplation of an unpleasant truth.

"What makes you say that?" I asked, curious. With his unquenchable cheer and boisterous humor, there was no doubt that Sam had the more sparkling personality. But that didn't mean I liked him better.

"It's obvious," Ted assured me, still sporting that strange half-grin.

"Not to me," I insisted. "What gives you that impression?"

"Well, maybe you haven't noticed..." he continued, "But you always sleep facing him."

"That's what makes you think I like him better?"

He shrugged. "I suppose you might just think he's better-looking."

"Ted," I chuckled. "Ted, you're right. I do always sleep facing Sam, and it's absolutely intentional."

He bore down harder on that grin and I heard the squeak of teeth grinding together.

"But it's not because I like him better than you. It's because he's shorter than you."

He frowned at me, more intensely than usual because he wasn't wearing his glasses. "What does that have to do with it?"

"Well, you've obviously never been with anyone taller than you," I said. "And at your size, it's not surprising. But I sleep on my side. And when you're snuggling up to someone like that, you have to stick your face somewhere, right?"

"Okay," he replied, unconvinced.

"So if I turn towards you, I get a faceful of back or chest. If I face Sam, my nose is nearer to his neck. It's a heck of lot easier to find breathing space around a neck than around a chest, you know what I mean?"

He looked at me silently a moment and then broke into a smile. A real one this time.

"I guess breathing is pretty important," he conceded.

"Totally overrated," I said. "But kind of necessary."

He pulled me closer; drew my body up higher along his until my nose tucked neatly under his chin. I could feel fresh wiener nudging my vagina but I pretended not to notice. I didn't want to ruin the moment.

It was pointless, though, because a second later he did it for me.

"So who do you like better?" he asked, leaning his face forward so he could look, twinkling, into my eyes.

"Who do you like better?" I countered.

"What?!"

"Who do you like better, me or Sam?" I repeated.

"I – I don't know!" he protested. "I like you in totally different ways."

"Well, there you have it," I said, looking meaningfully at him.

"Oh, come on," he protested. "You must like one of us better than the other. Even if only by a little."

"Don't tell me what I think, buster!" I threatened, poking him in the chest with a rigid index finger. "As it so happens, what I really like best is the two of you together."

The words had come out before I understood them myself. But the instant I heard what I'd said, I knew it was true. I didn't prefer Sam to Ted or Ted to Sam. I never had. Oh, I liked them both as individuals. I enjoyed the occasional moments I spent with each of them alone. But that wasn't what was drawing me to their apartment night after night. What truly kindled my desire, what was making me crazy about them, was the way in which they came together; the way they balanced and complemented one another. Even physically, the way they offset each other so perfectly: the broad with the slim, the tall with the short, the dark with the light. Somehow each one of them was a more appealing, more complete man when the other was around. It was those men that I wanted. On their own, they were great guys. But together, they were phenomenal.

"You know what I mean?" I said.

"Nope," he answered honestly, leaning in and kissing me tenderly on the lips.

"Hey, I want some of that!" Sam said, reappearing in the doorway and leaping sideways onto the bed. I smiled at Ted and he smiled back.

"Well, maybe I do get it a little bit," he said, kissing me once more before releasing me to the arms of his friend.

In the end, we made the decision in our usual way. The boys flipped a coin and I went to the wedding with Ted. But no one who didn't know specifically that Ted was my date could possibly have guessed one way or the other, because the whole evening panned out exactly as I'd predicted. We sat together at dinner, danced in a messy group like all of the other drunkards, said our sloppy farewells, and went home in the same taxi. In fact, the only people we even knew there were from hockey, and they were so used to seeing the three of us chumming it up that they probably didn't even think twice about it. Or if they did, it didn't show. Happens all the time, right? Three's company.

But although the wedding had gone off without a hitch, it did seem to have drawn my attention to a vague discomfort that was rumbling just beneath the surface of my conscious mind. Things were all but perfect between the three of us in the bedroom, and as long as our friendship remained solidly intact, until now it hadn't occurred to me that anything else mattered. And I suppose it didn't matter very much, so long as our private lives remained private. But when we were suddenly required to relate to one another in public, when I had to appear as someone's guest or someone's date, it was no longer so simple. They couldn't just walk around with me sandwiched between them like the odd-numbered groomsmen with the last, lucky bridesmaid. So what? I scolded myself. They weren't my boyfriends. We weren't a couple, and we shouldn't have been trying to act like one.

Yet as the months passed and the frequency of my visits to their apartment increased, I found myself wondering how long we could keep our private lives from intersecting with our public ones. And before the year ended, I had my answer.

CHAPTER 9

"What are you doing for Thanksgiving?" Sam hurled at me the second I crossed the threshold to their apartment on the second Friday in November. Normally it was his body that he hurled at me the moment I entered, so naturally I was surprised by this unexpected verbal assault.

"Nothing much," I answered. "You know I'm not one for holidays."

"Well, Ted always comes to my parents' house for Thanksgiving, and this year we think you should come, too." He turned away as if the announcement alone made it a done deal.

"Whoa, whoa, wait a minute, sweetheart," I frowned, my tone bearing none of the affection implied by the term. "Did you just say you want me to come home with you for Thanksgiving?"

"That was the gist of it," he replied deliberately, as if I were being more dense than usual. "Why, is that a problem?"

I didn't know where to begin. I mean, people bring their friends home for Thanksgiving all the time, especially when they're young and unmarried. Ted was a perfect example; since his folks lived out-of-state now, he was probably a regular at Sam's house on holidays. But a man generally doesn't bring a woman home for a family get-together unless it means something. I mean, you don't bring the woman you're casually fucking home to meet your parents. Particularly not when you're fucking her in concert with the best friend you've had since adolescence.

"Well, it's just a bit odd, don't you think?" I hedged.

"Oh, no, my Mom loves company. Plus she's dying to meet you."

"She's dying to meet me?!" I squeaked, wondering what on earth Sam had said to his poor dear mother about the old-lady pervert with whom he regularly shared a bed and a lover.

"Oh, yeah, I've told her all about you," he said nonchalantly, grabbing a twenty-two from the fridge and dividing it evenly among three pint glasses. "My dad, too. And my grandpa, of course." Sam and his grandfather were very close; I frequently overheard them chatting on the phone as if they were old friends and not merely relatives. "You'll have to meet him some other time, though; he's going to be off vacationing in Hawaii with his ladyfriend this year."

I searched my mind desperately for a reasonable response and failed to find one. "What does Ted say about this?" I spluttered finally.

"Hey, Ted!" Sam hollered. "Come and talk Kathy into coming to Thanksgiving with us."

Ted emerged from the direction of the bedroom, his hair damp and his goods covered only by a bright blue towel that was threatening to slide off of his lean waist, and for a moment I forgot my social consternation and indulged in my usual dirty thoughts instead.

"Sam's mom's a really good cook," he said, shattering my sexy almost-daydream. "And his dad's a riot. You should come; it'll be fun."

Helplessly I stared back and forth between the two of them while they looked at me and then at each other, evidently utterly clueless as to why this was a big deal.

Wasn't it, though? I'd only been brought home to the meet the folks once before. Talk about natural disasters – I'd have had a better chance of escaping unscathed from a forest fire. Never again, I'd vowed. But what was the alternative? Sitting home by myself as I did every other year while my boys partied without me.

"All right!" I finally exclaimed, exasperated. "I'll come to Thanksgiving."

"Sweet!" Sam said. "By the way, don't be surprised if my mom asks you a lot of pointed, personal questions," he added casually. "She's constantly trying to figure out what's going on with my sex life and she doesn't beat around the bush much."

"So I should tell her how much you've been beating around my bush, then?" I answered innocently.

He went purple from his neck all the way up to his forehead. "Let's save that for your second meeting, okay?"

This is great, I thought. It wasn't bad enough having to spend the day with Sam's family; somehow I was also going to have to evade an interrogation at a time in my life in which I had a lot I wanted to hide.

My anxieties were made no less when Sam informed me the following week that I should plan on spending the night.

"Mom does dinner late, by the way," he whispered, scrambling back into his boxers while Ted snored gently in my other ear. Sam was funny that way; always put his underwear back on after sex, as if he were afraid of being caught naked. "She always serves promptly at six. It's about three hours to get down there and she'll want us to stay awhile after dinner and then have breakfast with the family. So bring something to sleep in."

Seeing my opportunity, I seized on it. "And with whom will I be sleeping?" I said archly.

"Oh, you needn't worry about that," he assured me. "My folks are very old-fashioned about what goes on under their roof. You'll be sleeping in the guest room, all alone. Probably crying your eyes out because you miss us so."

"Probably," I agreed, thinking that if I wasn't even going to get laid, Thanksgiving was looking worse and worse.

We drove down in Sam's car, a compact little thing that got great gas mileage but was terrible for fooling around in, especially when there were three of you, as we'd learned on the last road trip we'd taken together. (It still worked better than Ted's commuter vehicle, though – a ten-speed bicycle without even a basket up front for balance.) As usual, I gave long-legged Ted the front seat and stretched out sideways in the back, trying to keep my mind on other things. I guess it was obvious what kinds of things I was keeping my mind on because after a while I caught Sam looking bemusedly at me in the rear-view mirror.

"Somebody's horny…" he sang out.

"You're horny!" I shot back automatically before realizing it wasn't an insult.

"Not as much as you!" he countered. "Trust me, I know that look. Doesn't she have that look, Ted?"

He glanced over his shoulder at me. "That's the look, all right," he agreed.

"So now what are we going to do about that? Hmm, let me

think…" Sam mused. "You know what, what with it being Thanksgiving and all, I'm feeling pretty generous here. If you two want to get it on in the back seat, I'll keep driving."

"No way!" I responded.

"I'm surprised at you, Kathy! For some strange reason I've never thought of you as the inhibited sort…"

"It's not that," I objected. "You'll end up watching us instead of the road and we'll all die tragically on Thanksgiving." Actually, it didn't sound like such a terrible way to go. At least I'd get out of this whole parent/dinner thing.

"I will totally behave myself, I swear," Sam replied in earnest. I leaned forward and ran my hand over the bulge in his crotch.

"Watch it!" Ted yelled as he swerved suddenly, narrowly missing a semi in the next lane.

"Oh, yeah," I agreed. "There's no distracting you."

"Okay, okay, you win. How about if you just kinda, you know, take care of things on your own and we'll promise not to watch?"

"I'm not making that promise!" Ted objected, chuckling.

"Well, since I'll presumably be taking care of things on my own this evening, I don't think I need to start now," I answered petulantly. "Had I known this was going to be a no-sex excursion, I might not have come."

"Always about the sex with her," Sam said, turning to Ted.

"I feel so used," Ted replied, wiping away a phony tear.

"Oh, please," I muttered.

"It's all right, sweetie," Sam said. "We know we're irresistible."

"You know she probably never even actually liked us? It was just an act, that whole 'I want to be friends' thing."

"Hey!" I protested. "I hung out with you guys all the time before…"

"She probably had it planned out from the beginning," Ted asserted, turning back to Sam.

"Was plotting to get us into the sack from day one," Sam agreed.

"I was not! I never even thought of you guys like that, you know, until that camping trip."

Sam swerved suddenly again, forcing Ted to grab the wheel to right it.

"Whoa, whoa, whoa!" Sam said, the back of his head turning a particularly violent shade of violet. "You mean that time somebody puked on your tent and you bunked with us? You were thinking about… you were thinking about doing us way back then? That was, like, ages ago."

"Well, if you'd been quicker on the uptake, it might have happened sooner!" I snorted.

"I was thinking about it," Ted blurted out suddenly.

"When?!" Sam asked. "That night?"

He nodded. "The second you two started arguing about whether Kathy was going to come and sleep with us."

I laughed. I was touched in a strange way. "Ted!" I said, squeezing his shoulder companionably. "Turns out I'm not the only one around here with a dirty mind…"

"I was thinking about it, too," Sam ventured.

"Oh, you were not," I returned.

"Sure I was. Actually, I'm the one who puked on your tent. I figured that would force you to come and climb into bed with us."

"Are you serious?" Ted asked, appalled.

"No," Sam answered. "But I guess I should be grateful to whoever did do the spewing because apparently, that's what planted the idea into Kathy's filthy little brain."

"What would you have done?" I interrupted suddenly. "I mean, if I had made a move that night."

There was a thoughtful silence disturbed only by the whine of the wind and the road before either of them answered me.

"Freaked," Sam said finally. "I would have completely freaked." Ted and I laughed. "I'm serious; I would not have been able to handle it. When I woke up and Kathy's arm was around me, I had no idea what to do. We were such good friends, you know? It had really never occurred to me that you would even think of us that way. I swear, if you had made a move, I think I would have leapt up and run screaming down the highway in my underwear."

"That's flattering!" I answered wryly. "Besides, you practically did that anyway."

"Not me," Ted countered. "I was totally ready."

"Oh, you were not!" I retorted. "You should have seen the way you jumped when you realized you'd put your hand so close to my goodies."

"Wait, what is this?!" Sam said with wonder. "Are you saying Ted felt you up that night? Like, down below?"

"No, of course not. He'd just put his arm around me in his sleep like I did with you. And it just happened to fall right across my pubes."

"Ted, you old horn-dog!" Sam said, giggling.

"That wasn't an accident, by the way," Ted said calmly.

"Get out!!" Sam yelled.

"Nope. I saw my opportunity and I took it. Pretty smooth, if I do say so myself."

"Then why'd you back off so suddenly?" I inquired curiously, not sure if I really believed him.

"I saw Sam lying there and I lost my appetite," he said seriously.

"Hey!"

"No, not really. I just don't think I was – I wasn't ready to be that guy." He didn't clarify but we all knew what he meant.

"And now?" I said quietly, thinking I'd learned more about my boys in the last ten minutes than I had all year.

"Now? Now I guess I don't think about it much. Or at least I don't question it anymore." He paused. "This is the happiest I've ever been."

"Pull over, Sam," I said. For once he obeyed without making a smart remark. He parked on the shoulder and I climbed into the front seat between them and hugged and kissed them each in turn.

"I – I want you both to know…" I began, not quite certain what it was that I was so anxious to tell them. They both leaned intently towards me and I grew flustered; it was logistically impossible for me to look at them both at once.

"I really like you guys," I finished lamely, my eyes fixed on Sam's fuzzy dice. Without giving them a chance to answer I cleared my throat and continued, "Now we'd better get going before we're late. I want to make a good impression."

It wasn't until I'd settled myself back in the rear that I understood the implications of what I'd said. I did want to make a good impression, not just for my sake, but for theirs. It was crazy, I knew, because there was no way that what the three of us shared was ever going to turn into a real relationship and in the long haul it didn't matter what Sam's folks thought of me because I wasn't his girlfriend or his wife and never ever would be. But somehow I cared anyway.

I cared.

That was too weird to think about so I stopped.

An hour later we were pulling up to Sam's parents' place, a sprawling ranch-style house that seemed to have been accidentally dropped in the middle of an abandoned apple orchard. Bare brown branches pierced the landscape in all directions, appearing ominous and threatening against a sky heavy with clouds. They stood in stark contrast to the fresh snow blanketing the landscape, the drifts pure and white and unblemished by traffic or smog, and unseen creatures shook and rattled their branches as we crept slowly between them.

"Well, here we are," Sam said in a whisper, letting the car drift to a halt at the end of the long, winding driveway and switching off the engine.

"Here we are," Ted agreed in a hush.

We got out. The mists of my breath swirled sinisterly around me in the chill air, transforming the atmosphere into the backdrop of a bad horror movie. I swallowed. Sam turned to look at me, then reached out and cinched my wool scarf tighter about my neck.

"You ready?" he said quietly.

I shook my head.

We stood for a moment and watched the clouds creeping eerily across the sky.

"How about now?" Ted murmured, shivering slightly.

I shivered, too. Then shook my head again.

"We have to… we have to go in eventually," Sam reminded me, inching closer to my side.

"Uh-huh," Ted concurred, shivering more violently and likewise moving closer to my other side.

I looked at one, and then the other. And suddenly a picture came into my mind, an image of two penises, one on each side of my face, and I felt myself flushing. How could I…?

And then the front door burst open and a plump, gray-haired woman nearly old enough to be my grandmother came bustling out exclaiming, "Well, my word, are you three going to stand there admiring the view all afternoon? You'll catch your deaths, I do declare!"

All at once I understood where Sam got his sometimes old-fashioned turns of phrase and I smiled in spite of myself.

"You must be Kathy," she stated matter-of-factly, working her way around behind us and shoving us in a huddle towards the open door. "Very lovely to meet you; now come inside and get warm at once."

She led us resolutely into a rustic kitchen filled from floor to ceiling with the most delicious smells imaginable and then tut-tutted while she hustled us out of our coats.

"Come look who I found on the doorstep!" she hollered in the direction of the parlor, and then clasped Sam and Ted each warmly in turn.

"My boys," she murmured, holding their hands in hers while they grinned back in goofy gratification.

"Hi, Dad!" Sam said, turning to the doorway to greet a sturdy white-haired man of about seventy with a friendly, wide-open face and big hazel eyes.

"Howdy, Samuel," he boomed, reaching out to embrace his son with the still-tough, tenacious arms of a longstanding military man before turning to Ted. "Good to see you, too, Ted," he said.

"Thanks for having us," Ted nodded.

"And this must be the Kathy we've heard so much about," he said, coming over and crushing me between those massive arms as if trying to extract a confession. "Not too delicate, I see!" he joked when I failed to cry out.

"No, sir," I squeaked, my breath failing me.

"Now, now, we're all civilians here," he reprimanded me. "You can call me Ken, and please feel free to address my wife as Barbara."

Barb and Ken? Really? I thought. I came so close to chuckling that I had to bite down on my tongue to hold it back. I wondered if they'd gotten married before Barbie was invented.

"Of course, my dear," Barbara chimed in smoothly. "The Colonel and I are on a first-name basis with all of Samuel's friends." She winked slyly at her husband and he winked back.

"Thank you," I said, tasting the blood of my tongue-bite and swallowing it with effort.

"Stop that!" Barbara scolded suddenly. I froze.

She inclined her neck towards the floor, and I followed her accusing finger to the face of an ancient, weary-looking hound dog who was snuffling about the oven door as if hoping to get first dibs on the turkey inside.

"It's nearly two hours yet until dinner, and you darn well know it, Gracie," she admonished severely. "Now come and say hello to our guest."

Gracie wobbled over and began nosing around my knee. I bent over and rubbed my fingers between her ears. Her tail thumped the linoleum weakly in response.

"That's a good girl," Ken said, scratching Gracie's hindquarters affectionately.

"How you doing, Gracie?" Sam said sweetly, caressing her beneath her slobbering chin. Ted bent down and began stroking her tail, and all at once I was overcome with a sensation of déjà-vu. Maybe the boys had it, too, because suddenly they both glanced up at me and smiled. I smiled back. Then I caught Sam's mom eyeing us curiously and the grin fell from my face like the walls of a newly imploded building.

A bell rang out like a whistle and I whipped my head around, startled. Everyone else jumped to attention as if it were a call to arms.

"Time for the basting," Ken announced in a voice that shook the rafters. "Want me to get it, Barb?"

"Actually, if you don't mind… Do you think you boys can mind the kitchen while I get to know your friend?"

Sam shot me a meaningful glance and subtly crossed his fingers together as if wishing me luck.

"Sure thing, Mom," they chorused.

"Good." I stood expectantly still as she rendered instructions on the sweet potatoes and banana bread. "Would you like to take a walk with me?" she proposed at last, in a manner that suggested I had little choice in the matter.

Suddenly I had the unpleasant sensation of being on a job interview and the familiar sweat began tickling my armpits. But I hadn't landed all those jobs for nothing. My highly developed interview instincts kicked in, and I responded automatically, "Oh, yes, thank you, that would be lovely."

"Fetch our coats, would you, boys?" she commanded. They, too, obeyed without thinking, like new recruits in the face of a screaming drill sergeant, only without the panic and fear. They flew to the coat closet and returned in seconds with thick winter jackets laid over each of their arms.

"Such gentlemen they are," she observed with pleasure as her son helped her on with her coat and Ted assisted me with mine. I pretended not to notice his fingers brushing gently against my bottom as he did so.

"Careful," he whispered into my ear. "She's a tough old nut."

I turned to look at him, surprised.

"You'll be all right," he said softly, fixing my scarf about my neck. "Just don't let her intimidate you."

"Thanks for the warning," I whispered back, wondering why he'd thought it was necessary. As I turned to the door, I saw that he, too, had crossed his fingers. That was when I started to worry.

"So what do you think of it?" she demanded as soon as we stepped outside, gesturing vaguely about with her arms in reference to the land.

"It's very…uh, very quiet," I observed tactfully.

She chuckled deep in her throat. "You should have seen it when the boys were growing up! Nothing but noisy children running through the house and about the grounds. Gracie was just a pup then, too, and I think she made a greater racket than the two of them combined."

I tried to imagine it: Sam and Ted as children, full of mayhem and merriment, chasing each other through flowering fruit trees with a big dog bellowing at their heels.

She strode briskly towards the narrow snow-free stone path that wound through the orchard and I followed close beside her. "We bought this property while Ken was still in the service," she explained. "It was the perfect place for him to retire. The orchard keeps him busy and my father lives nearby. Ninety-three years old and he still drives. Can you believe that?"

"Amazing," I agreed.

"Of course, he is starting to slow down some, and his health is not what it used to be. But he's very attached to Samuel. They're quite close, you know."

"I've noticed," I said, nodding.

"And we were so fond of Ted's folks…they lived right down the road from us." I nodded again. I knew quite a bit about both of my boys' family histories by now. "We missed them terribly when they moved a few years back, but when Ted's sister had her baby, they wanted to be nearby. We still see the boys pretty often, though," she added brightly. "As inseparable as ever. We never doubted for a moment that they'd be lifelong friends. Even when Ted went away to college, we knew he'd be back and they'd end up together again."

I looked at her curiously. There was a touch of something romantic in the way she'd said that. Almost as if she thought…

"They couldn't have stayed here, of course. Boys like that, they're better off in the city, I suppose."

I grunted unintelligibly, not wanting my answer to be interpreted as either confirmation or denial. If she was in fact saying what I thought she was saying.

"The employment opportunities, I mean," she added quickly. "Not much work out here in the country."

"I suppose not," I agreed.

"And they are getting older." She laughed a tinkling little laugh, as if she were amused by something inside herself that only she could see. "They might even start to think about settling down. Not that either of them was ever a – what's the word they use for it nowadays – a player. Both very nice boys."

"Yes," I agreed again, wondering what she'd think of her very nice boys if she'd seen them ravaging my body a mere eighteen hours before.

"Although I admit that until recently I thought maybe…" she began, then shrugged away the unfinished thought as if it wasn't important enough to elucidate. "My boys seem awfully taken with you," she observed. I thought it was funny that she also referred to them as "my boys."

"They've been very kind to me," I concurred.

"It's a little surprising. How well the three of you seem to get along, I mean," she continued, glancing at me sideways with her eyes narrowed. "You're an attractive woman… One would think that… jealousies, of sorts, might spring up?"

"Oh, no," I said, suddenly feeling as if I'd been dragged down to headquarters for questioning without knowing what the charges were. "It's not like that at all. We're all very good friends. And Sam and Ted, you know, are like that," I said, holding up my two fingers squeezed tightly together.

"Well, they always were. Two peas in a pod." I felt my cheeks coloring and I gazed out over the field, trying to forget that I was now the pod into which the peas made a habit of squeezing. "My son is certainly very fond of you. But if your relationship is merely friendly, as you say…"

I unzipped my coat in an effort to let out some of the heat that was rising within me. Again I felt as if I was defending myself against charges unknown and I wondered if I should refuse to answer any more questions in the absence of counsel. Was she perhaps offended that I wasn't dating her son?

"Oh, you know," I interceded as her sentence trailed away. "Perhaps under other circumstances... and besides, the age difference... Sam's going to want a family some day, isn't he?"

"Oh, I should think so," she agreed. "He's always simply doted on children. Of course, I was about your age when we had him. How happy we were, after trying so long! It's not too late for you, either, my dear," she hinted.

"Oh, well, you know," I said with all of the confidence I could muster, which at the moment didn't seem to be much. "What will be, will be, and all that jazz."

She suddenly stopped walking. I stopped, too, one step ahead of her, then swiveled around to look back. "You don't B.S. much, do you, dear?" she said shrewdly.

"I'm not very good at it," I conceded flatly. Her eyes glinted as she looked me straight in the face. Remembering Ted's warning, I stared right back.

"What exactly is the nature of your relationship with my boys?" she said abruptly. All at once, all pretense of civility had vanished. She hit me with a stare so cutting that I felt as if I'd already spilled my guts all over the walkway and was just waiting for her to come in with those dagger-eyes for the kill.

I inhaled sharply and hoped she wouldn't notice the flush creeping into my cheeks. "H-how do you mean?" I stuttered.

"My son insists that you're not romantically involved," she snapped. "But it's rather unusual, isn't it, for a woman to spend so much time with two men and not be sleeping with either of them?"

I gaped at her. Apparently she didn't B.S. much either.

"In fact, such a situation might cause one to wonder whether the woman had somehow managed to ensnare them both."

Oh-my-god, oh-my-god, oh-my-god, I thought, panicking. She knows, she knows everything!

"Yet I find it difficult to believe that my son, who is an excellent judge of character, would speak so highly of someone who had insinuated herself between him and his closest friend," she continued, crossing her arms defensively over her chest. "And you don't seem cruel or petty enough to keep them hanging while you make up your mind."

"While I make up my mind?" I echoed.

"Which one of them you want."

I was so relieved that I laughed out loud. She stared at me quizzically.

"I'm not choosing between them," I said firmly. "Sam is telling you the truth; we're not romantically involved. It's not like that between us."

Well, it wasn't, was it? Romantic was about the last word I'd use to describe that relationship.

Abruptly her eyes left mine and gazed out over the orchard instead. She let out a faint sigh, almost as if she were disappointed, and I didn't understand it; surely she didn't want me involved with her boys?

She began walking again at a slackened pace, her shoulders hunched forward, and I lurched along beside her, wondering what to say.

"I had rather given up on ever having grandchildren," she continued after a moment, glancing around at the stark, barren trees. "I confess that until recently I rather suspected… Well, I suspected that perhaps my son was gay."

So she'd finally come out with it. I couldn't help myself. I turned to her and smiled. She smiled back, the corners of her eyes crinkling merrily.

"Ted is such a sweet boy. He would have made a wonderful in-law," she sighed.

"You couldn't do better," I agreed.

"Hard to understand how they could both still be single… they must make quite an irresistible pair to the ladies. Of course, perhaps it's just as well. As close as they are, they'd probably end up falling for the same girl and end up in a heap of trouble over it. And I'd pity the woman who'd have to pick one over the other!" She eyed me appraisingly, and I wondered if she were giving me one last chance to confess.

"I wouldn't want to have to choose between them," I answered honestly, smiling to myself.

"A wise policy," she said, laying a hand amiably on my arm as if we were old pals now. "I'm sure you've been a very good friend to them. They certainly both seem very happy and well-adjusted. I suppose the right woman will come along some day."

I was tempted to say that maybe the right woman already had come along, then decided it was a thought best kept to myself.

"Well, we'd better get back to the house," she said, pivoting on her heel on the slate as if it were a well-practiced maneuver. "The turkey will be ready soon and the table still needs setting."

We marched back in silence, our breath fogging in the cold November air and shrouding me gratefully in mist. I gazed around the dismal, lonely winter landscape and thought that this must have been a dreary place in which to grow up. And then the door to the house burst open, releasing a cloud of magnificent aromas into the yard, and Sam and Ted stood on the doorstep, waving us cheerily inside.

"Mom! Kathy!" they called. "Dinner's almost ready!"

Dinner was pleasant and the conversation bright. Listening to Sam's father, I understood at once where Sam had gotten his personality and sense of humor. Ken regaled us with one amusing anecdote after another about his life in the Army while we stuffed ourselves with Barb's delicious dishes and tried not to spit up from laughing. After Barb's earlier inquisition, I'd been worried that they'd spend a lot of time interrogating me about my life. But as it turned out, they didn't have to. They already knew all about me, it seemed.

"Don't worry, dear," Barb said reassuringly when I faltered in response to a question from her husband regarding my job. "We know you haven't quite found your niche yet."

Not only did they not seem perturbed by my lack of career, they were equally unruffled by my seeming dearth of serious relationships.

"Aw, heck," Ken said, waving away his wife's query with an impatient hand. "The girl can wait if she wants to. Besides, maybe not everyone is cut out for marriage, eh?" he said, winking slyly at me and causing me to flinch involuntarily.

"I'm sure Kathy will settle down eventually," Ted said with a smile.

"What does she need a husband for, anyway?" Sam objected. "She's got us."

But if his parents noted the oddity of that remark, they gave no sign. In fact, they chit-chatted quite merrily with the three of us as if they, too, thought of us as a couple. "So what are your plans for the

New Year?" they said, and "When will you be taking vacation next summer?" Routine questions. The kinds of questions you might ask of people you assumed made their major life plans jointly.

After dinner we retired sleepily to the living room, where Sam and Ted plopped down beside me on the couch, one on each side of me, as was their custom. I was just congratulating myself on my self-restraint in refraining from snuggling up to them, as was my custom, when Sam caught my eye. The meaning behind his expression was so apparent that I glanced quickly around to see if his folks were watching, but they were tinkering with the fire and hadn't noticed.

"Wipe that look off your face," I hissed. "You look like a pizza delivery boy at the Playboy mansion."

He chuckled. "You're coming into our room tonight, right?"

I gaped at him. I'd already been shown my sleeping quarters for the evening, a rather prettily decorated guest room with floral bedsheets, a handmade quilt, and lace curtains lining the windows. Its only serious flaw was its location, down at the far end of the hall from Sam's old room and right next to his father's study.

"How are we going to get away with that?" I said, recollecting his mother's lecture. My stomach turned over queasily merely at the thought of it.

He ignored me. He was too busy rubbing his hands together like a mad scientist who'd just invented a dangerous new potion and couldn't wait to test it out on an unsuspecting populace.

"I always wanted to sneak a girl into my room while my parents were asleep," he admitted gleefully. "And with Ted there, they'll never suspect a thing!" He cackled and suddenly I was transported back a quarter of a century to when being naughty meant making out and maybe a hint of second base. It made his plan for the evening seem filthy indeed.

"Wait half an hour," he blew the words coyly into my ear. "My parents sleep like the dead."

"Thanks for dinner, Mom and Dad," he said aloud. "We're beat; do you mind if we head off to bed?"

"Of course not, dear," his mom answered. "We'll be going soon, too."

"Reveille's at oh-four-hundred," Ken said, winking at me.

"Oh, hush, Ken. Don't you listen to him, dear, you go ahead and sleep until six if you like."

"But not a second later," Sam said. "Or you won't get breakfast!" he and Ted chorused, as if it were a household catchphrase.

"Ah, now I understand why Sam's such an early riser," I said without thinking.

The silence that fell was so deep it made the Carlsbad Caverns seem like a miniscule dent in the desert. Horrified, I cast my eyes frantically around the room. Everyone was staring at me like I'd just confessed to the Kennedy assassination.

"Sometimes Kathy uses him as a wake-up service," Ted said smoothly, coming to my rescue. "Since he has to be to work at seven."

"That's right," Sam said, catching on, "I recite limericks to her over the phone until she gets out of bed. It doesn't take long; she never seems to want to know what became of the man from Nantucket."

Barbara gazed severely at him, but the accusation had fallen from her eyes and I breathed a silent sigh of relief.

"And on that note…" Sam said, getting up and strolling over to give them both a hug. "Good night!"

He shimmied ostentatiously out of the room like it was his final performance of the evening, mumbling something sing-song fashion under his breath. I groaned and wondered how long I was going to be punished for my indiscretion with lusty limericks.

I turned to Ted, trying to convey my gratitude with my eyes.

"You're welcome," he whispered, then sprang energetically to his feet, evidently unencumbered by the pound of turkey and two pounds of pie he'd just stuffed into that flat stomach of his. "Good night," he said aloud, giving Sam's folks a little wave. "Good night, Kathy," he added meaningfully, winking at me as he disappeared down the hallway.

With a flurry of thank-yous and good-nights, I graciously made my own exit. I hurried to the guest room, grateful to have gotten out of there without incriminating myself further. I undressed slowly, mulling over Sam's invitation and listening to the faint sounds of Barb and Ken readying themselves for slumber. It was a bad idea, I scolded myself severely, trying to ignore the yearning in my loins. Here you've spent the whole day trying not to give yourself away, and now you're going to take such a terrible chance?

This is ridiculous, I thought as I tossed and turned in my own solitary bed, anxiously watching the minutes pass on the glowing analog clock on my nightstand and feeling my lust increasing with each one that ticked by. I'm a grown woman; why am I acting like a naughty teenager?

Because it's fun, a little voice from inside my head whispered back.

It can't be helped, I concluded desperately an hour later as I cautiously swept the covers aside and searched in the darkness for my robe. We'd spent practically the whole day together without doing it once. I wasn't a machine, after all. I couldn't be expected not to be aroused by such virile, attractive young men, could I? And what about them? It was almost cruel to leave them hanging like this, after all. Lying awake, all alone in their twin beds, wondering if I was coming. Probably horny, too. Maybe even almost as much as I was.

Even as a teenager I'd been very cautious, particularly when I was being naughty. I crept softly to the door and then stood there a full five minutes more, breathing heavily into the quiet before I tiptoed down the hall myself towards the room in which my men were likely already peacefully asnooze.

Suddenly something rough and furry bumped my ankle and instinctively I thought "Rat!" and had to muffle the scream that threatened to burst out of my jaw-opened mouth. But then something wet dropped onto my foot and I heard a faint wheezing and I remembered Gracie and sighed with relief.

"Shhh!" I whispered. "You don't want us to get caught, do you?"

She whacked her tail against the carpet and I assumed that meant we had her blessing.

"You stand guard, ok, sweetie?" I said, giving her a friendly scratch beneath the chin. She drooled on me in response. I took that for assent.

Carefully I creaked open their door and wiggled my way inside. For a moment I stood there with the door ajar, listening to the sound of Gracie's breathing, and then squeezed myself in and closed it silently behind me.

It was black, pitch-black, and for one horrible moment I had a terrible fear that I was in the wrong room and would shortly realize that I was about to climb into bed with Sam's father, or worse yet, his mother. But then I heard a soft voice calling "Over here!" from somewhere nearby and I turned towards it and felt my way cautiously with my foot across the carpet until my knee banged up against the edge of a short twin bed.

"Hi!" Sam said, reaching up with an arm to guide me. I took it and climbed in beside him.

"We started to think you weren't coming," he whispered. "I think Ted might have fallen asleep."

"I'm still awake," Ted called quietly from the far side of the room. "Hi, Kathy!"

"Hi, Ted!" I called back. I turned back to Sam. Although I couldn't see him in the darkness, something in his tone or his manner told me that he was smiling broadly.

"What are you grinning about?" I said.

"How did you know?" he replied, surprised.

"I don't need to be able to see you to know when you're wearing that shit-eating grin," I chuckled.

"Why shouldn't I smile?" he said seriously. "I'm here with my family and my closest friends and a beautiful woman just crawled into bed with me. What more could a man ask for? You might even say – I'm thankful."

On most days the Sam I knew would have followed that up with a wisecrack or a stupid joke. But he merely held me tighter for a long moment so I held him back and decided for once to take him at his word.

And of a sudden he pulled back and kissed me, long and hard and soft and wet all at once and I admit it, I melted as I never had into his kiss before. And somewhere in the back of my mind I wondered if maybe that was because for once no one else was watching, and I didn't have to wonder how silly I looked with my mouth open and my tongue out and my eyes all bulging because it felt so good. Then he stripped me out of my nightie and made love to me in a very slow, very quiet, very ordinary fashion, and it was so lovely that once again I wondered if that was because there was no one else watching. And writhing there beneath him, I couldn't help but think how much I still liked plain old missionary-style sex, and how great normal one-on-one nookie could be when the mood was just right. I even wondered if maybe it really would be nicer if there were only two of us; if I didn't have to worry about who was on which side and whether I was paying enough attention to each of them and how often I should jerk my head around to keep the conversation even. And for a moment I even wondered what it would be like, if I had chosen between them from the start; picked one to be my lover and one to be my friend.

I lay there quietly for a long while after it was over and enjoyed the space and the silence until I heard his breathing grow deep and heavy, and then I rolled over to look for Ted but of course he wasn't there. And I chuckled to myself because in that instant I knew that I never could have chosen; I wouldn't even have wanted to try. It would have ruined everything.

"You coming, Kathy?" I heard him call out softly and I gathered up my robe and my nightie and made my way carefully over to the other bed. And oh, they felt so good around me, too, those supple arms slung across my backside, and those lips, so different from Sam's against mine. And then he climbed inside me and made love to me in his own slow, quiet and ordinary way that was so like Sam's but entirely different, too. And after it was over I lingered there in his arms and stared at the darkness and wished that it would never grow light.

"It was worth the wait," he said at last.

I sensed him smiling at me and I smiled back, hoping he could sense it in turn. I guess he did because he pulled me closer and pressed his lips tenderly against my forehead.

"Sam always takes this bed," he remarked, chuckling. "It was his when he was a kid. But tonight he insisted on being by the door."

I laughed softly. "Was it his turn to go first?" I said.

"Nah, it was mine," he answered. "But I don't mind. Sometimes it's nicer to be second. You get more time to relax afterwards."

He lay back with his arm on my hip and I listened to the sound of him breathing until I was sure he had fallen asleep. Then I stole my way back to my own room, patting my aged canine guardian, who still sat quietly thumping her tail against the plush carpet of the hall at the door of the bedroom. And for a long while I lay awake thinking of my boys sleeping so peacefully by themselves in the room down the hall and I decided that maybe it wasn't really so bad, after all, going to your boyfriends' house for Thanksgiving. And then I wondered what kinds of questions Sam's mom might come up with the next time, and vowed never again!

CHAPTER 10

Fortunately, there was to be no return visit to Sam's parents' house for Christmas. His grandfather was still travelling, and his folks would be going to Florida for the holidays, as they did every year.

"I thought you said your parents were old-fashioned!" I objected upon hearing this news.

"My dad was stationed there before I was born," Sam explained. "And a number of their other friends have retired down there. Once a year they go down and party it up for two weeks and then come home after New Year's. One time I picked them up from the airport and I could swear that my mom had a hangover and my dad was still drunk."

"Imagine that!" I marveled. "Do you think we'll still be partying like that thirty years from now?"

"We don't party like that now," Ted pointed out. It was true. While we did drink a lot of beer, it was very rare that any one of us ended up in the drunk stage. I took this as a sign that we'd actually learned something from our past experiences with excessive intake of alcohol. I knew I had.

"Well, we're definitely going to party this Christmas!" Sam declared. "I wanna do the whole kit and caboodle this year – chestnuts roasting, stockings hanging, mistletoe…" He shot me a leer.

"You're kidding, right?" I protested, aghast at the thought of yet another festive occasion coming upon us so soon. "I haven't celebrated Christmas in twenty years!"

"You haven't?" Sam said, surprised. "How come?" Ted gave him an elbow to the chest and shot him a look that silenced him instantly.

"We know how you are about holidays, and we don't have to

LORI SCHAFER

make a big thing," Ted said, eyeing Sam as if to make certain he maintained his quietude. "But we would like to celebrate the holiday with you, even if it's only on a small scale."

I was thoughtful for a moment. "How small a scale?" I inquired.

"About eight feet oughta do it," Sam answered.

He wasn't kidding. Ten days before Christmas they brought it home, tied to the roof of the car, a tree so large that its boughs drooped halfway down Sam's windshield. I'd stayed at the apartment to mind dinner and ran outside when I heard them pulling up to find Ted leaning out the passenger-side window, shouting out directions, his tan cheeks pink with the cold.

"Now is that a tree or is that a tree?" Sam said with admiration an hour later, when they'd finally managed to get it hauled it up the stairs and installed successfully in the living room.

"I wouldn't know," I answered, catching a whiff of the unfamiliar scent. "We always had a fake tree."

"Well, fake trees are nice, too," Sam conceded. He'd been tiptoeing around the subject of Christmas ever since the day they'd first brought it up, exercising a level of discretion with which I was duly impressed.

It wasn't really a big deal, I thought. I mean, nothing bad had ever happened to me at Christmastime, and I didn't get depressed around the holidays or anything. I'd absolutely loved Christmas when I was a little girl, and I still, yes even I still got a little misty-eyed when I watched Christmas specials on television, which I made a point of doing every year. It was more that as I'd gotten bigger, the holiday had gotten smaller on me. My mom had had no living relations worth speaking of, and once my last stepfather had moved out, it had been just her and me gathering around that giant tree to open our handful of presents, which somehow didn't have a very festive ring to it. And once she was gone, that left only me to make merry. Oh, I tried, those first few years. I even bought myself one of those miniature table-top trees and hung it with blinking lights and a handful of ornaments I'd salvaged from the attic before I'd left home. But once I finished college and started moving all over the place, it seemed silly to keep packing the stupid thing over and over and trying to make room for it in my ever-diminishing apartment space, and that had been the end of Christmas as far as I was concerned.

"Well, let's get some lights on this puppy!" I said, my spirits

94

rising. It might be nice to have a tree again, at that.

"Blinkers or no blinkers?" Ted inquired, raising the alternative strands in succession.

"I like some of each," I said.

"Me too!" he answered, tossing Sam the end of the first string and setting the other aside for safekeeping. "This was my dad's favorite part, hanging the lights; he wouldn't let anyone else touch them. He'd spend, like, an hour moving the strands around until every single light was in the perfect position, equally spaced from all of the other lights. It drove my mom crazy. 'It's a Christmas tree, Hal!' she'd say. 'It doesn't have to be perfect!' "

"My dad was the same way," Sam responded, passing his end of the strand back to Ted. "Mom and Ted and I would be standing around practically drooling in our desire to hang the ornaments and he'd still be trying to get them all arranged in an orderly fashion, like little soldiers in formation." He grinned at the memory and then shot me a glance. "Did your dad hang the lights in your house, too, Kathy?" he said warily, as if uncertain whether he ought to be asking.

"No, my mom always did it," I answered.

"So what did your dad do?" Ted asked.

I shifted uncomfortably and fingered my necklace. Besides my mom, we hadn't talked about my family much. There wasn't really much to say. "Um, well, let's see… You know, I'm not really sure I remember. One of them was really tall, so he got put in charge of the tree-topper, but that was only like a year or two… And the second-to-last one, he was funny; he always made a big thing about putting out milk and cookies for Santa even though I was way too old to believe in that by then… The others…Well, maybe they weren't around for Christmas or something, I don't recall."

"How many fathers have you had, exactly?" Sam said, bending to pick up the next string and not really looking at me.

"Seven," I answered, then laughed when they both dropped the lights they were holding in surprise. "Mom liked to get married a lot, I guess. Who knows how many husbands she would have had if she'd lived!"

They'd encircled the tree with arms outstretched again and seemed focused on the task at hand.

"She had, what, lung cancer, right?" Sam asked.

"I'm glad you've never smoked," Ted remarked.

"Neither did she," I said. "It was small cell, not related to tobacco use. I guess it moves very fast. Even with the chemotherapy, she didn't really have a chance."

They'd gotten about halfway down the tree and they paused to connect another strand.

"That's when you went out on your own, isn't it?" Sam said.

"Well, I didn't have much choice, did I?" I laughed. "There was enough money for me to finish school, but that was about it."

"What about your dad?" Ted inquired, furrowing his brow. "I mean, your biological father? Couldn't he have helped out?"

I shrugged. "They split up when I was five and I never heard from him again."

"You're kidding!" Sam said indignantly, standing poised with a jumble of lights in his upraised hand. "Why, if I had a daughter…"

"I think it was a little different back then," I interrupted, feeling like a member of another generation. "It was much more common for the dad to walk away when a marriage ended. The support laws weren't what they are now, and I don't think fathers had the rights they do now, either. Anyway, it never bothered me any; I barely remembered him, anyhow. I always pretty much thought of our family as me and my mom; her husbands were more like guys she was dating than fathers."

"So that's why you've never gone home for Christmas?" Sam said.

"I wouldn't mind seeing the old hometown again one of these days," I admitted. "But I don't think of it as 'home' anymore. I mean, it isn't as if I've got relatives there or anything."

They had finished the lights. Sam fetched the power strip from the pantry and Ted plugged the string's end into it.

"Oooohh!" Sam cooed as the tree lit up.

"Ahhhhh!" I said in admiration.

"Look – blinking!" Ted remarked as the bulbs warmed up and began winking their many colors at us.

"I was really mad at first," Sam said suddenly. "When my folks started going out of town for the holidays. It felt like they had ruined Christmas."

Ted nodded. "Me, too. It was around the same time my parents moved."

"So we decided to celebrate it ourselves from then on. And you know what? It hasn't been so bad."

"No," Ted agreed. "I guess we all have to move on at some point; make our own celebrations."

"I suppose that's true," I said.

"And you know, with you here now, Kathy, to share it with us? I think this is going to be a great Christmas," Sam said, nodding to himself.

"The best Christmas ever!" Ted agreed.

For a moment we didn't speak, but merely watched the lights twinkling calmly all around the tree while I wondered if I were really sentimental enough to celebrate the holiday with two such softies. And then Sam came around behind me and threw his arms around my waist.

"Especially when I get out that big red Santa suit and pull you up on my lap…" he said with zeal, nudging his pelvis into my backside.

"Hey, where did you hide that mistletoe?" Ted inquired. "Oh, never mind!" he said, getting in front of me and planting a big wet one on my lips.

Best Christmas ever, I agreed, as they took me on the sofa beneath the blinking multicolored lights of the giant Christmas tree. It was difficult to argue with such potent and powerful persuasion.

CHAPTER 11

Here we go, I thought as we tumbled out of bed on Christmas morning, following the worst night's sleep I'd ever suffered between them. I'd been awakened after midnight by the two of them sneaking out of bed for some undoubtedly nefarious purpose that I strongly suspected had something to do with impersonating Santa. But upon emerging into the living room, I was pleasantly surprised to find only a smattering of packages beneath the tree and three stockings standing full and erect on the windowsill. It seemed they'd respected my wish not to overdo it, after all.

"Oooh, let's see what Santa brought us!" Sam exclaimed, going over to the window and grabbing my stocking for me.

"Spiced Christmas beer!" I said, reaching my hand into it. "This would go well with my coffee."

"Why not?" Ted said, tossing me the bottle-opener from his key ring. "It's Christmas, after all!"

Hmm, I thought, sipping on my decadent breakfast beer. Christmas might be worth celebrating after all.

We examined the beers in the other two stockings and then Sam shoved a long flat box across the carpet towards me.

"It's from both of us!" he said.

I ripped open the package and lifted the top off of the shirt box inside. It was lingerie; very pink, very sheer, and very crotchless.

"Um, you know this is really a present for you, right?" I said.

"Mm-hmm!" they said happily.

"Well," I said seriously, "I think you're going to like the real presents I picked out very specially for you guys." I reached behind my back and scooted two boxes towards them. With gleeful expressions they tore open the packages and yanked out their contents.

"Lingerie?" Ted said bemusedly, holding up a pretty blue silk teddy with matching panties. "I dunno, Kathy, I think this may be more Sam's color."

"I'm not trading!" Sam replied, clutching a black lace body stocking tightly to his chest. "I'm wearing this to work on Monday; I don't care what the guys think."

"Unfortunately, I don't think that's going to fit you," I said, snatching it away. He pouted at me. "You'd better not pout," I warned, "Or I won't model it during breakfast!"

He sat back complacently and took a swig of his beer. Then I saw him catch Ted's eye and watched as Ted delved into the deepest reaches of the tree trunk and came out with a very small, flat box. That it was a jewelry box was obvious, and my heart leapt into my throat in spite of myself. I mean, logically, I knew it couldn't be. They wouldn't dare. How could that even work?

Besides, it was too soon; even for a regular couple it would have been too soon. But it would be just like them, the sentimental fools, on Christmas, I thought. Yet I betrayed no sign; I carefully peeled aside the shiny silver wrapping as if I had no expectations whatsoever.

And it was well that I did so, because otherwise I'm sure the disappointment would have shown all over my face. It wasn't a ring. It was worse, much worse. It was a necklace.

As my heart dropped out of my throat, a lump rose up into it, and I stared unseeing at the gift, appalled. How could they? I thought. How could they have done such a thing? I already had a necklace that I loved, that I wore always, that I had worn as long as I could remember; that, for my own very personal reasons, was important to me. What was this supposed to be, a replacement? Was I now supposed to remove this essential piece of myself and exchange it for something of theirs?

My heart sank further and I found myself unable even to look at them. Did they really know me so little? I wasn't my mother. I didn't have to have a man to feel complete. I was a whole person all on my own, and I didn't need them stepping in trying to change me any more than I'd needed any of the other men who had tried.

This was the whole problem with relationships, I thought. You always had to give up something of yourself to be with someone else.

"So what do you think?" Ted said at last, interrupting my

thoughts.

"It's um, it's lovely," I said trying and failing to feign enthusiasm. "Thank you."

"It goes perfectly," Sam said, getting up onto his knees and scootching over to me. "We tried it out with your pendant one time when you fell asleep with it off."

Perplexed, I peered down at the necklace in the box and saw that it wasn't a necklace at all, but a link chain.

"We thought it would be nice," Ted said, "For you to have something more permanent, you know, than those cheap chains you keep buying."

"It's sterling silver," Sam said proudly. "Probably last you forever."

Carefully I drew the chain from its velvet lining and studied it closely. It was very similar – in fact, nearly identical – to the one I was wearing, featuring the same coiled design and a fancier clasp, but it shone, shone like the sun beaming in through the living room blinds.

"We went with the same length, too, since that's how you seem to like it," Ted added.

"You, uh, want some help putting it on?" Sam said hopefully. I nodded.

They gathered around me. I felt Ted's hands on my neck, detaching the old clasp and slipping the chain delicately off my neck. He passed it to Sam, who removed the pendant and strung it through the new chain, then leaned towards me and handed it around each side of my neck to Ted, who secured it again.

Ted came around to my front side and they both knelt there on the carpet, smiling and evidently pleased with the effect. I gazed down at my chest and fingered my old pendant where it hung on my glistening new chain. I was pleased with the effect, too.

"Thank you," I said again. This time I meant it. I would have liked to have kissed them, but since I didn't know who I should kiss first, I settled for a hug instead. That I could give them both at once.

"You're welcome," Sam said, his big eyes going all misty again. Ted just smiled shyly and then turned his attention back to the tree.

We all sat watching the lights blinking for a long moment. I'd forgotten how pretty they always looked, the rainbow of colors flashing against the ornaments, turning silver balls to purple and then to green. The neat reflective pattern the sparkling tree-topper formed against the ceiling as the sun shone through it. The tinsel that always ended up everywhere, stuck to the floor and the soles of your shoes, reminding you that it was Christmastime even when you were at work or the gym. It didn't seem like too much to ask, did it? Even I could be sentimental one day out of the year.

Suddenly Sam jumped up, whacked his hand against his forehead, and dug one more package out from underneath the tree. Although it was quite large, it was wrapped in shiny dark green paper and had blended almost perfectly into the real tree's boughs.

I didn't really need to open it. I could tell from the expression on his face what it was going to be.

"I thought you were joking!" I said, drawing a furry red Santa suit out of the box.

"That has to go back next week!" he said hastily. "I borrowed it from a friend. So we can't spill anything on it!"

"Then what's the point?" I argued, downing what was left of my beer in one swallow.

He chuckled. "Oh, I think we'll manage," he said, grinning at me as if I'd just illustrated an important point. "Come on, Ted, let's go get this sucker on."

They scampered off towards the bedroom, leaving me to wonder which one was going to appear in which half and what I was going to do with those halves when they did appear. I knew one thing for sure. Whatever was going to happen with that silly Santa suit, I wasn't going to remove my necklace.

CHAPTER 12

Funny, isn't it; no matter how much you hate the holidays, you can't ever seem to get away from marking time by them, especially when you're in a relationship. Christmas passed with New Year's following hard on its heels, and before I knew it, we were coming up on the worst special occasion of all. I was dreading it more than going back to work after a four-day weekend, but since I didn't think, in good conscience, that I could get out of it without causing offense to the mushy men in my life, I'd steeled myself against this horrible, inescapable fate. So I couldn't decide if I was being punished for my lack of romance, or rewarded for my efforts in faking it, when, on the day before Valentine's Day, Ted came down with a terrible case of the flu.

"I'm sorry," he mumbled, his forehead a welter of scarlet and sweat. "We wanted to do something special."

"Don't worry about it, sweetie!" I said gently, pressing a cool washcloth against his brow. I'd come straight from work to see how he was doing. "I hate Valentine's Day, anyway."

"I know you do," he answered. "But you know what a sucker Sam is for romance."

I chuckled in an effort to silence that strange but growing suspicion in my gut that I'd somehow gotten myself into a relationship here. "I guess I can let him wine and dine me, if he wants to."

"I'm not sure that's what he has in mind."

It wasn't. The next evening I went by their apartment. Ted's fever was down, but he was still achy and listless, and Sam looked so hopeless and melancholy that I thought for sure that he must have caught the bug, too.

"I'm fine," he assured me as he closed the door to Ted's

bedroom partway and followed me down the hall. "It's just kind of a bummer that he got sick now. We had this whole big thing planned..."

"It's really okay," I assured him as I sat down on the living room sofa. "Personally I could skip the whole thing and not lose any sleep over it."

He collapsed in a heap beside me and rested a weary head on my shoulder. "Oh, but you wouldn't say that if you knew what we were going to do! See, first..."

"Stop right there," I warned, holding up a hand to silence him.

"I can't even tell you about it?" he squealed, his jowls drooping lower than Gracie's.

"Nope," I said. "If you don't tell me now, you can save it for next year and I'll still be surprised."

For a long moment he sat still in silent contemplation, so unusually still and silent that I wondered if he were sick after all and had passed out on my arm. Then he broke into a smile and kissed me tenderly on the cheek as if I'd said something uncharacteristically sweet.

"Okay!" he answered buoyantly. "We'll save it for next year."

He was still gazing at me with that goofy grin, looking so much like the world's jolliest jack o' lantern that it started to spook me a little. But then he sat up, slapped his hands against my knees, and said, "So what do you want to do tonight?"

"I don't know," I shrugged. "We probably shouldn't go far, with Ted being sick and all."

"Right," he said. "Plus it wouldn't seem right, leaving him all alone on Valentine's Day."

"Well, let's just stay home then. We can order take-out, and I know you've got beer," I managed to answer before exploding into an unexpected sneeze.

"Gesundheit! Well, if you really don't mind hanging around the house..." He brightened. "Hey, you know, this will be the first time we've really been alone together!"

"That's true," I conceded. It was. Except for the odd intervals when one of them was in the kitchen or bathroom, there were very few moments in which I wasn't with them both simultaneously.

He looked at me expectantly and I sneezed again, louder this time.

"Gesundheit!" he said again. "I hope you're not getting sick!"

"I don't think so," I replied tentatively as my throat grew scratchy. "It feels more like allergies, but I don't usually get them in the winter. You haven't been bathing in pollen, have you?" I joked.

"Not since yesterday," he kidded back. "That's how I keep my hair this lovely golden color."

I sneezed again and my eyes started watering. "Boy, this is going to drive me crazy," I said, sniffling. "It's strange; I've never had this kind of reaction in your apartment before."

He paled suddenly. "What exactly are you allergic to, Kathy?" he said.

"Oh, nothing specific, just the usual plant-type stuff, I guess," I answered. "Flowers sometimes trigger it, too."

He got up and went around to the back side of the recliner. "Like these?" he replied, squatting down to lift up a massive multi-colored assortment of fresh flowers bursting out of its shiny green wrapping.

I sneezed again by way of response. "They're lovely," I sniffed.

"Glad you think so," he said skeptically. "Would you like me to take them outside?"

"If you don't mind," I wheezed as my nostrils swelled shut.

"Well," he said when he returned, smacking his hands together as if to cleanse them of the deadly flower-dust, "Next year we'll know to skip the flowers."

"Ungh," I answered.

"Come on, let's get you out into some fresh clean air for a bit. I just need to make a quick phone call."

I went and took a quiet peek at Ted, who was sleeping soundly, his hair askew, his mouth agape, his usually neatly trimmed beard rough and ragged after two days in bed. The air in the room was stale with sweat and germs and I thought of how many nights I'd spent bundled up in that bed next to that man and how this would not be one of them. And then he snorted loudly, sending me scurrying down the hall, anxious to keep my thoughts a secret.

"Yeah, we won't be able to use them after all," I overheard Sam saying. "So if you still want 'em…Well, we're gonna step out for a bit but I'll leave them under the mat, okay? Nah, don't ring the bell, Ted will probably still be sleeping. All right, later."

I had come to a stop in the kitchen, and he didn't see me as he sighed and went back to the front door, clutching a small white envelope in his fist. I watched as he stepped outside and returned a moment later without it.

"There you are!" he said brightly. "Ted all tucked in?"

"Sleeping like a log," I replied.

"Sounds like Ted," he agreed. "Tall, dark, and always stiff as a board."

"Sam!" I protested, glancing over my shoulder as if expecting Ted to be standing behind me, ready with a clever comeback.

"What? It was a compliment!" he said. "Me, I'm more like a hedge. Kinda short, and thick and bushy." He ran his hands over the blond bristles of his head. "But on the plus side, I do poke in all directions."

He winked at me and I groaned, then shoved him out ahead of me into the hall.

We walked. That was one of the things I liked about Sam and Ted; I don't know if it was the native northerner in them or what, but they never hesitated to take a walk down the street even in the dead of winter. There was a great Chinese restaurant just a few blocks away and we headed for it automatically; it was our standard place for take-out on the rare occasions when we bought it. Sam was quieter than usual and so, I guess, was I, because halfway there he turned and said to me, "You don't seem very talkative today."

"Funny," I replied, "I was just thinking the same thing about you."

In fact, something seemed off with the whole situation. Here he was walking beside me as he'd done a hundred times before, but something had changed. He hadn't taken my hand or put his arm around my waist like he usually did, but was striding briskly along with his hands in his pockets as if they were cold.

Well, it was cold, I thought, gazing up the winter's early night sky and steeling myself against the chill wind that was nearly blowing me sideways.

"Brrr!" I said. "This must be the coldest night this year!"

He shrugged. "Seems the same to me." Then he laughed. "Maybe it just seems colder to you because your other windbreaker's at home in bed!"

I laughed, too, but I wondered if he was right.

We ordered several dishes and then beat it back to the

apartment, but the food was still cold by the time we got there.

"I'll warm this up," Sam said, chafing my hands with his in demonstration. "You wanna go see if Ted wants any?"

Once again I tiptoed down the hall, sneaked into the bedroom, and leaned over the ragged form of the sick man. He greeted me with a sleepy gurgle and then rolled away into oblivion.

"Let's just save him some," I told Sam.

We plopped down on the couch with our plates and our beers and smiled shyly at one another. And then Sam said, "How about a movie?" and I said that sounded good so he flipped through the stations on the satellite until he found us one.

"I love this movie!" he cried, cranking up the volume with the remote and nearly spilling his noodles in his exuberance.

"What is with you and romantic comedies, anyway?" I asked disgustedly, glancing towards the front window and wondering if I should attempt escape before I was provoked into a Valentine's Day massacre.

"Ha! I've got your number now, lady. I don't care what you say, you are just as sentimental as the rest of us."

"That seems unlikely," I said drily.

"Oh, really?" he said, squinting at me as if I'd thrown all my chips down on the table and he was about to call my bluff. "What was it you said earlier this evening? About Valentine's Day?"

"Oh, I don't remember," I answered. "That I hated it, or that I thought it was stupid and pointless?"

"You said we should save our special celebration for next year!" he gloated.

"So?"

He shook his head and chuckled.

"So what?!" I said again.

"That means you're still planning on being with us a year from now! Which would make us your longest relationship ever! By like, a lot! And if that's not romantic, I don't know what is!"

He gazed at me triumphantly and for a moment I felt beaten.

Then I said, "Hmph! Shows what you know. I am so going to dump you guys before our anniversary."

"You mean of the first time we…?"

"That's right!"

"Oh, really?" he said archly. "And when exactly is our

anniversary?"

"June twenty-second," I answered promptly.

"Not even close," he sighed, shaking his head and gnawing off a hunk of his teriyaki stick.

"Okay, I give," I snapped in return. "When is our anniversary? Tell me so I can pencil in our break-up for the day before."

"April the tenth."

"Are you just making that up?" I inquired suspiciously.

He smirked at me with superiority. "Ask Ted if you like. He's got it marked on his calendar, too."

"Marked on his...! Listen, bub, I don't know what kind of girl you guys think I am..."

"Oh, trust me, we know what kind of girl you are!" He looked me up and down appraisingly. "Beneath all the smut and sex-talk, you're really awfully... sweet."

I snatched the last potsticker from his plate and stuck my tongue out at him. "Says you!"

"I know what I know!" he said, again with that annoying air of superiority.

"Oh, shut up and watch your movie!" I retorted, turning my own attention to the drivel onscreen.

Near the end of the movie Sam broke out the box of chocolates that was supposed to have accompanied my flowers and we plucked away at it, taking half-bites and then sharing the good ones with the other.

"This is totally unsanitary," I remarked, chomping my half-eaten chocolate.

"Oh, yeah," Sam said. "I know you don't want my germs."

"Not in the least," I sighed, leaning over to give him a kiss. He lifted his arm and draped it around my shoulder and I snuggled in closer, wrapping my arm around his waist.

The movie ended and Sam turned off the television but still we sat there, almost holding each other, and with an odd thrill of anticipation I caught myself wondering what was going to happen next.

That's silly, I thought to myself. Would it really be anything new?

Except that it would be the first time we'd really been together one on one. Even at Thanksgiving Ted had been right across the room. What would it be like, just him and me? It was such an intriguing novelty that as I ran my hand over his thigh I felt myself getting excited. Really excited.

I guess it showed, because he kissed me on the forehead and then whispered, "Do you want to go to bed?"

"Uh-huh!" I said, feeling my good places getting squishy with my juices.

"We can sleep in my room," he offered. "The bed's smaller, but it's still plenty big enough for the two of us."

"Okay." Small was good. Small was cozy. Small was appropriate for only two, count 'em, two lovers.

"I'll just go check on Ted."

He wiggled his way out from underneath my arms and I tiptoed down the hall to his room.

I hadn't gone in there much. With its king-sized mattress, Ted's bed was definitely the place for three, and I'd only been in Sam's room briefly while we were waiting for him to get dressed and things like that. This was just as well because it was always a mess; piles of clothes on the floor and tools scattered all around his desk. I stepped over these and amused myself by examining the dozens of photographs he had posted, everywhere, it seemed: up and down the walls, in the niches of the mirror, on the rear of his door. Pictures of him and his family and friends and of course, lots of him and Ted and even of me and him and Ted. Indeed, I was stunned by the sheer volume of pictures that had been taken of the three of us in the few years of our acquaintance. But there we were at the bar after a hockey game, me all sweaty and disheveled, them only sweaty. There we were arm in arm at Ted's company picnic, and standing side by side in our swimsuits on that infamous camping trip that had started it all. And even there, toasting one another at the wedding, the boys so handsome in their tuxes while my own modest figure seemed lost between them.

"Quite the collection, isn't it?" a voice said behind me and I started.

"You've got a lot of pictures of us!" I remarked.

He nodded happily. "This one here is my favorite." He pointed to a small, simple photograph of us at our bar. There was nothing really special about it – it was just the three of us with our beers against the plain backdrop of the yellow wallpaper – except that we were sitting very close together and smiling broadly at the camera.

We all seemed to be shining.

"That was after our – you know – our 'first' time," he said, smiling shyly.

"That would explain the glow," I said wryly.

"You always glow like that, afterwards," he said. "That's the best part about it."

I didn't know what to say to that so I turned towards the wall over the bed. Over the headboard hung two large paintings, one a brilliant summer landscape, the other a close-up portrait of a butterfly in flight. "Where did those come from?" I asked. "They look similar to the ones Ted's got in his room."

"Ted painted them," he said, surprised. "I can't believe you didn't know that. He's quite the artist beneath that business suit."

I stared, stunned, at the paintings, and remembered how Ted had shown me his, long ago, when we were still merely good friends. How he'd asked my opinion without revealing who the artist was, as if only casually interested in my appraisal.

"Well, I don't know anything about art, of course," I'd said. "But this one here, the seascape? Kind of bores me."

"How come?" he'd asked without a hint of emotion.

"Well, it's a good rendition, but there's nothing all that interesting about it, if you know what I mean. It's well-done, but I just don't get anything out of it, I guess." I'd turned to the other painting, a side view of a sleeping barn owl, the figure nearly filling the frame. "Now this one is much more compelling. See the way the artist has delved into the detail of every line, every feather? It almost looks three-dimensional, as if it's about to explode off the canvas. And the colors, they're way brighter than those of a real owl, but they make you feel – they make you feel as if the artist has put something of himself into the painting, you know?"

"Interesting," he'd said, and then Sam had barged in and we'd gone out for our usual beer and had never spoken of it again.

"I can't believe I didn't know that, either," I said to Sam now, looking again at the landscape and the butterfly. They had the same strengths and flaws as the other pictures I'd seen. Or I thought so, anyway.

"He's actually working on a whole series now, when he has time. The first one is really neat; it's a picture of … Well, I guess you can ask him about it if you want to," he hastily concluded.

They did still have their private lives, after all, just like I did. I suppose even the closest of partners have their little secrets.

"Anyway, are you ready for bed?"

I went and used the bathroom, got my sexiest nightie out of my bag, and slipped thoughtfully into it. But when I clicked off the light and crawled into bed, I wasn't quite as much in the mood as I had been before.

Sam didn't seem to be, either. Instead of embracing or fondling me as he usually did, he merely lay close beside me holding my hand, and after a long while he said, "It's a little strange, with just the two of us, isn't it?"

"Different," I agreed. "I keep sort of expecting…" I trailed off.

"… Ted to be here, I know," he finished my sentence for me. "I don't know if this is weird or not, but it doesn't seem right somehow, you know, for us to…"

"Right," I said, taking my turn to complete the thought. "I mean, I know it's not like cheating or anything, but somehow…"

"It feels like something's missing."

"It would be kind of mean," I suggested. "I mean, for us to screw around while the poor guy's sick in bed."

"That's true, huh?" Sam said, seeming to take comfort in the morality of our no-sex position. "Well, maybe we should just go to sleep then."

"All right," I said, rolling over to kiss him on the lips. "Good night."

I kissed him once more for good measure and he kissed me back, hard. Instinctively I pulled in closer and kissed him again, wrapping my upper leg around his body as I did so. He chuckled and placed a hand on my breast and squeezed it. I swelled all over in response.

"I thought we weren't going to…" he whispered.

"Well, I…" I began, but just then there was a loud, frightening thump on the wall behind us and we both jumped up out of bed and ran into Ted's room. Hurriedly Sam flicked on the emergency nightlight so we could catch a glimpse of our friend.

He was still sleeping, but his long arm was now over his head, and it appeared as if he'd whacked the wall in his slumber.

Sam sighed with relief. "Go on back to bed," he said. "I'll be there in a minute."

I went back to his room and climbed back under the covers. I heard faint rustling noises from the room next door and imagined that Sam was tucking Ted in. And then he came back to his room, ambled over to my side of the bed, and tucked me in as well.

"Good night, Kathy," he whispered, leaning over to kiss me on the forehead. "Happy Valentine's Day."

I didn't answer. I merely rolled over onto my side away from him and thought how strange it was to find no one on my other side. And stranger still to realize that I didn't like it very much.

CHAPTER 13

"I can't believe you're fighting over this!" I said irritably, shoving them both away from my chest with a grunt.

Lately it seemed all they did was argue, although I couldn't for the life of me figure out why. It seemed to date back to our anniversary, which had turned out to be an even greater failure than Valentine's Day. I'd been forced by my work to attend some team-building seminar in the city that week, and couldn't get away. So their big production had to be put on hold once again, and my lack of real disappointment didn't seem to have helped matters any.

"Can't you at least try to get out of it?" Sam had pleaded. He'd still been reeling from my refusal to endure a party for my fortieth birthday the week before.

"It's mandatory. And this isn't exactly a family emergency."

What would I have said, anyway? I can't attend the conference because I have to celebrate the anniversary of the first time I slept with my boyfriends?

Sam had sighed heavily and Ted had spoken up, I thought, on his behalf. "We know you're not very sentimental, and we're cool with that. But sometimes we wish you were a little more interested in, you know, celebrating our relationship."

"Listen, I celebrate every morning I wake up with you guys," I'd said in a rare display of emotion. "I'm not going to get all upset because we can't be together on our three-hundred and sixty-fifth day."

That had seemed to reassure them, because they hadn't mentioned it again. But ever since, there seemed to have been some underlying, unspoken friction between the three of us, and while that made for some fantastic sex, it also created some irritating moments. Like this one.

"What is with you guys tonight?" I demanded. "You never argue over who's going to go first."

"Well, that's because we normally take turns," Ted answered. "Except that Sam's forgotten whose turn it is!"

"No, I haven't forgotten; you've forgotten, Ted! Don't you remember the night I had that bad sushi and you stepped up into my place?"

"Of course I remember! But we already squared up on that, dipshit. Remember that morning you had to leave early so I gave you my turn?"

"Okay, okay," I broke in. "Why does it matter so much, anyway? I mean, really?" Under the circumstances, why did it matter? I wondered. Someone was pretty much always "going" after someone else.

"Well, I guess it doesn't, really," Ted reasoned. "It's just that, you know, when you're prepared to do – something – right away, and then you have to hold off…"

"Oh, like you ever have any trouble getting 'prepared' again!" Sam howled.

"We're never exactly sitting around waiting for you to spring back to life, either, you horny hound-dog!"

Quite suddenly I felt like a mother to two small bratty children and I didn't like it; it was ruining the mood.

"Well, fellas," I interrupted again. "Speaking as one of the three of us who is not going to get laid as long as the two of you keep whining…" I glared at them both in turn. "I'm going to make a suggestion. Why don't you both go?"

"Aw, come on, Kathy," they protested, suddenly on the same side again. "Don't kick us out!" They seemed to have forgotten that we were in their apartment and I had no right to make anyone leave.

"No, I mean… I mean, you could both go at the same time."

There was an excruciating pause in which they both stared, astounded, at me and for a moment I thought I'd taken it too far.

"You mean," Sam whispered, as if afraid that someone might overhear, "You mean like one in front, and one… behind?"

"Lots of people do it," I contended, as if I were the undisputed expert on the mating rituals of the horny-backed Homo sapien. "When there are three together, I mean. It's almost customary," I argued, as if they'd been shortchanging me all this time.

Actually, I had no idea what was customary in this regard. It seemed like a fairly common scenario in the internet pornography I'd seen, which, granted, isn't a representative slice of how actual people do one another. No one ever actually screws two guys at once in real life, right? Ahem. Well, very few, I'm sure. And anyway, now that I'd said it, I wasn't certain I wanted to make that a part of our custom either. But at least my boys had stopped complaining; they were too busy lying there with their mouths hanging open at my suggestion to argue any more.

"Um, Kathy?" Ted said, in the manner that foretold he was about to ask me an incredibly direct and potentially embarrassing question. "Let me see if I'm understanding this right... Are you saying you want us to fuck you up the ass?"

I couldn't tell you if Ted blushed beneath that olive skin when he said that, but Sam turned his most scarlet shade of red and began sweating violently, while I choked on my own spit and had to have Ted slap my back until I stopped coughing.

"Well, I don't know," I gasped finally, raking my eyes over each of them in turn. "I've never actually had one – you know – in there before."

Both of Sam's heads perked up at once. He tilted his neck slightly and stared towards the underside of my open legs, almost as if he were trying to pinpoint the location of the hole in question where it lay concealed beneath the flesh of my ample buttocks. Maybe the thought of penetrating my virgin asshole didn't sound so bad after all. In fact, when you put it that way...

"I've heard," I whispered conspiratorially, "I've heard that it's actually pretty good as long as, you know, you lube it up right. I mean, millions of gay guys can't be wrong, can they?"

They glanced at each other, evidently unable to deny the logic of my reasoning.

"You do like being spanked," Ted observed, closing his eyes briefly as if working out the rationale in his head. "No, don't bother to deny it!" he said over my feeble, half-hearted objection. "Sam and I both know we wouldn't be here today if it wasn't for that."

"It is sort of like a spanking," Sam contributed hopefully. "Only deeper. And a lot more painful."

But of course, even that distressing observation couldn't turn me off once spanking was mentioned. In fact, I'd already stuck my ass out helpfully sideways where Ted was caressing it lightly, bringing back fond memories and sending shivers up and down my cracks. Sam must have caught the look in my eye because he reached over and whacked me hard with the flat of his hand, causing my cheek to redden pleasantly and my natural lube to come flooding out through my best-oiled doorway like an eager assistant.

"Okay," Ted said, banging the edge of his fist down on the mattress with all of the conviction of a Supreme Court justice who's just participated in a momentous, history-changing decision. "So who's going to take the back door?"

For a moment there was silence and I was afraid they'd start quarreling all over again.

"You should take it first," Sam said at last.

"Why?" Ted said, surprised. "You don't want to?"

"No, not because I don't want to. Because I got to go first you know, the very first time. When we flipped a coin. This will make us even," he said magnanimously. "More than even, really, because you'll be the first guy who's ever been in there." He swallowed uncomfortably, and it struck me that he might be jealous of Ted's privilege.

"Wow, you're right," Ted said softly. "Hey, thanks, man. This really means a lot to me." He let go of my butt and reached out a hand to Sam, who shook it warmly. I was moved. What had I been worried about? Not even my most deeply buried treasure could rupture a friendship as solidly built as theirs. And then Ted rolled me sideways with one arm, grabbed a great fistful of my buttcheek and squeezed, and I forgot about everything but the impending penetration.

I'd never found the idea of anal sex especially appealing. I mean, sure, I was curious about it. I'd had a finger or two pressed cautiously in there and it was by no means a turnoff, but no one had ever tried to take it any further than that, and I'd never been interested enough to say I wanted to give it a try. Of course, I'd also never really been in a relationship that had lasted long enough to stray that far off the beaten path, so to speak. But I did figure there had to be something to it, at that. Too many people were doing it and liking it for me to believe that it was a freak perversion that only the rare few enjoyed. Besides, my boys were right; there was no denying that most kinds of ass-play were guaranteed to get me going, and there was no reason to doubt that this would work just as well. Of course, in my mind, it wasn't all about the butt, either. Although the feminist in me loathed to admit it, there was a very tiny part of my erotic brain that was sexually submissive. And whenever I pictured anal sex I always imagined myself lying helplessly on my stomach, my ass exposed and vulnerable, hands grabbing hard onto it, gripping it, pounding it while balls slapped happily against it, giving me their own little light spanking where I lay at the mercy of a man and his cock.

Well, maybe the idea was somewhat appealing.

"Um, Kathy?" Ted said again, causing me to turn bemusedly half-backwards to look at him where he was again manhandling my asscheeks, pressing into them with his palms as if it were a very dirty, very riveting massage. "I know you said we should both go at once, but I was thinking that since you haven't, you know, done that before…"

"Oooh, good idea, Ted," Sam said approvingly, scooting across the mattress and kneeling down by my head, his erect penis wiggling enthusiastically in my face. "We should warm her up first."

"Right," he agreed. "So, um, how do you want to…?"

"Like this," I said, rolling flat onto my front with my face in Sam's lap. My lips were practically on his dick and I was nearly overcome by the urge to suck it, but I refrained. I didn't want to take a chance on biting down if the impending poking proved to be painful. Instead I just gave it an affectionate lick and he shivered appreciatively.

"In the behind from behind, eh?" he said with a goofy grin, running his fingers through my hair, where they twitched with nerves or excitement or both.

"If being flat doesn't work, I can get up on all fours," I offered. "But I'd definitely prefer to be like this, on my stomach. And sort of, you know, pinned down. Not too much!" I added hastily as I felt Ted's elbows pressing into my backside. "Just enough to make me feel like… Like, you know…" I trailed off, too embarrassed to say it.

"That's funny," Ted said, chuckling behind my back. "Usually you like to be in charge."

"Oh, hush," I snapped back. "And scoot over a little so I can see us in the mirror." That'd show them who was in charge here.

"Ooh, kinky!" Sam exclaimed, gently disengaging my head from his lap, clambering up behind me next to Ted, and checking our group reflection for size and clarity. "I thought I was the only one who used the mirror."

I felt probing in my hinter regions and turned sideways to look. Sam was holding my cheeks spread wide apart while Ted was very delicately fingering the area around my asshole. Both of them were peering at my hindquarters as if attempting to divine the mysteries of a dark, mysterious, and unexplored cavern.

"So what are we supposed to use for lubrication?" Sam inquired. In the mirror I could see him glancing towards the kitchen as if wondering whether he ought to fetch the butter from the fridge.

"Pussy juice?" Ted answered. After all this time, I was still amused when the subtle, serious Ted I had once known came out with such a straightforward yet crude remark. Pussy juice. Like orange juice, maybe, only stickier.

"I think that will work," I agreed. "There's plenty to go around."

And there was. It was rare that we prefaced sex with so much dirty talk, and already I could feel it dripping out of me. This will be convenient, I thought with satisfaction, nodding to myself as if I'd just developed a new and improved company policy on reuse and recycling. I'm way too slippery to fuck in the usual manner, anyway. I thought it again as a solitary finger slid smoothly into the heart of my pussy and emerged warm and wet and ready to explore my far more impenetrable hole. With agonizing slowness he gradually worked it in, like a cork being forced back into the top of an open wine bottle; my rectum expanding only slightly to admit the intruder and then collapsing tightly around it. The finger wiggled slightly and I moaned; glanced at the mirror and saw them smiling delightedly at one another. And then the finger withdrew cautiously from its tight tunnel and another was plunging deep into my pussy and then carefully but triumphantly into my ass. And then they got into it. They took turns, sliding their fingers into me longer and harder and faster while I moaned and groaned and made other ridiculous noises, and then they switched to two fingers at a time and that made me howl even louder. Finally I heard Sam say, "Okay, Kathy, now check this out," and as if on cue they each stuck one well-oiled finger into my asshole and sort of pulled slightly sideways in opposite directions, expanding it.

"Oh dear God," I said, my tongue curling in my mouth.

"I think she's ready!" Sam said.

"Yeah? Are you ready, Kathy?" Ted said, bending over to whisper in my ear. I felt his chest hairs rippling against my back and found it comforting somehow.

"As ready as I'm gonna get," I said sleepily. Somehow all of the fingering had relaxed me, like a deep tissue massage of my very deepest tissues.

"Okay, here goes," he said. I heard the familiar sound of a condom wrapper being ripped open and the reassuring thwack of rubber. And then he pressed his hips up against my butt, nuzzled his cock in between my cheeks and said, "One... two... three!"

I suppose it was kind of him to give me a countdown, but really, no number of numbers could have prepared me for that.

"AIEEEE!" I yelled.

Instantly he withdrew and I felt my asshole snapping shut, repelling the cock invasion.

"Are you all right?" he said, his penis nuzzling cozily into my crack again.

"Yup," I said, panting and no longer in the least bit either sleepy or relaxed. "Try it again."

"Are you sure?" Sam inquired. I could see him goggling in the mirror. "That was some yell!"

"You stuff a cucumber up your ass and see if it doesn't make you yell," I retorted.

"A cucumber?" Ted repeated, obviously flattered by the comparison. "Why, this is no more than a carrot at best..." he continued modestly.

"All right, Ted, we all know you've got an amazing dick. The lady says she wants to give it another go, then give it another go."

"All right," he answered reluctantly, shaking his head. "Ready?"

I nodded and tried to relax. I was about as successful as a skydiver making a first jump. In fact, the way I was clenching the pillowcase in my fists, you would have thought it was a parachute-cord – my sole defense against certain death.

"Unghh!" Ted said, pushing it slowly back in, one inch and then two before I let out a yelp.

"Do you want to stop?" he asked the back of my head, holding his steady where it had paused, unmoving, just inside the rim of my ass.

"Nope," I said. Sam was watching me in the mirror, his face lit

118

up with something like admiration. It inspired me to greater determination. "Spread my cheeks, Sam," I ordered.

He obeyed, getting up onto his knees and pushing my cheeks apart, widening the opening. I felt a whoosh of air rushing past the hole and it gave me that peculiar and deliciously nasty feeling of being exposed again. I raised my butt higher, spread my legs wider, and steeled my resolve.

Ted gave me no warning this time, but, meeting less resistance, plunged it all in at once, sending shockwaves through my belly and bowels and causing me to gasp for air.

"Oh, dear God," he moaned, pulling his cock slowly out of my ass and then pressing it firmly back in again. Each new thrust caused my asshole to shriek in agony and I began to be afraid that I wasn't going to make it.

"It's all right, sweetie," Sam was saying. He'd removed one hand from my ass and was brushing it awkwardly against my cheek instead. "You can bite down on it if you need to," he offered anxiously.

But just when I had decided to tell Ted to stop, the pain and burning seemed to ease, and I found my panicky screams turning into mere whimpers of protest as my hole expanded. And all at once it seemed to relax and open up, taking in that cock so sweetly and smoothly that after a few minutes I unexpectedly found myself squealing with astonished delight.

"I think she likes it!" Sam exclaimed excitedly.

"Do you like it?" Ted asked me.

"Unghhh!" I answered. It was the closest I could come to forming words that other humans might comprehend.

"Here it comes!" Ted boomed, more loudly than I had ever heard him speak. His cock stiffened hard inside me and that was it, right there, the moment in which I really, truly, perhaps for the first time in my life, felt utterly full of a man.

He had barely slipped out of me when I heard Sam shouting, "My turn! My turn!" He clambered up behind me and shoved Ted unapologetically onto the floor, where he landed with a ground-shaking thud.

"Watch it, dumbass!" Ted said, tossing Sam a fresh condom and rushing off to dispose of his own before the action resumed.

It went in smooth and easy this time, and I watched sideways in the dresser mirror while Sam fucked me, his cock dividing the curves of my ass neatly into halves. I couldn't stop staring; the look of it fascinated me, the way his cock was probing right between my cheeks, the slightly upward shift of position the only outward sign that his cock was in my ass and not my pussy. The sight of it was just as arousing as the sensation and I couldn't help myself; I wanted to play with my pussy, to stroke myself into orgasm, but Sam had me pinned hard to the bed and I couldn't reach it. And then I felt that stiffening inside again and he moaned like a pack of wolves in a patch of moonlight and collapsed in a clump on my backside.

"I'm in love," he announced into the sudden silence. "With your asshole."

"Shut up, dumbass," Ted replied, climbing back up into the bed, lying down beside me, and stretching his arm across my back. "Did you come?" he said to me. "It was hard to tell, it was so, um, loud in here."

"No," I said. "But I enjoyed it. Once I got used to it."

"But wouldn't you like to...?"

"Oh, well!" I answered, "I mean, I wouldn't turn it down or anything."

"My turn! My turn!" Sam yelled, his enthusiasm apparently undiminished although the beet-red color of his face finally seemed to be fading. He grasped my hips with his sturdy arms and rolled me heartily sideways, and then frontwards. Taking hold of my legs, he gleefully spread them, opening up my pussy to the room at large as if it was a sculpture he was unveiling. He dove into it like it was as smooth as a chocolate crème pie and twice as tasty, and in seconds I was so close that I almost told Ted not to bother when he interrupted.

"Make some room, will ya?" he said, pushing Sam up to the top part of my clit and lifting my hips as if to get to the pussyhole proper underneath.

Except he didn't go for my pussyhole. Instead I felt his rough wet tongue sliding across my asshole and I was suddenly very conscious that I was being eaten on both ends and I burst like a firework into screaming rockets of heat and noise and light and then fell in a flutter like so many burnt-out ashes to a welcoming earth.

Outside, night had fallen. My heart pounded as I looked out the window at the darkened sky and I wished that it was later; that I could lie down to sleep right then and there with them; drift off with the feel of their warmth clinging to my body like soft winter flannel. And then wake again to a morning bright with their faces still smiling up at me from my most wonderful of spaces.

I smiled, too.

"Come here," I said, patting the mattress on both sides of my naked body. They rose, dragged me gently up to the head of the bed, and settled themselves beside me with sighs of contentment.

We lay like that a long time, together, side by side, the three of us, enjoying the coolness of the evening air.

"I'm thirsty," Sam announced after a while. "Can I get you guys a beer?"

"Thanks, buddy," Ted said gratefully. Sam rose; turned his butt towards us and gave it a playful shake.

"Don't worry, I'll be right back," he said, wiggling his way down the hall.

"He's really a good guy," Ted said to me when he had gone. "I know I call him a dumbass a lot, but it's just a term of affection, you know what I mean?"

"I know," I said, smiling and rolling over to embrace him.

"And that was really cool of him, offering like he did, you know."

"Um-hmm."

"You really liked that?" he repeated.

"Did you?" I replied.

"Actually, I did," he answered, scratching his beard as if puzzled by the fact. "I mean, I didn't really expect to. Not the kind of thing I'm really into. But I dunno, once we started talking about it... And what you seemed to want, and the way that you wanted it..."

He cleared his throat. "There are many sides to you, Kathy. And I want to know them all."

He gazed thoughtfully into my eyes and I was overcome by the peculiar suspicion that this reserved young man who wanted to know all about me already did know more about me than anyone else I had ever known.

"Um, and what about what I did there at the end?" he said abruptly, his eyes glinting with mischief. "Did you like that, too?"

"Yowsers!" I answered, reaching down to fondle his still-sticky cock, which immediately began to grow again beneath my hand.

He laughed. "Don't tell Sam, though, okay? I'm not sure he

would approve."

I doubted seriously whether Sam was in a position to approve or disapprove anything any of us might do when we were naked together, but I agreed. Even the closest of partners have their little secrets, don't they?

Then Sam returned, precariously balancing three pint glasses between his outstretched fingers, and Ted jumped up to help him.

"Thanks, man," Sam said, plopping down on the bed, taking a big gulp of his drink and belching loudly in consequence.

I turned to Ted expectantly, awaiting a snide remark on the subject of Sam's lack of manners, but none was forthcoming. Instead he merely sipped at his beer. And then opened his mouth and sent an even louder, more onerous belch rippling across the room.

"That's so rude!!" Sam said with horror and evident admiration. "You know there's a lady present! Although, to be frank," he added, turning to me, "You didn't seem all that 'ladylike' when we were fucking you up the – hey, watch it!!"

Ted had punched him forcibly in the arm that was holding his beer.

"You almost made me spill!" Sam huffed.

"Serves you right!" Ted replied.

"Oh, I don't mind," I said quickly, hoping to avert another quarrel. "I've never thought of myself as much of a 'lady.'"

"Well, you are," Ted insisted. "No matter what position you're in."

"Personally, I like you with your ass up." Sam chimed in. "Always have. Like doggie-style, you know? In a very lady-like way, of course," he hastened to add.

"Oh, yeah," I agreed. "I'm sure you've noticed the way I always keep my pinky out when I'm getting fucked from behind."

"I do that, too," Ted answered. "I always stick my pinky out when I've got my hands on your ass."

"Like this?" Sam said, reaching a hand underneath the cheek that was closest to him and getting four fingers underneath it.

"No, more like this," Ted said, demonstrating the maneuver on his side. They were each pulling in opposite directions, and although I could sense that my asshole was already going to be sore come morning, the feel of it opening up like that made me wonder if I could stomach a repeat performance.

I guess it must have showed in my face, because the next thing Sam said was, "See, now look what you did!"

They were both staring at me as if I were the center attraction in a three-ring circus and I glanced back and forth between them defensively. "What?!" I said.

"You are totally turned on again!" Sam cried.

"I am not!" I retorted. I made to roll away from them in disgust, but since one was on each side of me, of course I couldn't. I compromised by rolling over onto my face instead, which, of course, didn't do much to support my claimed lack of interest.

"See?" Sam howled, slapping his hand against my ass as if it were evidence.

"Be nice," Ted warned. "It's okay," he said to me confidentially, gently patting my butt right along its exposed crack. "But we'd better not overdo it, first time out. Would you mind rolling over?" he inquired politely.

I obeyed. I never could turn down any of Ted's oh-so-polite requests for my compliance. They cuddled up beside me and I sighed with contentment. I felt contented, too.

I stretched out my hands and sought theirs; took hold of the firm fingers in my firm grip and looked over the two men by my side. Their penises were lax now, shriveled into sexless oblivion and I reached for them; stroked them tenderly with aching fingers and thought, What a wonderful invention this is, the wiener.

"What are you thinking about?" Sam said, grinning as he glanced down to where I'd cupped his balls gently in my palm.

"Wieners," I answered truthfully.

Ted laughed. "Is that all you ever think about?" he teased.

"It is when you guys are around!" I retorted, not unkindly.

Ted bent his face towards mine, then tricked me and bent to my breast instead. He kissed it, cupped it in his palm and kissed it again. I smiled and turned my face towards Sam, who took the hint and took my other nipple roughly into his mouth as if he'd merely been waiting for an invitation.

We played together like that for some time, their lips tickling my breasts in tandem while my fingers rambled carelessly over their nether regions, waiting, waiting for the moment that must inevitably come, when I would feel the stiffening beneath my fingers that meant those wonderful wieners were popping back into life. The moment in which they would both make love to me again in their sweet and usual way. The moment in which at last my wish would be fulfilled, that of falling into deep and pleasant dreams in the comfort and warmth of the bed that we shared. One of many such magical moments in my life with Sam and Ted.

CHAPTER 14

I didn't, however, let our new sexual experiment progress beyond that; not yet, anyway. I told my boys I wanted a little more practice on the anal alone before we moved on to the logical next step, but in fact I'd made what was for me a momentous decision. I'd decided to go on the pill. It was crazy-stupid, I knew. Who waits until they're forty to start using birth control? I'd always figured that as long as I was single, I'd have to keep using condoms anyway, so why bother with the drugs? But now here I was at last, in a committed relationship, such as it was, and even if it couldn't quite be described as monogamous, I was pretty confident that my men weren't hitting the hay with anyone else, and I finally felt safe in abandoning safe sex. Not that using protection was a big deal – I mean, I'd been doing it my whole life, so I was totally used to it – but I thought it might be nice for us to do away with that extra, and in my mind, now unnecessary precaution. Plus, I was curious to know what it was like. I'd never once had sex without one, and at their age and levels of experience, I doubted that they had either.

I didn't tell them at first, though. I wanted to be darned sure that it was working before I took any chances. Even though I was willing to lay pretty long odds on me getting knocked up at my age, they were still way better than the odds of me getting into a three-way with my two closest friends, and we all know what happened there. Plus I'd never been much of a one for medications, and since I was afraid of side effects, I wanted to see how my body responded before I committed to doing it in the real wild.

As it turned out, the pills only seemed to affect me in one spot: the gut. Through all these years and all those beers I'd managed to keep my tummy largely under control, and now here it was, bubbling up over the waistline of my pants, a distinct roundish bulge that protruded ironically from my waist like that of a pregnant lady who was just beginning to show.

One Saturday morning I was ruefully examining this unwelcome addition to my wardrobe in the bathroom mirror when I heard the faintest of whisperings through the door that stood ajar behind me. I whipped my head around like I'd been caught masturbating and found them both standing at the door, peering through the crack one on top of the other like adolescent boys trying to catch a peek into the girls' locker room.

"What?" I snarled, dropping my silk robe hastily back down over my disfigured form. It disguised my gut about as well as a maternity dress and with far less pizzazz.

"Good morning, sweetie!" Sam said with unwarranted cheerfulness.

"Can I make you some coffee?" Ted chirped.

"Thanks," I grunted.

"Still half and half, or would you like all decaf today?"

"No, I do not want all decaf," I barked back, baffled by the absurdity of the question. I'd only switched to half-caff because my doctor had made me. The real thing gave me the sweats and jitters if I drank more than a cup of it nowadays, and I needed my morning java to last longer than that.

"Let us know if you change your mind," he sang out, and they both retreated, skipping, towards the kitchen.

I finished my toilette wondering if maybe they needed to cut down on the coffee, too.

I emerged from the bathroom to the aroma of bacon frying and went into the kitchen.

"Here's your coffee, sweetheart," Ted said, pouring out a cup untainted with milk or sugar into my favorite mug, setting it down on the table, and then pulling out my chair for me as carefully as if I were somebody's great-great-grandmother.

"Don't worry, we've got breakfast!" Sam called out from the stove, where he was monitoring the bacon and eggs.

"I'm making my world-famous pigs-in-a-blanket," Ted added, moving over to the electric griddle he'd set up on the counter.

Bacon and sausage? Maybe it wasn't the pill that was making me fat after all.

"Exactly how many people are you guys expecting for

breakfast?" I queried, but they ignored me and continued humming around the kitchen with their pots and pans while I stared around the little table, already set for three.

"Could you move your elbow there, dear?" Sam said, approaching me with his big arms sagging under the burden of two gigantic serving bowls.

I watched while they crowded their dishes onto the table and then doled out a mountain of lard-laden breakfast foods onto a platter and handed it to me.

"I can't eat all this!" I protested. It was two days worth of food, at least.

"Now, now," Sam clucked, "If you don't eat your meal, you won't get any dessert!"

I heard a whistling noise and turned to find Ted filling a bowl with a can of whipped cream.

Internally, I groaned. I was definitely not in the mood for that today. But then Ted retrieved a huge bucket of strawberries from the refrigerator and plunked it down in front of me as if it were a statue erected in my honor.

"You're always saying we should eat more fresh fruit!" he said, smiling and dipping one of the berries into the cream as if it were merely there for culinary purposes, after all.

I grunted again and began snapping off tiny bites of my pancake with my fork. Another woman might have refused; might simply have admitted that she was trying to lose weight, not gain it. Not me. I was too busy foolishly hoping they hadn't noticed my burgeoning belly.

"How's your breakfast, honey?" Sam said, resting his hand on my knee and squeezing it in an utterly non-sexual manner.

"What is with you guys today?" I burst out, dropping my fork to my plate with a clanging clatter. "I've never been called dear and sweetie and honey so many times in my life. What's with all the –" I flapped my hands in the air while I searched for the right word – "niceness?" I concluded, failing to find a better term for the sappiness with which they were grinning at me.

Slowly the smiles faded from their faces and they examined one another seriously and then turned back to me.

"Actually, there's something we'd like to talk to you about after breakfast," Ted said quietly.

They had both stopped looking at me and were staring at their plates as if they contained the most solemn pancakes ever made.

"All right," I returned, bowing my own head to my meal and diving into it with greater zeal.

We finished our breakfast in silence while the pall that hung over the room grew thicker and more palpable, enveloping me in an air of insurmountable melancholy that I suspected would only grow deeper when I learned the subject of this dreaded conversation.

They're breaking up with me, I thought hysterically. Wasn't that always the topic of discussion when someone needed to talk?

At last I shoved my plate aside, vowing to run six miles after breakfast if that's what it took to burn off that enormous pile.

"Well?" I said expectantly.

They glanced at each other and nodded as if by prearrangement.

"It's not so much that we wanted to talk to you," Ted began. "More that we were wondering if you had something you wanted to talk to us about," he said enigmatically.

"I don't think so," I answered slowly. "Why?"

"Well," Sam said, taking over for Ted, "We've noticed that there's been a – a change in you, lately."

"What kind of change?" I queried suspiciously, instinctively sitting up straighter and sucking in my gut.

"In your body. You know," he said, holding his hand out in the air over his belly.

I couldn't believe it. I'd spent more than a year allowing my body to be repeatedly ravaged by shallow losers who thought it was necessary to have a "talk" over a measly five pounds. I couldn't decide who to slap first.

"You still look great, by the way," Sam assured me.

"Absolutely," Ted concurred. "And we're sure you'll still look great as – things progress."

"Listen, fellas," I snorted contemptuously. "Let's not kid ourselves here. Any progression that happens in this body is not going to be an improvement. I'm forty years old, for heaven's sake. Gut or no gut, I'm only going to get worse-looking as time goes on. And if you're not willing to accept that, then maybe we should just end it now."

I stood up suddenly, trying to blink away the tears that had risen unbidden into my eyes, and rushed into the bedroom to gather up my clothes and get the hell out of there, thinking I'd stayed way too long in this place as it was.

Heavy footsteps thundered after me and in a moment I was standing again between them, as I had done so many countless times before. They leaned in towards me and that made it hard to avoid their eyes. I succeeded by looking at their chests instead. It did little to decrease my upset.

"Come back to the kitchen, Kathy," Sam pleaded.

"Let's sit down and talk about this," Ted suggested. "Come on, huh? I'll pour you a fresh cup of coffee."

I was barely half a cup into my morning and that offer was too good to refuse. Oh well, I thought. I can always make my escape afterwards. If I listen to their lecture then I'll really know what gigantic jerks they are. Reluctantly I let them lead me back to the table and set me down on my chair as if I were a set of fine china.

"You don't have to go through this alone," Sam said, scooting his chair towards mine with a loud scraping sound that set my teeth on edge.

"We want to be involved," Ted agreed.

Really, I thought, I'd only put on a few hormone-induced pounds. There was no need for a full-scale intervention.

"Actually, we think it's great."

"Unexpected," Ted added. "But we've been talking it over, and we really think we're ready."

"We've got it all worked out," Sam continued, rubbing his hand across my back reassuringly while my annoyance changed to confusion. "We'll have to get a bigger place, of course."

How big were they expecting me to get?

"But it'll be cool, don't you think?" Ted said. "So much easier with the three of us."

"Oh, yeah," Sam said. "We can totally take turns watching it so you can get some rest."

"What the hell are you talking about?" I blurted out at last.

"You know… the, um, bun in your oven?"

"The bundle of joy?" Ted volunteered.

"You think I'm pregnant?" I said, stunned. Granted, my periods were no longer as regular as they once were, but I hadn't thought they were that far off. Not that I could have expected them to notice. These were men who were surprised every month to find something else occupying what they seemed to believe was their own private territory.

Ted reached out to rub my new little tummy. "Aren't you?" he said.

"Um, not that I know of." I stared bewildered back at the two of them. Had I not known it was crazy, I would have thought they seemed disappointed.

"Oh," Sam said, his chin drooping a little. "Well, that's okay, too, I guess."

He winced abruptly and I knew that Ted had kicked him underneath the table.

"He means we're happy for you. We know you don't really want children."

"But if you changed your mind, we'd totally stand behind you!" Sam said quickly.

"If that was what you wanted," Ted added.

"You know, just because you're not this time, that doesn't mean it might not still happen," Sam said, crossing his fingers absentmindedly and tapping them on the table.

"Condoms are only ninety-nine percent effective, after all," Ted agreed.

"Right. And with two such virile young men as us…"

"It could be hard to beat those odds."

"Besides, you're not getting any younger, you know. What if you wake up a few years from now wishing you'd had a kid when you had the chance?" Sam was studying me earnestly, and something about the glint in his eye made me suspect that he wasn't really considering my best interests.

I looked back at their maturing faces and got a mental image of the two of them huddled over an infant, rocking and making cooing sounds at it while I sat in a corner, reading my book with cotton plugs tucked into my ears. And suddenly it struck me that my boys were growing up far faster than I was.

"Were you, like, hoping I was pregnant?" I said bluntly.

Ted was first to break the ensuing silence. "Well, not hoping exactly. I guess… I guess we wouldn't have been sorry about it."

"Listen," I said urgently. "Listen, you guys aren't even thirty…You have plenty of time for families and children."

"Oh, sure, sure we do," Sam agreed.

"Absolutely," Ted said.

"Of course, they won't be as beautiful as you are."

"Or as smart."

"Or as funny."

"Or as good at hockey."

All at once I was overcome by a strange suspicion that I couldn't quite define. That maybe my boys were seeing this relationship in a way I wouldn't have dreamed it was possible for any man to see it.

It scared the hell out of me. So naturally I did what any rational woman would do under the circumstances. I changed the subject.

"I went on the pill," I blurted out.

"What?" they said. And then, "Why?"

I shrugged. "I just thought... Well, we've been together for quite a while now... I guess I thought it might be nice to, you know, dispense with the condom thing. I mean, you guys aren't seeing anyone else, are you?"

"Of course not," Ted assured me, reaching out to take hold of my hand and shaking it gently. Sam just shook his head and I guess my imagination was still acting up because I could have sworn he'd grown a little misty-eyed.

"Anyway, that's why I've put on weight recently. It's one of the potential side effects."

They were still scrutinizing me curiously and I began to wonder if I'd done the wrong thing.

"It's... okay, isn't it?" I said uncertainly. "I mean, you're not upset?"

They looked at one another again in that way they had of communicating without talking.

"We're not upset," Sam replied. "It's really very sweet of you."

"We thought... I mean, you've always said that since you don't plan on getting married, that you'd probably be using condoms forever."

"Right, but we've all been tested and stuff, and if we're not... I mean, if it's just us..."

"It's just us," Ted said quickly.

Sam nodded and gave me that misty-eyed look again and suddenly I wondered if it wasn't just my boys who were guilty of reading more into this relationship than there was supposed to be.

CHAPTER 15

"You ready?" Sam said. His pint glass stood empty on the nightstand, but his eyes were still bulging with apprehension.

"I think so," I answered. How did you get ready for something like that exactly?

He swallowed nervously and lay back on the bed, not quite reclining, motionless except for his cock, which swayed gently before me, like a flagpole in a breeze. I clambered awkwardly up on top of him, feeling his naked penis sliding across my clitoris as I straddled him up to the waist.

"How about you, Ted?" he squeaked. "Are you ready?"

"Let's do it," he said, moving up behind me and pressing his cock temptingly against my buttocks as if he did this every day.

"Here we go," Sam whispered.

"Here we go," I agreed, moving my pussy up into position but not quite pushing him into me. Apparently his fear was contagious.

"Do you want to… I should probably go in first, right?"

"I would think so," I agreed. "It seems… more manageable."

I wasn't even sure why we were having this conversation, really. I didn't doubt that they'd already planned it out amongst themselves, as they had every other major event in our lives together thus far. Indeed, the second I'd announced I was finally ready to take the plunges they'd jumped into position as if they'd rehearsed it. I wouldn't even have been surprised if they'd practiced it beforehand, like a fire drill, complete with an alarm, a stopwatch, and an evacuation plan. And a couple of weeks before, Sam had asked me for the name and number of my OB/GYN.

"It's for a friend of mine," he'd claimed without looking me in the eye.

"What friend?" I demanded suspiciously. Besides me, there

weren't really many women in Sam's circle of acquaintances.

"No one you know," he'd maintained, but I was still suspicious, particularly when I saw him programming the information I gave him into the emergency numbers category of contacts on his phone, "for safekeeping," he said. Was he worried that they might break me? I wondered. Should I be worried, too?

"You two okay down there?" Ted said, interrupting my thoughts. He leaned over my shoulder to look at us and slapped his cock sideways against my buttcheek in the process.

I tilted my neck over my shoulder. "Getting impatient, are we?" I said.

"No, of course not," he answered simply. "I'm just ready. Really, really ready," he said, leaning his dick hard against my butt.

"All right, all right," Sam said. "We'd better not keep Ted waiting; you know what an animal he turns into when he has to wait."

"That's right," Ted agreed. "So up you go!"

And with that he grabbed me about the hips and plunked me down so neatly upon Sam's cock that I only had to shift slightly to let it in. It was the first time I'd had a naked dick inside my pussy and although it wasn't really that much different, I liked it.

"Shit, I'm gonna come," Sam groaned.

"No, you're not," I answered severely.

"I don't think I can help it," he heaved. I felt his cock tensing inside me as if he was trying to keep it from leaking.

"You can and you will," I insisted. "We've put this off long enough, and no one is going anywhere until the two of you have dp'ed me."

And then I felt hands hard on my ass and Ted's cock was squeezing into my hole and for half a minute they were both inside me and crazily I thought, This is it; we are one. The three of us are one.

And then one after another they yelled and I felt warm, wet gizz bursting into both my vagina and my anus and I could smell it all around me, the sweet sex juice of my two men coagulating on my grateful body, and then they both reached for my pussy and sent me flying without hardly even trying.

I lay panting between them, my skin sweating freely in the crease of flesh all around me. How quickly it was over, I marveled, this act we had so long anticipated. Yet in some way I knew, knew that it was only the beginning; that this would mark a new start for them and me.

They were both still holding me, snuggling into me like lovers do. I looked into the big mirror on Ted's dresser. They were both shining brightly and so was I. And as I gazed upon their blissful faces, one before me and one behind, my only wish was that I could give them both a kiss with as much fluid ease as I could take them both into me.

For a long time we didn't speak; merely snuggled up together quietly catching our breath, my head on Sam's chest, Ted's chin on my shoulder, as afternoon dimmed into evening. And then my stomach rumbled hungrily, spoiling the silence.

"Let's get you something to eat," Sam said softly, stroking my hair where it had fallen about his face.

"I'd like a beer," Ted ventured, and of a sudden we all rolled in opposite directions, toppling over and away from each other like alphabet-blocks, laughing crazily as our limbs mingled and intertwined and at last, parted.

"Last one ready buys the first round!" I shouted, groping in Ted's closet for one of the spare dresses I kept there.

They both jumped up from the bed and leapt across the room towards me, fumbling for their own pants and shirts and underwear on the floor where they'd fallen. Giddy, I tried to struggle into my bra and failed.

"Here, your straps are all twisted," Ted intervened kindly, coming over to rectify them.

"I want to help, too!" Sam said, leaping to my other side and fussing with the other half of the brassiere.

How ordinary we were, I marveled as I stood between them, for all the world like an average wife whose husbands were helping her get ready for a night out on the town. How like a regular couple, I thought as we walked arm in arm in arm on the sidewalk beside all of the other couples enjoying the late summer evening. And sitting between them half an hour later at our local pub, it struck me again. Not the kinkiness, not the filthiness of what we had done, but rather how sweet and natural it seemed, one moment to be pressed naughtily between them, and the next to be chatting and enjoying a beer and a snack together as we so often had. Just like any other average, happy couple you'd meet on the streets of our town. Maybe more so.

We tried it again when we got home. They switched positions so that Sam was behind me. I can't explain how amazing it was, being rocked between them like a see-saw, one going in as the other went out, me trying to hold steady between them as I took them both into me, for much longer this time. How wonderfully it almost hurt when they thrust into me together, their penises seeming to meet in the middle of my body, in the center of my being; the extraordinary fullness that I felt in having them both, in bringing them together within me. I only knew that I wanted more; did not know if I could ever go back now, to having only one man. I couldn't imagine that I would ever want to. Not only one lover, or even two others besides them.

Perhaps I should have known then that it was the beginning of the end; that things had gotten too perfect, too magical between us now to go on indefinitely, but of course I didn't. I guess no one ever does. Still, I was grateful for the months that so blissfully followed before disaster struck. My boys filled me with many happy memories, memories that were to be my sole source of solace in the months that I would soon spend alone.

"No, no, come in my asshole," I said to Sam, who was rapidly speeding towards his inevitable conclusion in my more accommodating void.

"Really?" he said, slackening his pace slightly. "Didn't Ted just...?"

"That's why," I said hurriedly, afraid he would finish without finishing the job to my satisfaction. "I like the way it spills out of there when there's a lot of it."

Even now I could sometimes still manage to make Sam purple in the face.

"Boy, you really..." he spluttered before recovering his composure. "You still want it from behind, I suppose?"

"Yes, please," I said. He grabbed my butt and torso and flipped me with an audible plop over onto my knees. I loved the way he did that; as if I was a very naughty but very compliant rag doll. Ted was more of the supervisory sort, and I liked that a lot, too. "Could you please roll over?" he'd say, making a twirling motion with his finger that I instantly obeyed. "So I can fuck you from behind? Thank you." Of course, I did my share of commanding, too.

"Go, go, go!" I shouted. Eagerly I reached back with my hands and spread my cheeks. I groaned loudly as Sam slid his cock between them.

"Did you get it all in there?" I inquired anxiously when he was done.

"Didn't spill a drop," he answered, amused.

"You are really enjoying the no-condom thing, aren't you?" Ted said with a mischievous grin.

"I had no idea semen could be such fun," I answered seriously.

"So, what, it feels good sliding out of your tushy or something?" Sam said. "Doesn't it slide out of your, you know, the same way?"

"Not exactly," I answered. "It's all diluted when it comes out of my pussy, because of all the moisture."

"Your hoo-hoo is very moist," Ted agreed. Sam glared at him.

"Plus it isn't as tight. It stays in my asshole longer. And then later on when I'm just walking around doing my thing, I'll feel it come sliding out, this gooey glob of cock juice."

"Cock juice?" Sam said with wonder.

"Cock juice," I affirmed enthusiastically. "You have no idea how awesome it is to have it ooze out of you hours later when you're not expecting it. And that smell! Suddenly surrounding you like cock sprung fresh from a man's pants. That is how you know you've been fucked but good."

"Cock sprung fresh?"

"Ode to a Fresh-Sprung Cock, by Kathy Morris," Ted sniggered.

"You were kind of waxing poetic," Sam agreed.

"Well, it is poetic!" I huffed. "That's the best part of the whole thing, when you guys unbuckle your belts, drop your trousers, and let your cocks loose. That's when I know without a doubt that I'm about to get laid. It's the last perfect, pristine moment of pure anticipation."

"But I don't wear belts," Sam said, pouting abjectly. "You must be so disappointed!"

"Fortunately you have other redeeming qualities," I replied. "I've learned to accept this one shortcoming as part of the wonder that is you."

"I wear belts," Ted said proudly.

"That you do," I replied, nodding my affirmation. "That's why you always catch me drooling just before you're about to give it to me."

"Huh. I just thought that was because we're always doing it before breakfast."

One morning I lay in bed naked and alone, sighing contentedly and thinking about how great my life was. They'd fucked me simultaneously again and it had gone really smoothly this time; so smoothly that it wasn't even uncomfortable anymore, taking both of them at once. As if I felt full, but not overstuffed. There really was an art to it. You had to get a particular rhythm going on both ends for it to work well for all parties, and that required considerable coordination among the three of us. If someone slipped, or got off the beat, it took time to get back on track and I'd lose the lovely build-up I'd had going and almost need to start from scratch. Not that they weren't game about that, of course. They still had the stamina and enthusiasm of young men and it didn't take much to get them to take another crack at my cracks.

Sam was showering and Ted had gone to fix our coffee. I'd already taken my turn in the shower and was stretched out on the bed, my face planted in my pillow, waiting for my hair to dry. I was fondly recollecting the pressure of Sam's chest against my backside and the clutch of Ted's hands on my ass and feeling entire satisfied and rife with well-being when suddenly I felt something warm, wet and pointy snaking its way into my ass-crack.

"Ted?" I inquired, instinctively spreading my thighs apart.

"Mmmph," he said, his answer muffled by the oh-so-sensitive fat of my ass. He was running his tongue all along my crack up and down and suddenly something within me reared up its horny head and I was no longer completely satisfied.

He withdrew for a moment and I felt his sticky saliva drying cool between my cheeks. "Do you mind?" he said.

I turned my head to look at him. He was the same Ted I'd met several years before: a little quiet, a little reserved, but now his chin was resting on my ass and his long-fingered hands were poised over it as he looked at me in silent query and I couldn't help but laugh.

"If you please," I said with dignity.

And he took those hands and used them to spread my vast cheeks apart and then buried his face in between them.

I felt that muscular tongue probing my asshole and I gasped, spread my legs wider, and wondered what on God's green earth I had done to deserve this. He pressed into it further, working the surface

137

and then thrusting, penetrating into it, that tight little hole still somewhat stretched by its recent action and I writhed with pleasure and let out a moan that had to have been heard halfway to downtown.

Sam burst out of the bathroom, nakedly fresh from the shower, towel-less and dripping all over the carpet. "What the hell was that?!" he said, and then, taking in the scene, cried, "Are you licking her asshole?"

Ted retreated, leaving me lost in lust and lascivious agony. It was first time since I'd met him that I'd ever been unhappy to see Sam.

"Not exactly," Ted answered.

"Sure looked like it," Sam said dubiously.

"It was more like… a tongue-fucking," Ted replied icily, glaring at Sam as irritably as I was. "Do you have a problem with that?"

"Well, of course I have a problem with that!" Sam shot back. "How long has this been going on?" he demanded, cold accusation in his eyes.

"About five minutes, until you interrupted," I retorted.

"No, I mean…" He looked helplessly at the two of us, me propped up on my elbows on the bed, my breasts drooping dejectedly downward, while Ted sat sideways at its foot. "I just wish you had told me you were into that."

Ted shrugged. "Why is it such a big deal?"

"Well, because!" Sam said. "Look here."

And he came over to the bed, trailing shower-water in his wake, and yanked me up into a standing position, leaving Ted at my back. And then he got down on his knees and smiled at me and touched his tongue to my pussy.

I couldn't help it. I laughed and looked back at Ted, who was sitting quite comfortably now in a direct line with my bared asshole. He smiled at me sideways and, taking the cue, I bent over. I gasped again as he dug into it, even more forcibly than before.

By the time I was done I was dripping as if I, too, had just emerged from the shower, but they didn't complain about my slipperiness when they fucked me together again, harder and longer and with undiminished enthusiasm. What great guys, I thought, watching Sam's face harden into an orgasmic frown as he hung tight to my happy breasts and forced his cock into my box. What wonderful fellows, I thought as Ted removed his dick from my ass, rolled me over and slipped it into my sopping-wet pussy, too.

After that, it was no holds barred for any of us. It was almost as if some invisible line had finally been crossed, and whatever inhibitions or compunctions we might have had about any of the things we might do to or with one another had utterly vanished overnight. We couldn't go for a stroll in the park without me dropping to my knees to suck a cock or two, and get my pussy eaten if the spot was secluded, to boot. We'd make plans to go to the movies, and instead I'd sit on Sam's face in the backseat of his small car and Ted and I would watch while he ate me, and then I'd get up on all fours with my ass hanging out while they took turns fucking me doggie-style through the open door, one watching covertly around the deserted corner of the parking lot for mall security. We'd go out for a friendly drink and I'd end up slipping off my panties in the alley next to our bar and lifting up my skirt while they took turns holding me up for the other to fuck. And then we'd go inside and they'd both finger my naked pussy with one hand while drinking their beers with the other and I'd watch my face flushing in the mirror over the bar and try not to let on. Once on a late-night bus that we took back from a beer festival I even crawled up on their laps, stripped off my shirt and bra, and gave each of them a breast to suck on while they fondled my undersides and I made faces at the three strange men sitting slack-jawed and fascinated in the last row. And I don't think I'll ever forget the day we arrived at the rink extra early for our game and found the locker room empty.

"Oh, boy!!" Sam exclaimed, his eyes popping like firecrackers on the fourth of July as he turned excitedly to me and Ted.

"Right there with you, pal!" Ted grunted, lifting me up at the waist while Sam yanked my shorts down over my ankles.

"Hey!!" I cried. They ignored me. In a flash Ted had wriggled out of his sweatshorts and was standing in front of me, his hands under my ass, holding me up at waist height as I wrapped my legs around him. I could feel Sam's belly tentatively touching my thighs and knew that he, too, was pantless.

"A little lower," I heard him whisper as Ted slid effortlessly into me without any apparent exertion of his abundant musculature. "Lower!" he whispered more urgently as his cock tickled my asscrack. "Come on, Ted, I'm not as tall as you!"

Ted leaned forward, effectively dropping me down a few inches.

"Aha, that's more like it!" I heard Sam exclaim as he grabbed onto my hips and poked his dick unapologetically into my asshole.

"Yikes!" I yelled as they thrust simultaneously into me.

"Shhh!" Sam said, jamming his cock even harder up my ass while Ted rocked his hips towards mine. "Do you want us to get caught?"

"No, but I – oh! – it's impossible – ohh! – to be quiet with – ohhh!! – two cocks in your – Oh, my God!"

"So can we come again early again next game?" Sam proposed fifteen minutes later, as we were dressing in the locker room now packed with our teammates, several of whom had commented that it smelled "different" in there today. "Come on, Kathy... it'll help you get loosened up and relaxed before the game!"

I was already loosened up. These days I always felt relaxed. I had never in my life felt so happy to be alive. I had never before even felt so alive.

Mealtimes were the best. I guess something about the oral sex I was now so frequently getting formed the connection in my mind, because for some reason I was always horny at breakfast and dinner, meals that we frequently shared before or after a passionate night. Somehow I'd gotten into the habit of splaying myself out on the table, my legs spread gleefully wide.

"Breakfast-time!" I'd yell, plunking a cover over the French toast to keep it warm.

They'd emerge sleepily from the bedroom and find me waving my legs about like one of those dancing sign-advertisers you find on urban street corners. I guess I was a believer in hands-on marketing.

"You know you're like a nymphomaniac or something, right?" Sam would say grumpily. He may have been an early riser, but he wasn't much of a morning person.

"I've got pussy!" I'd offer tantalizingly, opening up again and wafting the scent of it towards them with my hand.

"I have to be at work in half an hour," Ted would say. "Why can't you wake us up earlier when you're in the mood?"

"You're right," I'd apologize. "Sorry, fellas. I'll take care of it this time."

And then I'd reach down and start stroking my pussy slow and smooth with my own fingers, gently making cooing noises as if it was the greatest feeling in the world, and they'd look at one another and sigh, and before the steam was even off the coffee I'd be getting laid or licked or both.

It wasn't always like that, of course. Some mornings if we'd been up late they wouldn't respond to the alarm at all, and I'd have to resort to drastic measures to get them moving.

"Well, I was hungry," I'd say when one of them woke to find his sleep-stiffened cock already balls-deep in my mouth.

And then I'd turn my backside to the one I'd started with and give the other a go, pretending not to notice that I'd gotten down on all fours and raised my pussy temptingly in the air.

"Rise and shine!" I'd say.

"You are so annoyingly cheerful in the morning, you know that?"

"It's hard not to be when I wake up with two such sweet and sexy young men," I'd say seriously, grabbing onto both cocks and giving them a fond shake. "Come on, now, I just want to suck you guys off, just a little bit, huh? Won't that be fun?"

And then I'd turn and give the other one the full view of my pretty little box while I sucked on the other, and even if I didn't get fucked I'd at least end up with two giant mouthfuls of gizz for my efforts, which was a pretty great way to start the day in my book.

As time went on, however, these incredibly amusing dalliances routinely began to be cut short, and it was obvious to all of us who was to blame. Ted.

He'd been sneaking off to work earlier and coming home later, and several times now, he'd even gone into the office on the weekend. He'd always worked fairly long hours, but now it seemed to be getting out of control, and it was actually getting to the point where sometimes I almost felt like I missed him. But when we pressed him about it, all he would say was that he was in middle of an important project and had to get it done as quickly as possible. It was so unlike him to neglect us that I even entertained the possibility that it was all an excuse and he was having an affair. I would have liked to question Sam about that, but I couldn't figure out how to broach the subject. Would it have meant that he was cheating on me, or that he was cheating on us?

I abandoned that theory, though, when one Saturday morning I woke up late to find them having a terrible row in the kitchen.

"What, again?" Sam said. He almost sounded angry. "This is the third weekend in a row already! I thought you were going to try to cut your hours so you'd have time for, you know, other things!"

He looked meaningfully at Ted and I got that strange sensation in my gut that I always got when I was made aware that they were keeping something from me.

"Well, I've been trying!" Ted replied. "It's just really busy right now with this big new client and –"

"There's always some big new client!" Sam shouted. "There's always going to be some big new client!" I was shocked to see him getting so worked up over this.

"And what, you never stay late at work?!" Ted shot back. "You never put in overtime to get a project done?"

"Of course I do! But I'm not like you, Ted! Besides hanging out with you and Kathy, I don't have anything else I'd be like to be doing with my time!"

Ted stood, shaking, and for a moment I wasn't sure whether he was going to storm out or burst into tears. He did neither.

"You just don't understand," he said at last. "People are counting on me. I can't let them down."

"But what about you?" Sam said softly. "What about what you want? You're thirty years old, Ted. You're not getting any younger."

It was an echo of something I'd often said, often felt myself, but I was stunned to hear the familiar phrase issuing from the mouth of one of my boys.

"Well, neither are you," Ted muttered, glancing briefly at me before marching to the door and flinging it open to a morning bright with beautiful sunshine. Then the door slammed shut and we heard footsteps fading down the hall.

"I'll be right back," I said, cinching my robe about my waist and tucking my feet hurriedly into my slippers.

I found him at the bottom of the stairwell, his face turned upwards as if he were debating whether to come back upstairs after all. He grinned sheepishly when he saw me.

"Thanks for coming after me," he said, circling his long arms tight around my waist and pulling me towards him. "I didn't say goodbye, and I couldn't decide whether I should go back or not."

"Thanks for waiting," I answered, grinning back. I gazed at him a moment. "You okay?" I said at last.

"Yeah," he shrugged. "I guess you're probably wondering what that was all about."

"Probably none of my business," I replied.

"You don't think what goes on between Sam and me is your business?"

"To a point," I conceded. "But you guys have your own relationship. I'm the newcomer here."

He brought his hand to my chin and lifted it, and then kissed me gently on the lips.

"I'll tell you all about it," he promised. "But not today."

I nodded, squeezed him one last time, and shuffled my slippered feet back up the stairs.

"I'm sorry about that, Kathy," Sam said the second I reappeared. "I shouldn't have gotten so mad in front of you."

"It's all right," I answered. "I'm sure you had your reasons."

"I did," he assured me. "But I'm not sure...I'm not sure Ted would really want me to talk about it..."

"Don't worry," I said, pulling clean underwear out of my drawer in the dresser. "I wouldn't ask you to betray the confidence of a friend."

I did wonder about it, though. And I decided that the best thing for me to do was to give them some space. Lately I'd gotten into the habit of going over there nearly every night, and I thought maybe they could use some alone time. I made my excuses and gave my own place some much-needed attention. And when I next saw them, the following Friday, it was obvious that they'd made up and I didn't want to stir things up by asking a lot of nosy questions, so I let it go. But I noticed that after that Ted didn't go in to work on weekends anymore, and I knew that whatever their argument had been about, Sam had won.

CHAPTER 16

Near the end of July, Sam's grandfather died. Sam was barely coherent when he called to tell me.

"Complications of pneumonia," he said, sniffling into the phone. "Very sudden. Nothing anyone could have done."

"I'm so sorry, sweetie," I said with genuine sadness.

"Funeral's tomorrow at my parents' place. Mom wants to get it over with. Driving down in the morning."

"Can I come with you?" I asked uncertainly, unsure whether this would be considered an intrusion on the family grief.

He sighed with relief. "I was hoping you'd say that." He paused. "I don't suppose you'd want to come over tonight?" he said.

Ted was out of town for a couple of days on a business trip. That meant Sam was at the apartment all alone.

"Just let me pack a bag and I'll be right over," I promised.

The door was unlocked and I let myself in. I found him in his own bedroom, perched sadly on the edge of the bed, lost in sober melancholy. He looked terrible. His eyes were bloodshot and puffed up like roasted marshmallows and he sat hunched over, more miserable than I'd ever seen him look. To see Sam not cheerful was a rarity indeed.

"Thanks for coming," he said gratefully, not rising to meet me but extending his arms in a half-hearted hug. Carefully navigating around the pile of tissues on the floor, I made my way over to him, wrapped my arms around his neck, and pulled him to my chest.

We stood like that a long time while he cried, me making soothing noises and stroking the bristly back of his head in what I hoped was a comforting fashion.

"Ted couldn't get a flight out tonight," he choked. "But he'll meet us there tomorrow."

I nodded.

"I'm exhausted, Kathy," he said at last. "Would you mind if we went to bed?"

"Sure," I said. "We'll probably want to get an early start tomorrow anyway so you can see your folks before the ceremony."

"Right," he agreed glumly. I went into the bathroom to get undressed. Somehow it just didn't seem like a night for getting naked in front of him. When I returned, he was already lying in bed. The apartment suddenly seemed very quiet and empty without Ted, and I understood why he'd wanted me to come by.

I lay down beside him; circled his waist quietly with my arm, and nuzzled my head against his neck. He stroked my hair thoughtfully.

"Why do people have to die?" he said, brushing his lips against my forehead.

I didn't answer. I had no answer for him. Instead I just squeezed his hand and caressed his stomach with my fingers until I drifted off into sleep.

I woke in the middle of the night and found Sam still tenderly stroking my hair while I slept. All I could see by the moonlight filtering in through the open blinds was a glistening in his eyes.

"Can't sleep?" I murmured.

"I dozed a little bit," he answered unconvincingly.

I wrapped my arm around him and hugged him reassuringly.

"Do you want a beer?" I said.

He turned towards me and blinked his big eyes at me. "Actually, that would be nice."

I padded my way across the apartment in my bare feet to the kitchen. I'd made this journey so many times that I could do it in the dark without stumbling. When I returned with our beers, I set them both down on the nightstand on his side of the bed.

"You can put yours over there," he ventured.

"Oh, of course," I said. I was so used to sharing a nightstand with one or the other of them that it hadn't even occurred to me to take advantage of Ted's temporary absence to claim my own space. Actually, I didn't mind the sharing much. It meant I had to lean over one of them any time I wanted a drink of water, but that was a perk in itself.

"Weird without Ted here, isn't it?" he observed.

"Different," I agreed.

"I can't remember the last time we were alone together."

"It's been a while."

We lay together silently a long while and sipped our beers. And then he propped himself up on one elbow and spoke, his voice shaking slightly.

"Do you think it would be all right if just this once, that we, you know – just me and you?"

I hesitated, but only for a second. "Come here," I said, taking him in my arms.

"Ted won't mind, will he?" he inquired anxiously.

"I'm sure he won't."

"It's not even that I really want to… I just need…"

"Come here," I said again, rolling him over on top of me and wrapping my legs tightly around him.

After we'd made love he did finally drift off into sleep, but I lay awake and finished the beers we'd neglected and watched the moonlight sparkling through his long dark eyelashes until dawn.

CHAPTER 17

Barb and Ken greeted us with hugs and tears.

"Thank you so much for coming," Sam's mother said, her eyes brimming over with grateful sincerity.

"Mom!" Sam cried, bundling her into his arms.

"I know, sweetie," she said, patting him hard on the back. "I know."

We whiled away the morning preparing for the reception that was to take place following the funeral. I made myself useful setting out dinnerware and helping Barb slice melons for her legendary fruit salad, while Sam and his father rearranged the furniture and set out chairs to accommodate the crowd.

"Thank you, dear," she said appreciatively as I dug into their cupboard seeking two final serving bowls. "I don't know what I would have done without your help!"

I shrugged. "It helps to have something to do," I remarked.

She stopped fussing with the cloth napkins for a second to glance up at me.

"It certainly does," she agreed, then went back to her work.

A little before one o'clock, we heard a car pulling up outside.

"Now who could that be?" Barb wondered aloud, marching to the door and opening it. The service wasn't for another hour.

But I knew at once who it was. I slipped past her and nearly ran outside to find Ted climbing out of a rented sedan and Sam already striding purposefully towards him.

"Glad you could make it," Sam said, pulling Ted into a half-embrace and a handshake.

"Wouldn't have missed it," he answered seriously before turning to me. "There she is," he said, drawing me tenderly into his arms.

"We missed you," I breathed into his ear as he enveloped me

with a smile. "Glad you're back."

"Me, too," he said, giving my shoulder a friendly pat and gazing warmly into my eyes. Then he turned to Sam and said, "How you holding up?"

Sam shrugged in answer. "Okay, I guess. I still can't believe it. He seemed so young!"

I heard his mom chuckling behind me and my attention was roused. It was the first laughter I'd heard all day.

"You think ninety-four is young?" she teased. "You must think your dad and I are real spring chickens!"

"Well, you are!" he agreed. "You guys'll never –" He stopped short and as I watched his face grow pale with horror, I knew what he'd been about to say.

"It's nearly time," Ken interrupted gruffly. "I think we'd better get going."

Ted and I were already dressed in our funeral clothes, and while the family retreated to their rooms to change we stood uncomfortably together in the kitchen, not speaking but only occasionally glancing at one another for reassurance. Finally they emerged, Sam taking his mother's arm and leading her out to the car, his dad trailing along behind them with me and Ted. We gazed at one another sympathetically, the three outsiders. I guess no matter how close you are to someone, you can't really understand their grief if you're not the one experiencing it.

The funeral was nice, as nice as a funeral can be. It was a non-denominational service and lots of the local folks came out to pay their respects. Nearly all of them knew Sam and Ted, of course, and some of them looked queerly at me as if wondering what my relationship to the family was. For once I didn't care. I knew that this was one occasion in which no one would even dare to think suspiciously of me for standing by my men. And I did. I stood shoulder-to-shoulder between them in my long black dress, my head bowed in quiet contemplation, remembering my mother's funeral and thinking how the sparkling sunshine had made that terrible day just a bit brighter, too.

"He was a wonderful man, wasn't he, Ted?" Barb said when it was over. "I know you didn't know him well, but..."

"He told the greatest stories," Ted answered promptly. "Remember that one about the giant swordfish on the mantelpiece?

How he always insisted he caught it in the lake on a fishing trip?"

" 'But Grandpa, swordfish live in the ocean,' " Sam recalled. " 'Not this one, my boy. This one was raised in Holy Water. The holy waters of Lake Michigan.' "

"Where did he get that swordfish?" Ken wondered.

"Tag sale, I'll bet you anything," Sam replied. "Remember how he used to love to go cruising through town looking for them? Always convinced he was going to find a hidden treasure in someone's old roll-up desk."

"I remember that!" Ted exclaimed. "You should check all of his old furniture. Wouldn't it be funny if he'd found something after all?"

"I wouldn't be surprised if he hid something in a desk himself!" Sam declared. "It would be just like him."

"Well, I don't know about that," his mom answered doubtfully. "But he did leave something for you, sweetheart."

"Eh, I don't need any of Grandpa's stuff. You should keep it, Mom."

"You'll want this. It's a letter he wrote to you shortly before he died. He made me promise to deliver it to you – afterwards."

We all stopped dead in our tracks. Sam wiped fresh tears from his eyes and when at long last he spoke, all he said, in a very small voice, was "Thanks, Mom."

We didn't stay overnight. All of us had to work in the morning, and even Sam didn't seem to want to be there anymore, either.

"I'll come back down next weekend," he promised. "To help you go through Grandpa's things."

"You don't have to do that, Samuel," Barbara said.

"No, I want to," he said. "It will help me get to know him better."

We stayed late enough to help Sam's folks clean up after the reception, and then we said our farewells and embarked on the long drive back to the city, me driving Sam's car and Ted in his rental.

"Have you read your letter yet?" I inquired when we were halfway home. I swiveled my head around to look at Sam where he lay sprawled out in the back seat in a hopeless attempt at napping and then re-glued my eyes to the road.

"Nah," he answered vaguely, and for a moment I thought it was strange. Then it occurred to me that maybe he wanted to save it for the right moment, and maybe driving back in the car from the funeral wasn't the best time for a heartrending venture.

We didn't speak much on the ride home. I could see Ted trailing along behind us and I wondered why; usually he was a much faster driver than I was, and I thought that he should have passed us long before. I appreciated knowing he was right behind, though. In some strange way it made me feel that he was with us after all.

"Hey, can we go to your place?" Sam said suddenly as we neared our exit.

"What?" I answered. "Why?" Never once had I had them over to the hole I called home. I wasn't even convinced that there was room for the three of us in there.

He shrugged. "I'd just like to see it, is all."

"Well, I guess that would be all right," I said doubtfully. "I hope you've got low expectations."

"Great, I'll call Ted."

I watched the sedan veering off the highway behind us and then following us down the avenue to my apartment. I took an open spot on the street in front of my mid-sized brick building and waited as Ted parked behind me. Then we all got out and I reluctantly dragged them the three stories up the rickety stairs to my apartment, convinced that this was not the most cheerful destination for three people just come from a funeral.

They stood in the doorway and stared horrified at the yellow shades half ripped from the windows, the broken tiles in what passed for my bathroom, the packing-boxes I used for my nightstands.

Sam whistled. "What a dump!" he said.

"You didn't do it justice," Ted agreed.

"It's not so bad," I said defensively. "It costs a quarter of what you guys pay. Some of us haven't quite managed to settle on a career yet, you know."

"You spend most nights with us, anyway," Sam observed.

"True," I said. "And it's not as if I'm having company here."

"You are tonight," he answered. "I think we should stay here."

"Why?" I said again, confounded as to why they'd want to cram themselves into this tiny shitshack when they had a relatively luxurious place right down the road.

"See how the other half lives," Sam replied.

"See how you live," Ted clarified. "You said it wasn't so bad, right?"

I supposed it would be rude to refuse. A man had died, after all. Wasn't I obligated to obey the wishes of the mourners?

"Okay," I agreed after a moment's hesitation. "If you think there's room."

"We'll make room," Sam insisted.

It wasn't easy. The three of us fairly had to crush together to all fit side by side on my full-sized bed, and every time someone had to get up to go to the bathroom, he had to practically step on top of the other two to make it the ten feet to the toilet. We made the most of it, though.

"Have you got any beer, Kathy?" Sam mumbled into my shoulder, his back crammed up against the partially papered wall.

"Of course!" I answered, attempting to struggle out from between them to my feet.

"I'll get it," Ted said, rolling off the other edge of the mattress and onto the cracked and creaky wooden floor. "It'll be easier."

He returned in a moment with two full pints, stepping gingerly across the floorboards as if fearful of taking a tumble.

"I guess we'll have to share," he said, nodding at the drinks in his hands. "Do you really only own two glasses?"

"Well, I don't usually need more!" I answered defensively.

"Seriously, Kathy, are you really this poor?" Sam inquired with sincere concern.

"No, not really," I replied. "It's just…You don't want to acquire a lot of stuff when you move so much. But I've been here so long now… I mean, I may live poor, but at least I've got money in the bank." I did, too. I always made sure I had enough stashed away for the next move if I decided to make it without warning. "I don't know; I guess I'm just used to living like this. I mean, who ever wants to come home with me anyway?"

I blushed. It wasn't often these days that I was reminded of the incredibly lonely life I'd led before Sam and Ted and I didn't like it much. They both gulped their beers silently and then handed me their glasses. I took a small sip from each and then handed them back without looking at either of them.

"We're always happy to come home to you, Kathy," Sam said, his eyes brimming with tenderness.

"Every day," Ted agreed.

"Oh, what do you know?" I answered crossly, reaching over him to flick off the light. But as I lay down between them, I sensed the stress of the long melancholy day draining out of my body, and as I felt myself relaxing in their cozy comfort I thought, well, why not, why not me, too?

"I like coming home to you, too," I whispered into the darkness, and, burying my face in my two-thirds of a pillow, dropped exhaustedly to sleep.

I woke before dawn to find Sam attempting to struggle his way out from between my hip and the wall with no inconsiderable effort.

"Sorry, sweetie," he whispered, tugging an arm out from beneath my thigh. "I didn't mean to wake you."

"That's all right," I answered, reaching up to caress his rough, unshaven cheek. Ted hadn't stirred beside me. "Couldn't you sleep?"

"Nah… nah, I'm gonna go back to the apartment and get ready for work. I'll be better once I'm doing something."

"Want me to come over tonight?" I asked, glancing out the window at the streetlights shining through my torn blinds and wondering how long it was until morning.

He paused for a moment, his face cloaked in shadow. "That'd be great," he said softly.

I leaned up on one elbow to kiss him goodbye and then watched his silhouette stumbling across the floor to the door. At my doorway he hesitated, and I wondered if there was something else he wanted to say, but then I saw him kicking the floor and realized he was getting into his clothes. A few minutes later he gave me a little wave, and with only the slightest of sounds, he edged open my door and slipped out into the hall, vanishing into the darkness.

I must have fallen back to sleep, because when I next opened my eyes, the sky had already transformed into a pale blue tinted with pink, and Ted was stretched out on his side, gazing over at me with inscrutable eyes.

"Couldn't sleep, either, huh?" I said, reaching up to caress his rough, unshaven cheek.

"I slept very well," he answered. "It's just more fun watching you sleep."

I rolled over into his arms and for a long while we lay there close together, my head tucked under his chin while he stroked my hair up over my ears with his strong, gentle fingers.

After a time I propped myself up to peek at the alarm clock that sat on the floor by my bed. "I have to get up for work pretty soon," I sighed.

"Me, too," he replied, pulling me closer and tickling my earlobe with his tongue.

"Doesn't seem like it," I remarked.

"Soon is relative," he answered, leaning in to kiss me on the lips.

All at once I felt his hardness growing on my thigh, and before I could even come up with a clever observation of the fact, he had stripped off both my underthings and his and was penetrating me without a word or even a smile.

Afterwards he remained silent, and I lay in bed and watched him sliding that lithe body back into his shirt and trousers, wearing an oddly blank expression that betrayed nothing of what he was thinking. When he had finished dressing, he knelt awkwardly back down onto the mattress to kiss me goodbye.

"Thank you, Kathy," he said, squeezing my hand before heading for the door, and I couldn't help but wonder what it was about death that makes people want to love one another.

CHAPTER 18

"**We need to talk,**" Ted said, sliding my beer across their kitchen table towards me. I looked over at Sam, who nodded. It had been two months since the funeral, and in that time he had become a very subtly changed man. It was difficult to say what it was exactly about him that had changed, because on the surface he was as crude and comical as ever. But beneath the wisecracking exterior a different man seemed to lie, one who was a bit more thoughtful and intense; more serious and grown-up somehow. And some days, both sides became equally apparent, this day being one of them.

"I am not pregnant!" I joked. They laughed and I was reassured. I confess I wasn't really worried. I guess eventually you come to a point in a relationship in which you're so confident in its stability that even the dreaded "need to talk" phrase no longer alarms you.

"So what is it?" I said, taking a sip of my beer and reaching out to grab hold of their hands.

"Well... we've decided to move," Sam said.

My heart beat a little faster and I felt myself nervously squeezing their fingers. Wait a minute, I thought. I'm the one who moves. You're supposed to stay here.

"Where to?" I said, trying to keep the burgeoning apprehension out of my voice.

"Not far," Ted answered quickly. "We've found a place on the outskirts of town."

"What's wrong with this place?" I said, puzzled.

"Oh, nothing, really. It just isn't big enough," Sam explained. "See, Ted would like to set up a studio for his painting."

"Oh!" I said, brightening. "That's wonderful, Ted!" I beamed at him and he smiled back, warm and fuzzy, through his glasses. "Is it like a loft or something?"

They looked quickly at one another and then back at me. "It's a house," Sam said. "We want to buy it."

I gaped at them, astonished. They were buying a house already? At the ripe old age of thirty? Here I was, a decade older, and I was only a few steps up from living in my car.

"Pending your approval," Ted added hastily. "I mean, we want you to come and look at it. See if you like it."

"I'm sure I'll love it!" I responded enthusiastically, thinking that it wasn't my place to object even if I hated it more than ballroom dancing. But happy as I was for them, as the implication of the news began to sink in, my heart's beating transformed into an anxious flutter. I wouldn't be seeing them as much if they were out in the suburbs. But again, this was their decision, not mine, and I was determined not to let on that I had any concerns about it. "What's it like?"

"Oh, it's fantastic!" Sam exclaimed. "So bright and sunny, you can't believe it. And it's got a great big backyard."

"With a ten-foot-high wooden fence already built all around it," Ted added.

"Perfect for sunbathing in the nude!" Sam remarked, winking at me.

I chuckled. "I didn't know you were into that, too," I said, pretending to misunderstand.

"Oh, I will be!" he answered, rubbing his hand over mine and shooting me a leer.

"Combination kitchen/dining room," Ted said.

"Just the right size for us to bend you right over this table and…"

"And the master bedroom is enormous," Ted interrupted, glaring at Sam. "Twice the size of the one we have here."

"Think about it, Kathy! We'll no longer have to suffer with an ordinary king-sized bed. Now we can get nasty on a Cal King!"

"What is with you today?!" Ted exploded. "Here we are trying to have an adult conversation and all you can do is make crude jokes!"

"Househunting makes me horny," he answered simply, but he wiped the lascivious look from his face and adopted a more serious expression. It would have been more believable had he not concurrently reached under the table and thrust his hand between my thighs.

I wasn't offended, though. In the weeks that had passed since his grandfather's death, Sam had been melancholy and definitely off his game as far as bedroom stuff was concerned. The mood had affected us all, and the few times we'd made love had been straightforward, ordinary affairs, not the raunchy romps of which we'd made a habit of late. All someone peeking in the window would have seen was a plain old heterosexual couple going at it plain old missionary style. And then a slightly different couple going at it the same way a few minutes later. In any case, it was encouraging to see his enthusiasm for depravity rebounding.

"The best part," Ted continued icily, "Is that all of the bedrooms all have big walk-in closets. So we'll have someplace to stick Sam when he's being a dumbass."

"How many bedrooms are there?" I inquired. The place sounded huge from the way they were describing it.

"Three," Sam answered promptly, his cheek twitching a little as if he were packing away nuts for the winter.

"Oh, so one will be Ted's studio?" I said, thinking how fancy and artistic that sounded.

"No, the attic will be perfect for that; it's finished," Ted answered.

"Well," I said, shrugging, "I guess it never hurts to have an extra bedroom."

"We were thinking of making it like, a guest room," Sam said.

"Well, you do have a lot of guests," I joked. Apart from me, I couldn't recall anyone ever staying over at their place, ever. And when I stayed over, I sure as hell wasn't going to be willing to sleep in the guest room.

"Actually," Ted began, "Actually, Kathy, we thought we might use it for a more permanent guest."

"Huh?" I said, fear creeping into my heart as I glanced back and forth between them. Was this the real reason for the big talk? Were they trying to tell me they'd adopted a pet or a kid or something?

"Remember my grandfather?" Sam interjected suddenly, abandoning his cozy niche between my legs and digging into his own pants pocket instead.

"Of course!"

"Well, he left me this letter, remember? That he wrote just before he died. Most of it is – well, personal – but here, listen to this last paragraph:

" 'The most important thing to remember, Samuel, is to be yourself. It sounds like simple, maybe even stupid advice, but it is absolutely the only way to find happiness in this world. Accept yourself the way you are. Live the life you want to lead. Wherever that takes you. And if other people don't understand what you're after, I say screw them. Screw them! They're not going to be lying with you on your deathbed looking back on your life regretting the chances you didn't take because you were worried about what people might think. You've got great friends who understand you and they're the only ones you should care about.' "

"That's sound advice," I observed somberly, wondering if my grandparents had ever used such colorful language. "But what does it have to do with buying a house?"

He took a deep breath and glanced at Ted, who nodded encouragingly.

"See, Kathy, ever since we got together…Ever since the three of us got together, it's been great between us. Hasn't it?" he prodded.

"Sure!" I answered truthfully. "I love being with you guys."

He pointed at me as if I'd just made a profound observation and I stared at him quizzically.

"Us guys!" he said triumphantly.

I looked at Ted to see if he knew what the hell Sam was talking about. He was nodding in seemingly perfect understanding but, catching my bewildered eye, decided to come to my rescue.

"You don't want to be with me," he said matter-of-factly. "And you don't want to be with Sam, either. If you'd only met one of us, it never would have turned into a relationship, would it?"

"Well, I…" I wanted to object but I felt my cheeks coloring and knew that it would be a lie. I never had been able to picture myself with either one of them alone. "No, I guess not," I sighed.

"And we're okay with that," Sam assured me.

"Frankly, we're not sure if this relationship would work for us, either, if it was just you and me, or just you and Sam," Ted said.

That surprised me. I guess I'd always thought of myself as the one who was being shared because there was only one of me.

"Not that we don't like you, you know, alone," Sam added hurriedly. "But what we've got going here… It's more than that, if you know what I mean."

They were right, of course. Whatever it was that we had, it existed on a level beyond ordinary coupledom. The bond between the three of us was far stronger than the bonds between any two.

"And that's been the main source of our problems, hasn't it?" Ted continued. "The awkwardness of not being, well, a traditional couple."

"You know, like weddings, holidays, things like that," Sam said. "Most women don't bring two dates."

Most women? I didn't think any woman ever brought two dates, unless it was on a sitcom and she'd accidentally overscheduled.

"And all of the other things that regular couples do..." Ted continued, "Getting married, raising a family... it's hard to picture three people doing that together, right? Because even if they themselves were willing to do it, it would be difficult for society to accept it."

"Right," I agreed, puzzled. I couldn't even guess where this sociological discussion was going.

"But see here, what my grandfather is saying?" Sam said, slapping the back of his hand against the papers still clutched in his fist.

"I'm not sure I understand..."

"Screw 'em!" Ted roared suddenly, causing me to jump and bang my knee on the table leg and send half my beer flying. "Oops, sorry, sweetie, didn't mean to scare you," he continued solicitously, rubbing his hand tenderly over my kneecap while Sam threw a napkin down over my splattered drink.

"But he's right," Sam said, sopping up the spill and crumbling the cloth in his fist. "Screw 'em!"

They were studying me in earnest and somehow I felt that it was my turn to speak, although I still couldn't guess what I was supposed to say. Screw 'em? Sure, I could support that. It was nobody's business what I did with my private life, and if someone didn't like it, they could go to hell. But all attitude aside, it still wasn't reasonable to suppose that I could attend a formal function with two men on my arm and not expect anyone to notice. It wasn't reasonable to expect Sam's folks to be delighted about pushing Sam's and Ted's old twin beds together so that the three of us could snuggle and fool around. It wasn't reasonable to think that their other friends would congratulate them on the woman they were sharing. Was I ever going to make out with them in public? Would we walk down the street with both their hands on my ass? Would I ever not balk over introducing them as my boyfriends? I knew we weren't the only threesome in the world; we couldn't be. But I still couldn't imagine that the world was ready for the three of us together.

"Screw 'em," I finally agreed aloud. "But I still don't get what that has to do with you guys buying a house."

"We thought maybe it was time we got a place together," Ted said, barely concealing a smile.

I frowned, confused. "But you already have a place together."

They looked at one another again, their eyes bright.

"A place for the three of us," Ted clarified.

"We want you to move in with us, Kathy!" Sam burst out, as if it were the year's greatest news.

I set down what was left of my beer with trembling hands. I was dizzy with shock and stunned by my own stupidity in not realizing that this was where this was heading all along; had been heading for many months now.

It wasn't as if I hadn't been propositioned with cohabitation before. That nice fellow back in California, the one who'd wanted me to move in with him, even though it had only been six months. It was too soon; anyone would have said so. But this was different, somehow. I'd known Sam and Ted for nearly four years, and had been seeing them for two. It was the natural next step, and I knew it.

I should have been thrilled. It actually should have been my year's greatest news, and had they been one man or I two women, perhaps it would have been. I could almost picture what it would be like, too, living with them. No more nights lying alone in my bed at home, my mind and body aching for their conversation and companionship. Evenings whiled away cooking and doing housework together; chores that would become games, playtime; even the dull drudgery of household maintenance would not seem so dreary, so arduous when I knew what would be waiting at the end of it. Limb upon limb wrapped tight around mine; the heat of their bodies enveloping my skin, penetrating into the recesses of my body and the depths of my soul. The comfort of knowing that I would be with them while I slept, and again when I woke. No more separations; no more waiting two days to see them because I never wanted to admit that I didn't want to wait two days to see them. No more packing a bag, and choosing which outfits to leave at their apartment; no more milk gone bad in my own little fridge because I was never there to drink it. No late-night phone calls asking me to come when someone was ill or had died, because I would be beside them to see it, to live it, to experience it right along with them.

"I'm home!" I could hear myself calling out in my mind; imagine them rushing forward to greet me. Never again would I have to decide when it was time to go home, because I would already be there. I would always already be at home.

And it was obvious to me, looking at them smiling back, that that's how they saw it, too. That they, too, understood what kind of life we might have if we extended our commitment to one another; expanded our time together. How our intimacy would grow and flourish; how I could become more than their sex partner or even their girlfriend; how we might even build a household, a home, a life together. A crazy, shifted sort of life in which none of us could ever be truly happy.

I couldn't let that happen. To me, yes. I had nothing to lose. But not to them.

"You don't want to," Ted was saying, his smile fading.

I hesitated. "I don't think it's a good idea."

"Mind telling us why?" Sam said, stabbing the tablecloth with the tines of his fork.

"Because," I said, watching them both stare at me as if I hadn't properly understood the question. "Because it's crazy??" I said in reply.

"How come?" Ted objected.

"Because! Because..." I wanted to say because it isn't normal. Because it just isn't done. But nothing else we did fell under the category of socially acceptable either, and that hadn't stopped me yet. I needed a far more solid reason for refusing to move forward with the best romantic relationship I'd ever had.

"Because I cannot be responsible for keeping the two of you from finding wives, having children, and living happily ever after!"

"You're not keeping us from doing that!" Sam protested.

"Oh, really?" I said. "When was the last time you went on a date with a nice, normal girl, hmm? How about you, Ted?"

"Well, maybe we don't want to date anyone else," he said defensively.

"And you don't see why that's crazy?!" I answered. "I mean, come on, guys, you can't seriously... This isn't like a real relationship here."

"Not a real relationship?" Sam murmured. His eyes were glistening and I felt an ache in my chest and knew that I'd hurt him.

"Well, it's not... Not a permanent one, I mean," I said, attempting to soften the blow.

"So, what, you've just been keeping us around for laughs then?" Ted said to me with ice in his eyes. "Shits and giggles until you're ready to move on again? Which, knowing you, could be any day now?"

I was shocked. Ted had never spoken to me like that before and for a moment I was tempted to take back what I'd said. But I recovered quickly enough to snort back a response. "What's the alternative, Ted? What do you want us the three of us to do, get married? I'm pretty sure that isn't legal in this state, or any other, for that matter."

"It's not about that, and you damn well know it."

"No, it's not about that," I agreed. "It's not even about us. It's about everyone else. Listen, I know you guys. I mean, I know we've gotten ourselves into an unusual situation here, but the fact is, the two of you are really very... very normal. Very traditional. And you expect to lead normal, traditional lives, and I want that for you, too, I truly do. But the sad fact of it is that you're not going to be able to do that with me. And deep down, you know it. You know how I know? Because neither one of you has ever said that you love me. The most frequently spoken set of three words in the English language, and neither one of you has ever said it. Because you don't. Because you just can't. Not the way we are."

A lump rose in my throat and I fell silent. Until that very moment I had not realized how much their silence on that subject had wounded me. They glanced quickly at one another and didn't answer, and I knew I was right. That made it hurt even more.

Finally Sam said, "So does this mean you won't move in with us?" His voice sounded very small.

"I don't... I don't think I can," I answered.

Ted let out a bark of mirthless laughter.

"Why are you laughing?" I said.

"Because it's bullshit, Kathy! The whole thing. Since when have you cared about what society thinks? Look at the life you lead. You call that normal? You call that traditional? And now you're blaming us? When have we ever given you reason to doubt our feelings for you? No, the real problem is that you're too terrified to ever take a chance on sharing your life with someone, no matter how great you know it would be!"

He stared at me defiantly and I wanted to cry. I didn't think they'd ever been angry with me before.

"Well, maybe I don't want to settle down!" I yelled, losing my grip on my temper.

"You are settled down!" he yelled back. "You're just too stubborn and blind to know it yet!"

"Oh, what do you know?" I shot back. "You think everyone's like you, that everyone wants to get married and make babies and live happily ever after. Well, maybe we're not all cut out for that!"

"Nobody's asking you for a lifetime commitment here, Kathy!" Sam said urgently. "Listen, we know how you are, we know you're scared; that's why we've taken things so slowly. Have we ever pushed you into anything you weren't ready for?" He shook his head sadly. "But at some point... at some point we have to move on. This is just one step forward, just one little step forward in our relationship. The worst that can happen is that it doesn't work out, right?"

Ted was still breathing heavily and glaring at me in a manner that was not in the least suggestive of love or affection. Sam, for once, seemed to be the calm and rational one of the two.

I took a deep breath. "It isn't a matter of being afraid," I said. "And there are worse things that could happen. We start living together and it's going to become obvious what we are, if it isn't already. What are you going to do when your boss finds out?" I said to Ted. I turned to Sam. "Or your mom and dad?"

"They like you!" he replied stubbornly.

"Really? Do you think they'd still like me if they knew about this?" I gestured wildly about with my hands. "What would they think if they saw us sleeping all together in one bed? What would they think if they knew about – " I couldn't bring myself to say it.

"What, about the sex?" he exploded, jumping up out of his chair, his face a severe shade of scarlet. "Well, guess what? I don't care!!"

All of the fury seemed to fall out of Ted as he watched Sam

standing there, shouting and shaking.

"If my folks were able to deal with the idea of Ted and me sucking each other off and fucking each other up the ass until the end of time – and were able to be happy about it, no less – then I don't see why they wouldn't learn to accept this, too!"

"It's totally different!" I insisted. "Homosexuality, that's biological. But this, this is weird; it's not normal. I mean, I know it's not as if we planned it. We didn't go out looking for this particular arrangement; it just happened. It seemed almost natural the way it happened. But it's not. And most people – it's not even that they'll have trouble accepting it. They'll think it's disgusting. Even without knowing what we do, or how we do it... They'll think it's sick."

"Is that what you think, Kathy?" Ted said quietly. "You think it's sick when you're lying naked between us?"

"No. I think it's heaven. It's how I picture heaven."

It was my turn to be stared at, and as their eyes softened towards me I knew I had to act fast before I lost my moment.

"I'm sorry," I said. "I don't think we should see each other anymore."

And without even grabbing my jacket I stood up and strode to the door and walked out without looking back.

CHAPTER 19

I went home. Home to my lonely one-room apartment with its greasy kitchenette and its mattress on the floor. Home to my cardboard-box furniture and the two pint glasses I'd never intended to share. Home to the hollow silence that had never seemed to ring as long or as loudly as it did now.

Didn't seem right to call it home, really.

But did I break down? Did I dissolve into sobs at the thought of my lost sweethearts and the life I might have led with them? Did I consider going back and begging them, please, to be with me again?

No, I did not. I did what I knew best. I hid out in my apartment and went to work and forced myself not to think about them.

I won't pretend that it was as simple as it sounded. They'd left a gigantic void, one that I had no hope of ever filling now. It wasn't like the other times, the other failed relationships. You barely had time to grow accustomed to someone you only knew for a month or two. But Sam and Ted had been my nearly constant companions for years now and I felt their absence, every night and every day, in everything I did. Every meal I ate without them snuggled up beside me. Every beer I drank without first splitting it three ways. Every morning I didn't have to fight for my turn in the bathroom or a spot at the mirror. Every chilly evening in which I lay in my bed alone, patting the empty spaces beside me, still wondering why there was no one there anymore.

They didn't come after me. Maybe I'd thought they would; maybe I hadn't. Maybe they'd moved on. Maybe they thought I had, too. Or maybe they'd finally decided it wasn't worth the bother. That I wasn't worth the bother. Maybe I wasn't.

I waited a long time. I waited all through the autumn and into the winter for the depression, the sense of hopelessness to pass, but it didn't. It's the bitter winter weather, I thought gloomily, gazing out from my station at the heavy skies outside, imagining I saw them pressed up against the bank window like two angels in the fog. What else could it be? It had never taken me this long to forget before. Not even when Mom died and I'd gone out on my own. Even then I hadn't understood how crushing loneliness could be.

It was no good, I thought, sneaking by their apartment with my hood pulled down tight over my face, hoping for a glimpse of one of them coming in or out and never catching one. It was no good, I thought, skulking in the aisles of the grocery store where we'd so often shopped, the boys pushing me around in the cart and then covering me up with their jackets when the manager hurried by. It was no good, I thought, standing across the corner from Delaney's on a Friday night and wondering if they were inside; wondering if they still drank beer without me and if it tasted odd to them now, too, that I wasn't there to share it.

But at last I came around – to the same place I always did. I decided to move.

It ought to have been exciting, as it had always been before. Picking out a new town. Looking forward to leaving the old one. I flipped through my trusty road atlas, pondering all of the wonderfully interesting cities in which I had never yet lived. Memphis. Biloxi. Twin Falls. But somehow not one of them appealed to me. Maybe I was done with cities, I thought. Maybe I should move out to the country. Or at least to the suburbs. Maybe it was time for me, too, to live an average American life. But then I'd think of Sam and Ted and the house they'd intended to buy and I'd wonder if they were living there now. And the thought of living in the suburbs would lose its appeal and I'd go back to searching my maps again.

In the end I gave up trying to make a rational decision. In a fit of frustration I tossed my atlas across the room and chose the state to which it fell open when it landed.

Texas. Perfect, I thought. A thousand miles away. And it would be nice to be in warm weather again. Besides, Texas was enormous. I could work my way from one end of the state to the other and probably never risk running into anyone I'd ever known. No one would ever find me there. Not that anyone would be trying.

I moved fast, as I always did once I'd decided. I gave notice at the apartment. Gave notice at my job. Changed the oil in my pickup truck and I was nearly ready to go. Amazing how quickly it went. How easy it was, to leave it all behind. In just a few short weeks I found myself standing gazing around my one-room apartment at the half-a-dozen boxes that contained my things and my battered old suitcase and wondered how I had gotten there. And suddenly it came over me that I did want to cry, after all, here at the end I did want to cry because I still missed them, still, after all this time, my heart ached and I missed them as badly as I had the first month, the first week, the first day, the first hour, and I didn't see how that was ever going to go away no matter how far I ran away from it. And then I wanted a beer and I had none left; it was my last night in town and I had no beer and I couldn't take it; couldn't suffer through yet another move without even a pint to keep me warm and so I bundled up in my winter coat and galoshes and shuffled down the street to our bar.

It struck me like a hard right hook as I went inside, the place where it all began, and I reeled as it hit me, the blunt force of a thousand memories suddenly thrown in my face, a punch that rattled my skull and deformed my defenseless mind into cooked cauliflower. There, at the end of the bar, where we'd sat together so many times, their hands on my knees or my thighs or my forearms. There, by the jukebox, where we'd joked and flirted and argued over whose turn it was to choose and whose turn to veto. There, by the window, where we'd stood when it was too crowded to sit and watched the flow of humanity passing by in the street outside. And there in our corner, at our favorite table, where even now two young men sat side by side, enjoying a beer, with a young woman half-kneeling beside them, leaning over provocatively and touching them on the arms; perhaps uncertain which one of them she wanted. Perhaps even, like me, wanting both.

For a moment I stood there, enthralled, watching the unlikely trio, and then a roar erupted from the crowd watching hockey at the bar and the two young men turned to see who had just scored and I saw that they weren't just any two young men, they were mine.

I looked at them just long enough to see their faces light up with surprise before I turned on my heel and bolted for the door.

I didn't get far. Two steps onto the sidewalk I slipped on a patch of ice and fell with a painful thud onto my hip. For a moment I couldn't even move and I wondered whether I was old and fragile enough to have broken it. How old was the new girl? I wondered as I sprawled there in agony. Young enough to marry. Young enough to have children. Probably normal and ordinary enough to want both of those things. And perhaps unusual enough to want to do them with my boys.

And in the next instant I was surrounded and four strong arms were helping me to my feet and I was touching them again at last, my friends, my lovers; my Sam, my Ted.

"I'm fine," I snarled without looking at them once I was upright again. "You'd better get back."

"Back to what?" Ted inquired.

"Oh, I don't know," I replied, massaging my aching hip and straining my neck to peer over his shoulder. "Your new girlfriend, maybe?"

"What new girlfriend?" Sam said stupidly.

"Don't play dumb, Sam," I spat back. "I saw her hanging all over you guys."

"Oh, she means Maureen!" Ted said.

"Maureen, huh? Maureen who?"

I don't know why I wanted her last name. I suppose I had some vague vision of hunting her down like a dog and then politely asking her if she wouldn't mind staying away from my men.

"Maureen the waitress," Sam replied. "Don't you remember her?"

"If that was her, she's lost a lot of weight," I said skeptically.

"Yes, she has," Ted said. "She just got back from this boot camp or something."

"Oh." I had nothing else to say.

I wasn't mad anymore, but I wanted to be. It was better than what I felt now, sensing them standing so close beside me. I took a step back and caught a gust of bitter wind on my face. I shivered.

"Oh, we're sorry, Kathy," Sam said. "You must be freezing."

"Do you want to step inside and get warm?" Ted suggested.

"I have to go load up," I muttered through chattering teeth. "I'm moving. Tomorrow!" I vowed.

They gazed at me in silence, their faces shrouded by the shadow of the awning over the big front windows.

"Where to?" Ted said at last.

"Texas," I answered promptly.

"I see," he said while Sam stared at the sidewalk, kicking his heels against the ice that had assaulted me. "Have you found a job there?"

"Nope!" I answered defiantly. "Haven't even picked a city yet. I'll start looking when I get there."

"I see," Ted said again.

We all stared at one another without speaking for a moment. I thrust my hands deep into my pockets and tried not to move closer to them for warmth. It wasn't easy.

"It can't be very comfortable," Sam said suddenly, his voice breaking slightly in the cold. "At the apartment, with everything packed."

"You can come home with us," Ted said softly. "Just for a little while? We... we were really hoping you'd get to see our new house."

"You did move after all, then?" I said. That explained why I hadn't seen them around the neighborhood in a while. Not that I'd been looking.

"It's a great place," Sam confirmed. "You really oughta see it before you go," he urged.

"You're not in that much of a hurry to pack up, are you? I mean, it can wait until morning?"

No, I thought, gazing into their gentle eyes. I'm not in a hurry to leave.

We walked half a block to where Sam's familiar small car stood patiently waiting at the curb and climbed inside. I sat stiffly upright in the front seat and watched the road signs racing by like seconds on a stopwatch. It seemed strange, driving back to their place from the bar from which we'd so often walked home. In fact, it really wasn't very convenient anymore and I wondered why they'd kept going there.

"Kinda far now, isn't it?" I remarked as we got off the highway.

"Don't worry," Ted assured me, his hands firm on the wheel. "I only had one beer."

"Why do you even keep going there?" I asked. "I mean, it's a nice place, but not that nice."

There was a moment of silence in which no one spoke and I wondered what it was that neither of them wanted to say.

"We thought..." Sam began at last, "We thought maybe one Friday night you'd come looking for us." Even in the rear-view mirror I could almost see his cheeks changing color.

"And we wanted to be there if you did," Ted confirmed.

Now it was my turn to debate whether to speak my mind or not. "I didn't," I said with defiance. "I didn't come looking for you. I was just out of beer."

"Oh, really?" Ted said. "Then why didn't you hit up that awesome liquor store that's right around the corner from your apartment?"

"I... Well, I guess I forgot..."

"Instead of walking a mile down the street in the freezing cold to some bar. You can't stand going to bars alone!" Sam reminded me.

I didn't answer. We were pulling up to a quaint two-story colonial, complete with wooden shutters on the windows and a white picket fence. It was such a silly-looking thing that I almost laughed, but something about the way the snow had lightly blanketed its slanted roof and lawn made it seem safe and secure; homey somehow. It reminded me of the small New England town in which I'd grown up.

"Well, this is it," Ted said. "What do you think?"

"It's cute," I answered noncommittally.

"Oh, we know it's old-fashioned," Sam said. "But trust me, it really grows on you."

"Wait until you see the inside," Ted said. He opened his door, got out, and came around to the passenger side of the car. Sam and I followed suit.

"Careful, it might be icy," Sam said, taking me by the elbow as we edged our way up the path. Ted came around to my other side, almost as if without thinking, as if it was still natural after all this time.

And as I walked between them I thought, you know, this does still feel natural after all this time.

They led me into the kitchen and Ted poured us a beer, dividing it equally between three pint glasses that he took from a cabinet over the stove.

"Still got it," he said, smiling at his perfect apportionment.

They gave me the tour. With a quiet earnestness that was unlike their usual boisterous eagerness; without their usual banter. Not just a, hey, come check out our new place. As if it were a serious matter.

They hadn't been exaggerating. The master bedroom was easily big enough for three, even with the sprawling California King bed that stood in the center of it.

"Check this out, Kathy – dual sinks. And the toilet's back there, so you can take a poo in private while someone else is washing up."

A long marble countertop ran along the wall next to the master bath, which was separated from the bedroom by a door. How many times had I griped about fighting over the bathroom with them in their old place, cheerful griping that inevitably ended in my shoving them playfully out of the way so I could get my turn in front of the mirror. How many times had they shoved me playfully back and forth between them in return.

We went into Sam's room next. I could tell because of all of the pictures on the wall. That and the fact that there were pajama pants on the floor and the bed was unmade.

"I didn't know you'd be coming over," he said unnecessarily as he hurried to straighten up.

"It's all right, Sam," I assured him. "I've seen it much worse."

"Well, living in a nice place like this makes you want to keep it neater," he said.

He took me over to show me the walk-in closet but I only half-listened to his lecture on the joys of hanger space; I was too busy eyeing the photographs that surrounded us. So many pictures, so many still shots of the way that we, not so very long ago, had been.

"What about Ted's studio?" I interrupted suddenly.

"Come on, I'll show you," he answered, taking me again by the arm and leading me down the hall and up a wide wooden stairway, Sam following behind us.

"Oh, wow," I said when he flicked on the light. I seemed to be surrounded by a hundred works in progress, although on closer inspection, I only actually counted a dozen standing easels.

"I cut a deal at work," he explained. "A lower level position for less pay and fewer hours. Amazing how much you can get done when you don't have to work late all the time, eh?"

"What's this one?" I inquired curiously, a strange shape catching my eye. Not waiting for an answer, I ambled over and looked more closely at it. It was an ear. A very close-up image of an ear. Looped around it was a delicate curling tendril of loose, chestnut-brown hair. It was a strange, striking image, but there was something about it that intrigued me. Something about the lines, the curves, was sensual, somehow. And then I examined it more closely and realized that between the curve of the ear and the loop of the hair was the outline of a woman's silhouette. And with a sudden inexplicable certainty, I knew that the painting was of me.

"Do you like it?" Ted said.

"It's fascinating," I replied. "Very unusual."

"He got an offer on it, you know," Sam interjected.

"What?? Really?" I turned to Ted, who was smiling shyly.

"Yep. Five hundred bucks."

"Wow!!" I said, both impressed and amazed.

"He turned it down, though."

"How come?"

"Eh… I guess I wasn't ready to part with it yet." He smiled again and self-consciously ran his fingers over his hair.

We examined the other paintings, which were in various stages of completion, and then Sam said, "Whoops! Look, Kathy's beer's empty."

And he was right, my glass was empty, and so were theirs. Meekly I trailed behind them back down to the kitchen, feeling… I didn't know how I felt.

"What do you think, Sam?" Ted said, holding up a large and very fancy-looking bottle. "Is this the night for it?"

"Absolutely, I think it is," Sam replied, fetching the bottle opener from the drawer.

I took the glass he handed me and tasted it. It was a barleywine. By the flavor of it, a very potent one. I took another sip and yawned.

"Uh-oh," Sam said. "Kathy's getting sleepy."

"Long day," I admitted.

"Well, you know you're welcome to stay over," Sam said seriously.

"You can sleep in the third bedroom," Ted said.

They were standing very close to me, and as I caught a hint of their warmth brushing against my skin, I wanted to suggest another sleeping arrangement, one that involved one bed and three naked bodies, but they were already leading me down the hall towards a closed door. When they reached it, they stood stock-still a moment and I felt as if I were in a game show, waiting on tenterhooks for my prize to be revealed. And then they nodded to one another and opened the door and we went inside.

It had clearly never been used, this room that stood in absolute pristine condition, fresh paint coating the walls and plush carpeting lining the floor. There wasn't much in it; a full-sized bed draped in plain white sheets and a soft blue comforter; an oaken dresser with a fleet of drawers; two familiar paintings hanging over the bed, one from Sam's old room and one from Ted's. A large wooden bookcase stood empty on the wall beside the windows, and beside it was poised a heavy-looking desk of meticulous construction.

"Check this out, Kathy," Sam said, pointing to a shelf with a built-in pint glass holder, and I knew at once who'd made the desk.

I stepped over to the closet and opened it. Two dozen empty hangers stood inside, along with one that was not empty, the one that held the jacket I'd abandoned those many months before. I reached out and touched its sleeve. The memory of that night, of that horrible fight, came rushing over me and I knew that Sam and Ted were watching me and I didn't dare to look at them, so I turned and walked over to another little door that stood off at the edge of the room.

"A half-bath," Ted said as I went inside. I unlatched the little cabinet that stood over the toilet and it was full of my things, too, the shampoo and deodorant and toothbrush I'd left behind when I'd left them; even the sunscreen moisturizer I liked to use on my face in the summer. I looked into the medicine cabinet mirror and saw them standing expectantly behind me, not frowning, not smiling, neither one of them speaking.

I turned. I still didn't know what to say. I went with the first words that popped out of my mouth. They weren't very profound.

"I'm tired," I said.

"We'll let you get some sleep then," Sam answered softly. He came over to kiss me on the forehead, and then walked quietly through the doorway. Ted reached out, pulled me close, and hugged me, oh, so briefly, and before I'd even managed to fight back my tears, he'd walked away, too, shutting the door behind him again without even speaking, and I was left alone.

I was tired. Tired and utterly drained from all of the months of misery, of wondering whether I'd done the right thing, of kicking myself without quite knowing why. And now here it was, the whole setup laid out neatly before me, and all I had to do was walk back into it and I could be back in their lives for good. And they could be back in mine.

I took another peek in the closet. My old nightie was hanging on a hook behind the door, as I had known it would be. I got undressed and crawled under the covers, cool and crisp in the unused room, and marveled at the pains they'd taken to preserve a place for me. They still want me, I thought with amazement. After the way I'd walked out on them, after the months of not speaking, of never even trying to get in touch, they still wanted me.

Yet they hadn't come after me. It hadn't made sense to me at the time; it had puzzled and hurt me, but I thought I understood it now. I'd needed space and they'd given it to me. Given it to me until I didn't want it anymore. Just like they'd always given me everything I'd ever wanted or needed, whether I'd asked for it or not. And they'd waited, patiently waited, one lonely week at a time, for me to show up in a bar some Friday night, or maybe no Friday night. How disappointed they must have been, all those nights when I didn't come. I could imagine Sam sighing with downcast eyes as the hours ticked by. "She's not coming, Ted." "Maybe next week," he'd answer with his eternal calm, patting his buddy's shoulder in reassurance. Or maybe they'd never spoken of it at all; simply sat and pretended that nothing had changed from the days when it was just the two of them going out for a beer at the bar.

I took a sip of my beer, the barleywine that had been selected especially for me, and suddenly it came over me how incredibly selfish I had been. All these months I'd done nothing but drown in my own self-pity without ever once thinking about what our breaking up had been like for them. They'd missed me just as much as I had missed them. They'd gone home night after night to their barren, lonely beds without ever knowing if one day I would be there to share one with them again. This house that they had bought together, with me in mind; how empty it must have seemed with that third bedroom standing vacant, populated only by the junk remnants of the woman who'd abandoned them after so much time. How carefully they'd set it up; how purposefully selected bedding they knew I would like and paintings to pretty up my walls; even a hand-hewn desk at which I might one day work at something. How melancholy it must have made them feel, walking by that empty room day after day, hoping against hope that one day I might successfully be installed in it. They hadn't moved on, either; from the looks of things, they hadn't even tried. As if they hadn't seen any point in even attempting to replace me. As if they'd known that I couldn't be replaced; that none of us could.

They loved me. They really loved me. I knew it now, although they'd never said it, not once in all this time. It wasn't because they were afraid to speak; of that I was certain. They'd probably simply never been able to agree on who would get the ultimate privilege of being the first to tell me so.

It was I, I who was guilty of being unable to speak; unable to commit myself. I'd spent my whole adult life moving on: to new cities, new apartments, new jobs, new men. But never once had I really tried to move forward.

I finished my beer and snuggled down under the covers and wondered if they were still awake, quietly talking over the evening's events; wondering what I'd do tomorrow. If I'd throw my boxes into my truck and leave them once again, for good this time. Because for me leaving was easy; staying was hard. Maybe that had been the truth all along. Maybe that was why I'd let it go so far with them, farther than I'd ever gone before, because in my heart I knew it couldn't last; it wasn't supposed to last. It was an impossible relationship, one that was predestined to fail, and maybe in some strange way that had made me feel safe, knowing that I would never be trapped with them; that I could walk away at any time and no one could ever blame me.

But if I'd been so determined to end it between us, then why hadn't I left sooner? Why had I stuck around all these months, knowing that there was nothing left for me here, if I hadn't, on some level, continued to hope that I would see them again? Were they right after all – was my righteous indignation just a mask I'd thrown on to pretend I had a real reason for backing away from them? Maybe I'd convinced myself that it was for their own good, my leaving them as I had, but maybe it wasn't about them at all, maybe it was about me; my inability to throw myself as wholeheartedly into anything as they threw themselves into everything.

Staying was hard. But maybe you got more out of things when you stuck around long enough to learn to appreciate them. How would I ever know if I didn't try?

And just before I dropped off to sleep, one final thought took root in my mind and planted itself there, a thought that grew and spread throughout my being like the branches of a well-watered tree in the bright summer sun.

I loved them, too.

CHAPTER 20

I woke to a shining winter morning, the kind that makes you forget that it's winter until you step outside and feel your boogers freezing. My window overlooked a great big backyard dotted with trees and crowded with snowbanks, off of which the pale white sun reflected with blinding brilliance. And leaping in bounds across the snow were Sam and Ted.

I laughed. They were out there in snowpants and galoshes and were making two-foot jumps all across the yard in seemingly random fashion. Then a wisp of a cloud drifted across the sun and in the growing shadow I saw that they hadn't been running around at random, but had rather written a greeting in the snow with their feet.

"Hi Kathy!" it said in eight-foot tall letters.

Goobers, I thought, but I smiled nonetheless. I made to lift the sash to return the greeting, but it stuck. I tried harder, but it still wouldn't give. Finally I banged my palm against the sash in the hope of loosening the wood, and they glanced up and began waving at me.

I waved back and they came running over, stopping directly beneath my window. "My window's stuck!" I yelled down but they shook their heads and cupped their ears as if they couldn't hear me and at last I gave it up and decided to wander down to the kitchen in search of coffee.

It was already made, of course. I could tell by the taste that it was the half-caffeinated stuff I drank nowadays but I wasn't in the least surprised, not any more than I was at finding my favorite old mug standing waiting for me on the counter. Whatever their other faults were, my men had always been very thoughtful.

I heard footsteps thundering through the front door and they came bursting in, their cheeks flushed with cold and excitement.

"Good morning, Kathy!" they shouted, waving energetically at me as they stripped off their snow gear.

"Hi guys!" I waved back. "I tried to yell earlier, but my window sticks; I couldn't get it open."

As if on cue they both stopped dressing and stood there gaping at me, dripping melting snow all over the foyer.

"It's not a big deal," I said quickly, unsure whether they'd taken my comment as a criticism of their new abode.

"Did you hear what I heard, Ted?" Sam said, turning towards his friend.

"Yup, I sure did. Her window sticks!"

"Her window sticks!" Sam repeated, breaking into a broad smile.

They both stood there grinning at me like idiots or madmen; I couldn't decide which. I stared back at them in bewilderment. Finally they snapped out of their strange mirth and Ted said, "We'll take care of it, won't we, Sam?" He nodded eagerly in agreement and they went bounding up the stairs as if they only had four minutes in which to save the world from the hazards of sticky window-sashes.

I started breakfast. Having been on my own for a while, I'd gotten away from deliciously lard-laden breakfast meats and I decided to make one of my new favorites, an oatmeal-based dish baked with brown sugar and bananas. It wasn't hard to put together and it wasn't too much trouble to make even for one, although I didn't cook much when I was alone.

I heard a noise and I turned to find Sam leaping across the kitchen with his arms out as if to catch me in an embrace.

"Sam!" Ted interjected and he stopped dead, nearly falling over in his effort to come to an immediate halt.

"Whatcha makin'?" Sam said, attempting to peer over my shoulder from six feet away.

"Oatmeal," I answered.

"What?" he said, as if he'd never heard of such an odd breakfast food.

"It's fancy oatmeal," I replied. "You bake it in the oven and it gets all crispy and junk. It's good; you'll like it."

"You did see that we have bacon, right?"

"And sausage?" Ted put in.

"Yup," I answered, rummaging around in the fridge for some fresh fruit. "But I thought we could go meatless for once. You guys aren't getting any younger, after all," I remarked, wagging a threatening finger at them.

"I guess not," Sam agreed, snagging a grape from the bag in my hand.

I snatched it back. "I haven't washed them yet!" I said.

"On that subject," Sam said, "Now that we've got this big sunny yard and all, I think I'm going to start my garden in the spring." He looked hopefully over at me as he set the plates and flatware down on the table.

"I've always wanted to do that," I admitted. "But I'm a terrible plant-killer; I can't even keep cacti alive."

It was true. Even this last-ditch effort at agrarianism had ended in miserable failure: two shriveled poky brown balls that very closely resembled a dead porcupine I'd once seen in the middle of the road but without the sad smile.

"Sam's pretty good with plants," Ted said. "He used to help my mom with her vegetable garden."

"That's right, I did!" Sam said. " 'Oh, you have such a green thumb!' she always said. That's why she liked me best!" he said, pointing at his chest as if he were God's gift to maternity.

"Can you blame her?" Ted responded, throwing his hands up in unanticipated agreement.

"Oh – oh, pshaw," Sam said, blushing. "I was just kidding you. But just for that I'm going to let you help me with my arbor. You'll love it, Kathy," he said, turning to me. "I'm gonna train vines to grow all over the top of it so you can sit under it naked and not have to worry about passing planes spying on you."

"I do often worry about that," I said, grabbing a pair of mitts and pulling breakfast from the oven.

"Well, you're hot – you can't blame them for wanting a peek."

"Yeah, yeah, yeah," I said, but I was pleased nonetheless. "Come eat your breakfast."

"Hey, Kathy," Ted said, vigorously digging into his baked oatmeal, "This is actually really good. We don't let her cook often enough, Sam."

"It's – mmph – delicious," Sam agreed, swallowing noisily. "Maybe this eating healthy thing isn't so bad after all. What do you say, Kathy, can you whip us back into shape?"

"What's that supposed to mean?" Ted retorted, sitting up straighter. He was as lean as ever.

"I know, I know, muscle-man, you're a bottomless pit," Sam snorted. "But some of us are starting to show our beer-bellies." He looked ruefully down at the gut that was protruding over the edge of his pants and sighed.

"Don't worry, sweetie," I said. "It only gets worse from here."

"Gee, thanks," he said. "You're so reassuring."

"It comes with age."

"You," Ted said, pointing at me with his fork, "Are still in terrific shape. Are you still playing hockey?"

"Yeah," I reluctantly admitted. I'd joined a league on the other side of town and I still felt guilty about it. "I thought it would be good experience to play with some new people for a change," I fibbed.

I plunged into my plate with greater ardor. Actually, not only was I not particularly enjoying playing with new people, I had rigorously avoided even making eye contact with any of the male members of my team. I knew it was absurd, but I couldn't get past my irrational and statistically unsupportable fear of lightning striking twice.

"Well, beer or no beer, at this rate you're going to live to be a hundred. Of course, women live longer than men, anyway," Ted said.

"Right," Sam agreed. "That's why you're lucky to have found guys who are younger, Kathy. No lonely old age for you!"

It was as if the door had closed on our own private bomb shelter. Darkness fell over my eyes and the silence was so absolute that I could hear my heart pounding in my ears and the blood rushing away from my brain. I was trapped, trapped here with the two of them, and the only alternative was the deadly post-apocalyptic landscape on the other side of the many tons of steel and concrete encasing us.

It was no contest.

I jumped up from the table and sprang for the door, losing my grip on my fork in the process. It struck my plate with a loud, ringing clang that seemed to echo endlessly in the silence, then bounced with a gentle thud onto the linoleum, where I promptly stepped down upon it.

"Ow!" I yelled as I crashed to the floor on that same badly bruised hip, and they rushed toward me. They surrounded me with their strong, warm bodies and their faces filled with concern but my head was spinning and I couldn't see them clearly; they were melting, dissolving like wax figures caught in a red-hot flame and I grew dizzy with terror.

"Stop!!" I cried and they let go of me and I buried my face in my knees and tried to blot out the terrible vision but it was useless; it had too strong a hold on me. And I didn't know what to do because much as I didn't want to be stuck with them for ever and ever, I couldn't bear the thought of losing them, either.

"Kathy?" Ted prompted when I hadn't spoken for a while.

"Mmm," I answered vaguely, peeking out at him from beneath my folded arms.

"Are you all right?"

I swallowed. Looked at each of them in turn. The way they looked back reassured me somehow.

"I never said I was coming back," I whispered hoarsely.

They glanced at each other, the barest hint of a smile playing about each man's lips.

"You didn't have to," Ted said, taking my hand and squeezing it gently.

I gazed at him querulously, then turned to Sam.

"We knew you'd decided," he said. "When you made that comment about the window."

"About it being stuck?" I answered, puzzled. "How did you figure that?"

"It was the way you said it," Ted replied. "My window sticks. Not 'the window sticks' or 'the window was stuck' but 'my window sticks.' Your window."

"In your room," Sam added, taking my other hand. "In what could be our house."

I snorted my contempt for their reasoning. "You're basing this on linguistics?" I said. "You're planning the course of our lives around some tiny accident of speech?"

Ted squeezed my hand again and I squeezed back in spite of myself. " 'Our' lives?" he echoed, shaking his head. "No, coming from someone else it may have been an accident. But not from you."

"Well, it's you guys' fault!" I burst out. "Setting it up like you did, with all my stuff there… Of course I was going to think of it as my room!"

"And we hope you always will," Sam said softly.

"Say you will," Ted urged.

I thought of my car, of the six boxes waiting back at my apartment for me. I thought of the job in Texas that I didn't yet have, and the one-room apartment I would have to acquire there. I thought of hauling my new mattress home in the bed of my truck, of laying it out on the floor with my poorly fitting sheets, and the single pillow that would sit at its head. I thought of me, sitting there alone, night after night, with no dreams left to keep me alive. With nothing but fading sweet memories of Sam and Ted to fill the multitude of empty days and nights of a vast, empty life.

And then I considered the alternative. Of the room upstairs, where I might live and work and even sleep if I liked. Of my morning coffee waiting for me in the kitchen in the special mug that I loved. Of the lively dinner-table conversation and the beers with which to close out the evenings. Of the three of us puttering around the house, Ted in his studio and Sam in his garden, and I... Well, there would be someplace for me. They'd made certain that there would always be a place for me. In their bed or out of it.

It seemed stupid now, when I thought of it that way. Kind of a no-brainer.

"Are you sure that's what you want?" I said, looking at them each in turn.

I felt their grasps on my hands tighten.

"Dead sure," Sam answered.

"Wouldn't have it any other way," Ted replied.

I took a deep breath, as if I was about to plunge into deep, deep water. I was.

"Then yes," I said. "I will."

With gleeful exclamations they took me in their arms and held me there, right around the knees, while tears of joy filled their eyes, and for once even I wept without shame. All three of us were smiling and laughing and crying and it felt so good, so right that for once I didn't even care if they knew how I felt and I shouted it, shouted it out loud and they shouted it back and it made me feel so warm all over that I couldn't even remember why I had been so determined to resist this moment. And when calm at last overtook us, and we were again gazing softly, lovingly at one another, they rose slowly from the floor and helped me up after them. And then they picked me up and carried me into the bedroom and made love to me until dawn.

CHAPTER 21

The following day we drove back to my apartment to pick up my things.

"I still can't believe you've spent your whole life in dumps like these," Sam said, shaking his head as he surveyed the dismal scene.

I shrugged. "It's not so bad," I countered. "Cheap, anyway."

"That reminds me," Ted said. "What are you going to do for work now? You quit your job, didn't you?"

"We're happy to put you up, of course," Sam assured me. "But we know you like to pay your own way."

"Don't worry about it," I said offhandedly. "I've got money to last me."

They exchanged looks of concern.

"We don't want you starving or anything," Ted said.

"Or running out of beer money!" Sam added, looking horrified at the thought.

"If you need some cash to tide you over..."

"Really, don't worry about it, fellas," I repeated. "I've got enough saved up to last me two, maybe three years if I pinch."

They gaped at me, stunned.

"How on earth did you save up so much money?" Sam demanded.

"Living in dumps like this," I answered promptly. "I figured there was a chance that one day I might actually get around to choosing a career, and I thought it would be useful to have some money to fall back on if I needed it for school or investment capital or something."

"And here we thought you were a drifter," Ted said with admiration.

"A lot of planning goes into being a drifter," I reminded them.

"Anyway, I don't think I'm going to go back to work for a while."

"So what are you going to do?" Sam demanded again.

"If you don't mind telling us," Ted added hastily.

Reluctantly I looked up at them. They were scrutinizing me closely, their eyes full of questions I didn't really want to answer. But they were going to know about it sooner or later, weren't they? If I was going to give this commitment thing a shot, the least I could do was try to put my whole ass into it.

"I've decided to write a book," I said at last.

They were, if possible, even more stunned by this revelation than by the knowledge that their poor relation was sitting on a fairly substantial stack of cash.

"What kind of book?" Ted inquired, creasing his brow as if trying to wrap his mind around the idea.

"It's an alternate history," I answered. "Based on an idea I've had for quite some time."

"You're going to be a writer?" Sam said, his eyes wide with wonder.

"Let's not go that far!" I rejoined hastily. "The odds of success for a writer are about as good as those for any other kind of artist – slim to none. But it's something I've wanted to do for a long while now, and you know, maybe it's about time I just did it."

"You're not getting any younger, you know," Ted said seriously.

"No, I am not," I affirmed. "But I sure feel like I am."

And they enclosed me in a big congratulatory hug as if I'd already done something really worthwhile. Indeed, they seemed entirely ignorant of the truth of the matter, which was that I hadn't done anything but announce that I was giving up my long career of making a living and was instead going to do the opposite. I guess that's what love does to people. It prompts them to make reality fit the fantasy, instead of the other way around.

"That's so great, Kathy!" Sam said, shaking my hand with as much pomp as if he were awarding me the keys to the city.

"It actually kind of makes sense," Ted said, scratching his chin thoughtfully. "You do have a lot of life experience to draw on."

"Hey, all those shit jobs may come in handy after all!"

"They may at that," I agreed.

And as we loaded up my things and brought them back to their new home – our new home – I thought that it really hadn't been so bad, after all, sharing that private little piece of me with the men in my life. I thought I'd grown accustomed to being on my own. But maybe if you tried, you could get just as accustomed to not being alone.

CHAPTER 22

It's been nearly two years now that we've been living together, the three of us, in our two-story house out in the suburbs. Maybe it's not your typical, everyday home. Maybe the mailman thinks it's strange to find three different surnames on the mailbox. Maybe the neighbors we've invited in for a beer think it odd to see the three of us together, so close, so affectionate, so unusually tender towards one another for such an unlikely trio. Maybe there's even whispering about town about the two no-longer-so-young men living with that older woman in the same house; maybe the locals are, even now, exchanging suspicions over beers at the new bar that we frequent on Friday evenings.

But somehow I don't think they are. Because once you get to know Sam and Ted, you can't help but like them. They're such ordinary guys that the thought never seems to cross anyone's mind that they could be involved in anything so... well, you choose your word for it. People see what they want to see, after all. Maybe we're ready for the world, but I don't think the world is ready for us. And if our setup is a little odd, a little unusual, people probably pass it off as natural eccentricity.

"Oh, that's Ted Sands, the artist!" they exclaim, raising a hand to their brow as if it explains everything.

"He's also an executive," I reply with a smile. Around here he's becoming better known as the artist.

Sam's got his own way of dealing with the curious questions regarding the nature of our relationship. He tells people the truth.

"We're lovers," he says, pulling me to him and kissing me tenderly on the forehead. "The three of us."

"Really?" the skeptical response inevitably comes back.

"It's true!" he avows, crossing his heart. "Sleep in the same bed

— the whole bit," he claims, smiling and winking at me.

No one ever believes it.

And what do people think of me? Not much, I'm afraid. Being with Sam and Ted hasn't transformed me into a ball of social fire all of a sudden. But at least I've got an excuse now for being reclusive.

"She's an author!" they interrupt proudly when someone asks what I do.

Technically I guess they're right. My book has been picked up by an obscure small press, but it remains to be seen whether anyone will actually buy it. In the meantime, I've begun a second book, a novel. I don't know whether I'll be able to finish it before I run out of money and have to go back to work, but you know what? At least I gave it a try. At least I didn't let the opportunity slip away because I was too afraid of losing my chips to ante up. And I know now that my boys will be there to comfort me if I fail.

Of course, you can hardly call them boys anymore. At thirty-two they are most definitely men, mature, very handsome men, in the flower of their prime, but they still haven't lost the boyish charm and wit that drew me to them those long years ago. I still worry sometimes that they'll be sorry one day for not starting a regular family, for not having a traditional American home with 2.6 cars and 2.3 children. But we may get one step closer to that after all. I've stopped using birth control, and we haven't gone back to using condoms, either. I know it's a long shot at my age, and I'm still not entirely sure how I'll feel about it if it happens. But I figure if six years with Sam and Ted could fly by as quickly and wonderfully as they have, then maybe a lifetime isn't so much to sign up for after all. Besides, I kinda like the idea of being the most spoiled mom in America.

It's peaceful here, in our little home out in the suburbs. Every afternoon this summer my men have come home from work to find me lying nude under the arbor that Sam built, typing away at my computer and basking in the late summer sun. And even after all this time, not a day goes by that they don't strip off their clothes and make love to me out there on the grass in our backyard, just the way I always dreamed they would. I've long since stopped worrying that the neighbors might see. Suburban life can be pretty dull, after all. Let 'em talk.

But we don't lie around naked for long anymore, relaxing in each other's arms and whiling away hours in the coziness of our hot, sweaty, commingled bodies. We've all got too much to do. But it's pleasant to me, to work there under the arbor and listen to Sam coaxing another tomato plant out of the soil of his expanding vegetable garden. I've even learned to pretend not to notice when Ted sets up his easel nearby and paints me in the nude, even though I've always hated having my picture taken.

And when we do finally trundle off to bed with our beers and snuggle close together, one of them on each side of me and me in the middle, I think that maybe it isn't really so strange after all, the three of us being together the way we are. Because two may be harmony. But three's a chord.

EPILOGUE
AND PROLOGUE TO
THE OTHER THREE OF US

I close the lid of my laptop with a sigh and glance around my tiny apartment, illuminated solely by a single lamp and not much better-looking for the shade. With effort I rise and meander over to the greasy kitchenette, then pull a glass from the cabinet and pour myself a beer.

I hear a knock on the door. Surprised, I walk over to answer it. I don't often have company. Especially so late.

"Hi, guys!" I exclaim with pleasure, embracing each of my friends in turn. "What are you doing this far downtown?"

"We brought you a beer," Sam says, extending it towards me with a smile.

"Thanks!" I reply. "I just opened one."

I select two more pint glasses and pour the rest of my bottle into them. Sam and Ted lean up against the counter, one on each side of me, sipping their beers.

"So, a funny thing happened to us today, Lori," Sam begins mysteriously. "We went to the bookstore."

"I've heard those places are riots," I answer.

He smirks at me. "We were cruising the women's section. Not looking for women," he adds hastily.

"You know what a sucker Sam is for romance," Ted explains.

"Right," Sam agrees. "So we're wandering through the romance aisle, and what do you think we find? A new novel by our personal friend, Lori Schafer."

" 'Hmm,' we said," Ted continues. " 'That's funny; Lori didn't tell us she had a new book coming out.' "

"I didn't?" I reply, warmth flowing into my cheeks. "How very strange. I guess I must have forgotten."

"So Ted and I, we decide we're going to buy a copy."

"Two copies, even."

"Because you know how much we like reading your books."

"Uh-huh," I say, downing my beer in one big gulp and cracking open the bottle they've brought as if it's headache medicine and I've got a terrible migraine.

"So we go back to our apartment…" Ted continues.

"And we start reading…"

"And we can't help but notice that there seems to be something awfully familiar about the characters in the book."

"As if maybe they were based on people we knew."

"Huh," I say, the kindling in my cheeks catching fire. "I didn't notice anything."

I turn my back to them and set their glasses down on the counter so I can pour the new beer. They lean over me, watching, their chests pressing into my shoulders.

"Here you go!" I announce, abruptly forcing the half-pints into their hands and stepping away from them.

"Thanks," they say. They move in closer, one on each side, and I shiver in spite of their warmth.

"See, the thing is, Lori," Sam continues, turning sideways into me, "We were actually kind of wondering if there might be something a little autobiographical in that book of yours."

"Oh, no!" I say, trembling harder. "It's just a story, you know, entirely fictional. No reality in it at all."

"You sure about that?" Ted says, stretching a long arm across my backside and drawing me towards him.

"Ungh," I gulp.

"Because it would be kind of a shame," Sam says, leaning in so close I can feel his breath on my neck, "To let an opportunity like that go to waste. If it happened to appear on your doorstep."

"In the middle of the night, say. Over a beer."

"Uh-huh," I whisper. They inch in closer, their thighs pressing against mine. I stand paralyzed between them, wishing, hoping, wondering… This couldn't really be happening, could it?

Abruptly, Sam breaks away. Ted looks at him questioningly.

He throws up his hands. "I can't do it, Ted!"

"Why not?!" Ted cries, gesturing towards me.

I can't speak. I droop down between them, hopelessly disappointed.

"Look at this dump!" Sam exclaims. "There isn't even room enough for three on that bed!"

"Well, we'll fix that!" Ted answers, hoisting my whole body up onto his shoulder and giving my ass a friendly little pat. "You get the car, Sam!"

"Good idea, Ted. Don't you worry, Lori," Sam says to me kindly, patting my ass in turn before heading towards the stairs. "You're coming home with us!"

"Just a second, guys!" I call out, giddy with anticipation. "Don't you think we ought to have a toast?"

"Sure, a toast!" Ted says, turning us both around, marching back to the counter, and grabbing our glasses. Sam follows behind him in turn.

"To the three of us!" he cries, lifting his glass.

"To the three of us!" we answer, hoisting ours.

We clink.

***

Everything turned out great for Sam and Kathy and Ted. Now find out what happens to the author when her real-life inspirations read her book…

The Other Three of Us
Coming in 2015

OTHER BOOKS BY THE AUTHOR

MY LIFE WITH MICHAEL

My Life with Michael: A Novel of Sex, Beer and Middle Age **is** an erotic fantasy for anyone who has ever wanted to have their beer and drink it, too. Surprisingly sweet, the story follows the course of an adulterous affair between two ordinary people confronting the changes that aging brings to the experience of love and sexuality. With humor and honesty, my novel explores the pleasures and pitfalls of the adulterous relationship: the crudity of the courtship, the raw sexuality that ultimately lapses into monotony, and, inevitably, the bittersweet farewell.

Now available in paperback (both standard and large print sizes) and in eBook at retailers worldwide.

Excerpt from *My Life with Michael*:

When I crept around the next corner, fingers clenched to the steering wheel as if it were a life preserver, the street sign told me it was the right one and there I was, driving into the hotel parking lot at last. I still had twenty minutes to spare. Why wasn't it over yet?!

I sat absolutely still for five of those minutes, mentally commanding my heart to cease its infernal yammering. I spent the next five gathering up my things and checking to make sure that all of the windows and doors were locked and the parking brake was set six or seven times. And then it was ten till and I still had to get to the tenth floor and I figured I'd better hurry because I didn't want to be late. What was this, a job interview?

Contempt for my own foolishness finally got me going. I made it through the lobby and all the way up the stairs to the tenth floor without hesitating, and then I was in his hallway and the room was right there, but I was panting and sweating and I couldn't go in just yet. Unless I was going up to the thirty-eighth floor or I had a lot of baggage or companions, I always took the stairs, and now I regretted that age-old resolve on my part because I was a mess and even worse,

I'd lost my physical momentum and had started thinking again about what was going to happen here. Big mistake.

The hallway was high-ceilinged and dim. Phony candle-type lanterns hung in iron brackets every ten feet along the walls, spilling what little there was of their eerie light onto the blood-red carpet. The only windows to the outside were at the very ends of the protracted hallways; I could barely make out the tiny breaks they carved into the pervasive gloom. I wondered whether they were large enough for me to jump through. Hoping for respite from the strangling sensation that clutched at my throat, I craned my neck skyward. The ceiling was decorated with some sort of bronze gilded pattern, and where a moment before it had given the impression of loftiness, now it seemed to be pressing down, ever closer to my unprotected skull, and the gilding wasn't an artistic design, it was a web of interlocking chains poised to drop down and trap me there, where Michael would undoubtedly find me the next morning, huddled in a whimpering ball and ready for the insane asylum. I peeked reluctantly back towards his door. It stood tall and ominous, a large black iron knocker dead in its center. "Boom! Boom! Boom!" I seemed to hear it clamor, surely in order to summon the damned spirits within. "Boom! Boom! Boom!" And then there was a slow creaking sound, like that of a poorly oiled door or the gates of hell opening, and I leapt into the air and from that elevated vantage point finally saw that there was a visitor entering another room down at the other end of the hall.

I exhaled. Somewhere in my head I heard chicken noises and that was annoying so I ran a brush through my now mostly dry hair, resettled my bag on my shoulder, and took a fortifying deep breath that I wished was a beer. I took the teeniest hold possible of that big black knocker and gave it the most timid tap I could muster. "Boom!" it resounded. I heard movement inside the room, and then a chasm was opening before my eyes, threatening to swallow me up, and I held my breath as the door separated slowly from its jamb. I don't mind telling you that in that moment I was scared out of my wits and not in the least bit horny. And when he finally appeared in the doorway the expression on his face told me that he felt about the same way.

"Hi," I said. As usual I'd chosen the best moment to show off my quick wit and brilliant conversational skills.

"Hi," he answered back, with equally impressive eloquence.

And then we stared at each other, motionless with fear.

"Can I come in?" I asked finally, speculating with some justification that the answer might be no.

"Oh, of course." He moved aside about three inches, and I wiggled my way out of the hallway and into the room.

ABOUT THE AUTHOR

Lori Schafer is a writer of serious prose and humorous erotica and romance. Her flash fiction, short stories, and essays have appeared in numerous print and online publications, and her first two books were published in November 2014. *On Hearing of My Mother's Death Six Years After It Happened: A Daughter's Memoir of Mental Illness* commemorates Lori's terrifying adolescent experience of her mother's psychosis, while *Stories from My Memory-Shelf: Fiction and Essays from My Past* is an autobiographical collection featuring stories and essays inspired by other events from Lori's own life. In the summer of 2014, Lori began work on a second memoir, *The Long Road Home*, during the course of a two-month-long journey across the United States and Canada. She anticipates that it will be ready for publication in 2016.

Lori's first two novels, *My Life with Michael: A Novel of Sex, Beer, and Middle Age* and *Just the Three of Us: An Erotic Romantic Comedy for the Commitment-Challenged*, were released in 2015. She is currently at work on a third novel, a sequel to *Just the Three of Us*. When she isn't writing (which isn't often), Lori enjoys playing ice hockey, attending beer festivals, and spending long afternoons reading at the beach in the sunshine.

For further information on Lori's upcoming projects, please visit her website at http://lorilschafer.com, where you may subscribe to her newsletter. You are also welcome to email her directly at lorilschafer@outlook.com with any comments, questions, or suggestions you may have. No requests for advice on your love life, though. She'll give it to you, but you probably won't be thrilled with the results.

"We Are All Miss America"

BOOK CLUB QUESTIONS

1. What was your favorite part of the book? Why?

2. What, in your mind, differentiates this book from others in its genre?

3. Which of the male characters did you prefer? Why?

4. What did you think of Kathy? Were you surprised that she was the commitment-phobe? How did her attitude contrast with that of Sam and Ted?

5. What did you think of the way the three characters got together? How did it parallel the way a two-person relationship develops?

6. What did you think of the age difference between Kathy and her lovers? How would the story have differed had they all been the same age? How would it have differed if Sam and Ted had been older?

7. Could you ever imagine being in a three-way relationship? Do you think it would be possible to sustain such an arrangement romantically?

8. Several of the sex scenes focus on the logistical difficulties of being in a threesome – who does what, who goes first, etc. Had you ever considered these kinds of problems before? How do you think such encounters would go?

9. The book addresses a number of the social and familial issues that would arise for a romantic threesome. In what ways did these resemble the difficulties sometimes encountered by real-life people with alternate sexualities – for example, homosexuals? In what ways did they differ?

10. What did you think of the Epilogue/Prologue? What do you think the plot of the sequel might be?

www.ingramcontent.com/pod-product-compliance
Lightning Source LLC
Chambersburg PA
CBHW020956180626
46814CB00003B/1119